THE HUNTER

The man stood alone in the midst of the vampires, like an island of jagged rock thrusting up from a cruel and cold sea. He was dressed all in black. His ebony skin seemed to absorb the strobe lights, and the black-lensed wraparound sunglasses he wore gave nothing away. His features showed only cruel contempt as he gazed at the vampires.

Dennis waited, shaking, not knowing what was going on. He didn't see how the hell the man dressed in black could cause a room full of vampires to freeze.

Then someone moved.

And all hell broke loose in the club.

BLADE

A NOVELIZATION BY
MEL ODOM

BASED ON THE SCREENPLAY BY
DAVID S. GOYER

HarperPaperbacks
A Division of HarperCollinsPublishers

HarperPaperbacks
A Division of HarperCollins*Publishers*
10 East 53rd Street, New York, NY 10022-5299

This is a work of fiction. The characters, incidents, and dialogues are products of the author's imagination and are not to be construed as real. Any resemblance to actual events or persons, living or dead, is entirely coincidental.

ISBN 0-06-105913-7

Cover photo © 1998 by New Line Cinema

First printing: September 1998

Printed in the United States of America

Visit HarperPaperbacks on the World Wide Web at
http://www.harpercollins.com

❖ 10 9 8 7 6 5 4 3 2 1

DEDICATION

Dear Shiloh Odom,

This book is dedicated to you, little guy, with all my love. It's filled with tough-guy heroes just the way we like 'em, and scary villains.

We've been through a lot of adventures together so far. We've saved the world with *Duke Nukem*, raided *Thunderhold Comics* on a weekly basis for years, and braved the rigors of every *Nate the Great* mystery ever written.

I've had nine fantastic years with you so far, and hope to have ninety more. Since you've been born, I've always had someone in my house who understood heroes and the importance of capes (even if they were just bath towels), and I've had a constant companion to help bring the toughest of computer games to their knees.

Thanks for sharing your life and interests with me, and rest assured if you ever get super-powers, you can trust me with your secret identity.

Love,
Dad

ACKNOWLEDGMENTS

This book represents a work of labor and love.

Love because I can clearly remember the day I picked up the *Tomb of Dracula* comic that Blade the Vampire Hunter appeared in. Thanks to the magic of comics, I find myself now curiously older than he is, but the fascination with the character remains. Marv Wolfman has created a lot of memorable heroes in his comics, and has been one of the best writers I ever read. So thanks, Marv, for all the fun and for the education I received flipping through the pages you scripted.

And now the labor part. Guys, really you don't want to know. The movie, as you know, got delayed a number of times. But that was because everyone connected with it wanted it to be the best it could be. And judging from the trailers I've seen, it's going to be a blast.

However, there were a number of incarnations along the way, and it just kept getting better. By the time you read this book, *Blade* the movie will be out, and I'm going to be one of the first guys in line.

But about those incarnations . . . Man, for a time there this script just kept coming back. More changes, more revisions. It became the novelization that wouldn't die.

My heartfelt thanks go out to Caitlin Blasdell, editor, for having one of the most charming personalities under fire that I've seen. And in the face of killer deadlines, unforeseen obstacles, a sense of humor even.

Caitlin, I swear it just wouldn't have been the same without you.

PROLOGUE

"I've got a female bleeder with complications!"

Balancing his latest attempt at a fresh cup of bad coffee during a shift that had gone into its twenty-first straight hour of pure white-hot hell, Carl Hunley glanced over at the nurse manning radio communications behind the Trauma Ward admissions desk.

"What complications?" he asked her. He set the coffee on the high wall separating them, picking a spot between a potted ivy and a ceramic lamb that had obviously been painted by a very young artist who loved rainbows.

Nurse Hightower picked up his interruption, managed to give Hunley a scathing look of reproach, and said calmly, "Explain the nature of the complications, TruCare Forty-two." She was twice Hunley's age, a heavy woman used to commanding respect because of her skills and her demeanor.

"She's pregnant," the excited male voice at the other end said. "Looks like she's ready to deliver at any time here."

"Can you check—" Nurse Hightower began.

The radio crackled, spat static. "Goddamn it, Hightower, I'm barely able to hold her throat together. Some sadistic bastard really worked her over good. Advise your trauma team we're coming in hot and messy with this one."

"What's your ETA?" Hightower asked in a calm voice.

"Fucking *now*!"

Despite the fatigue that had settled over him from the grueling shift, Hunley felt the excitement fill him. When a crash cart rolled through the doors of the Trauma Ward, especially in this city, there really was no telling what would be on the gurney.

The radio communications ended with an abrupt, staticky crackle.

Hunley, tall and lean, with long blond hair that flipped up where it hit his shoulders, took a final sip on his coffee. The competitive edge that had seen him through collegiate basketball with a near miss at the pros kicked in, waking up his system. Love the medical profession or leave it. He didn't know how many times he'd heard that from a variety of instructors and doctors.

"I've got it, Hightower," he told the nurse. "See

if you can get Couch up here. Stat. Bessel doesn't usually come apart like that."

And that was the truth. He'd known Martin Bessel for almost a year. The guy was a damn legend on the graveyard shifts at the Trauma Ward. There wasn't an accident around that Bessel hadn't worked. It would take a lot to shake the man.

Hunley moved for the double doors, his hands drifting over his white coat and green scrubs to make sure his stethoscope was with him and not with one of the other thirty-two patients he'd seen so far today.

But before he got to them, the doors opened with a shotgun blast of sound.

Broad and deeply tanned from the sun, Bessel manned the port side of the gurney, shoving with long strides. His dark brown eyes raked the reception room, nailing Hunley within a heartbeat. He wore his hair pulled back, but it hung down over one shoulder now, as blood-flecked as the rest of him. His white TruCare jacket had turned almost completely red from the arterial flow that continued to spray in a fine crimson mist from the woman's throat.

"Hey, junior," Bessel growled, "are you ready to rock and roll?"

Hunley grabbed the side of the gurney in front of Bessel's partner, Lyndon Meyers, who gave way at once. He was barely in his twenties, still learning in spite of a tour in Vietnam, to put on the hard edge that kept a pickup from becoming too personal.

"What about Couch?" Bessel roared at Hightower, as they passed the nurse. "He's senior on tonight, isn't he?"

"On his way," Hightower responded. No matter how short Bessel got with her, Hunley had noted the respect Hightower always gave the paramedic.

"Gonna need a full team," Bessel told her.

"I've got one standing by."

Hunley kept stride, pushing the gurney, watching other staff members rushing around them. Some of them merely got out of the way, others came to help. In heartbeats, too many of them against the woman on the gurney, they were inside the operating room.

Hunley reached up, flicked on the intense light above. The sudden illumination revealed the woman's wounds instantly. For a moment Hunley thought he was going to freeze up. Despite everything he'd witnessed, he had never seen anything like this.

Her throat gaped open, huge flaps of flesh peeled back to uncover the musculature and bones of the esophagus and trachea beneath. Every breath the woman struggled to take sucked some of the blood down into her lungs, creating even more problems. If she didn't bleed to death first, she was in real danger of drowning in her own blood.

"What happened?" a nurse asked in a hoarse voice.

"The police found her in the street," Meyers said. "Called us in."

"She was attacked by some kind of animal," the OR scrub nurse stated. "Look at that. Almost tore her throat out."

"C'mon, dammit!" Bessel growled from across the gurney.

"Get a Vacutainer into an artery," Hunley ordered. "And get her strapped down. Now, people!" He let one of the nurses help him get into mask, cap, and gloves as he pulled his arms from the antiseptic scrub.

The shock-trauma team crowding into the room went to work at once. They shifted the woman from the gurney to the OR table, finding their positions with practiced ease. But there were some startled exclamations when they looked at the patient.

"Handle it or get the hell out of my OR," Hunley ordered. The adrenaline beat a savage dance inside him now, thundering for release. He could only imagine what was going on inside the woman's body.

He studied her, listening to the stats as they were called out to him. She was in her early twenties, dressed in a maternity blouse that was so bloody he couldn't even guess what color it had originally been. Her face was torn by fear and pain now, but he knew she was pretty. Her ebony skin had gone pale and gray with blood loss and trauma. She was definitely pregnant. On her small frame, her stomach had ballooned out, heavy with the child that was so close to arrival. And blood continued to spurt from her throat.

A male nurse lashed a pressure cuff around her left arm, having difficulty because her skin was slick with blood.

"Where's the respiratory therapist?" Hunley demanded.

"Here." Mike Thorsland started setting up, quietly and efficiently.

Hunley didn't look up, sponging away the blood and trying to sort through the wreckage of the woman's throat. He didn't know what could have done all the damage, but around her neck he spotted what looked like—"Are those bite marks?" he asked Bessel.

The paramedic nodded. "Saw 'em, too. Gives you a fucking chill, don't it? Thinking about the psycho bastard that must have done it."

"She's not breathing," a nurse announced.

"Intubate her!" Dan Couch, the senior resident at the Trauma Ward, exploded into the room in a whirl of motion, his white coat seeming on the verge of catching up to him. He was short and wiry, with sandy hair mixed with gray, a full beard, and glasses. His eyes blinked like he'd just awakened.

The respiratory therapist nodded to a nurse, who rolled the patient's head back off the edge of the table. It took real effort to pry her jaws open. Then Thorsland fed the endotracheal tube down the woman's ruined throat. When it was in place, he attached it to an Ambu bag. "Ready."

Hunley checked the blood-pressure cuff. "Blood pressure's forty and falling . . ."

Couch nodded, fitting his hands into the gloves a scrub nurse offered. They snapped into place. He turned his full attention to the woman's throat.

Hunley knew they couldn't throw in the towel yet. Couch was a miracle worker when it came to breathing life back into the nearly dead. And there were two lives here to save.

He gazed into the woman's frightened gaze. Her lips moved around the endotracheal tube, and her attention was focused on Hunley, as if trying to tell him something. Instinctively, he knew what she was worried about. "We're going to take care of your baby," he said, "and we're going to take care of you."

Wrapped in the womb, the baby listened to his mother's heart beating. It didn't sound like anything he'd heard before. The rhythm was off, fast but somehow weak. And it was fading.

Her screams still echoed in the amniotic fluid. Those sounds had scared him more than anything. He'd never felt an emotion so sharp, so jangling from his mother. The vibrations trapped inside her womb were less now, but still coasting through the liquid medium.

He felt distance grow between himself and his mother, something he'd never experienced in the nine months of gestation. Pressure constricted around him. His space had grown smaller in the past few weeks, but he'd accepted that. This was different.

He shifted, trying to find a comfortable position. He didn't like lying like this. His mother already knew that because he had let her know. Instead of being able to move, however, he felt he was pinned.

Then he felt a constriction so tight it hurt.

There had been some warning signs of that during the last few days, but he hadn't worried about it. Everything that had happened to him seemed normal.

He moved again, wishing she would sing to him. But his mother seemed to pull away from him even more.

Then a cold, burning sensation filled his whole body. Some*thing* invaded him, fed down into him through the umbilical cord that attached him to his mother. It hurt so bad. He tried to scream, but he couldn't.

"Got a name for her," Bessel said.

Hunley looked back at the man, staring at the woman's blood-spattered wallet in his hand. "What?"

"Vanessa." Bessel wiped at the driver's license he shoved in front of Hunley. "Can't read the last name. Damn blood's soaked through and ruined it."

The woman's picture showed her beauty, and a smile that Hunley wished he could put back on her terrified face. A smile that he *would* help put back on the woman's face, he amended.

"How about an address?" Hunley asked.

"Got it."

Couch spoke without looking. "Get Hightower to send a police officer around to that address. If this woman has a medical history, I need to know it. Hunley, I'm going to need your help here. Trach's gotta be put back together."

Hunley slid his fingers down beside the senior resident's, feeling tissue give way.

Without warning, the patient came up off the table, fighting against the straps that held her down. A nurse went down, hit by one of the flailing arms.

Hunley pulled his hand out of the woman's throat and tried to find a grip to help hold her down. He couldn't believe she was so strong, not in her condition.

"Jesus, her water's broken!" Couch yelled. He called for more help, then looked at Hunley. "She's going into uterine contractions! Get Robinson down here! We'll have to do a C-section!"

Hunley moved, holding the woman down as more straps were added. He looked into her eyes as the spasms weakened, watching as the light died away. "Vanessa!" he said in a strong, clear voice. "Don't go. Everything's going to be all right! Do you hear me? You hang in there! You've got a baby who's going to need you!"

Pain wracked the baby. Part of it was from the constrictions that wrapped all around him, pushing him, pushing him. His head shifted sizes, shapes. The light he'd been able to see through his mother's stomach blurred.

He listened for her heartbeat, trying to hang on to the sound of it.

But the other part of the pain flooding him made it impossible to focus on the rhythmic noise all of the time. The burning cold sensation continued cycling through his bloodstream, fed directly into his system by the umbilical cord. It attacked him, a predator that fed from the inside. He was changing, becoming different.

And his mother was going away. He felt her grow more and more distant, till it was impossible to feel or hear her heart at all.

For the first time since he had been conceived, he was alone, locked in the deadly embrace of the husk that had been his mother.

CHAPTER

1

Dennis Tohler sat in the passenger seat of the black Mercedes 850 convertible and watched the night-draped cityscape speed by. He was tall and tan enough that is platinum-white George Clooney hairstyle really stood out. His agent had suggested he go with the new hairstyle since Clooney was pricing himself out of the market.

Dennis hadn't been keen on it at first, but a few more gigs had dropped into his lap lately, so maybe the agent was right. He'd died as a plague victim on a recent *X-Files*, been killed on a *Silk Stalkings*, and showed up as an office worker on *Suddenly Susan*. His agent also had a movie deal working with the USA network, an indy domestic-terror screamer that needed an infusion of cash if it was going to make it to the screen.

And tonight he had managed to capture the

attention of the woman driving the Mercedes.

He glanced over at her, amazed at how long she'd been driving without speaking to him. Usually the pretty ones were all over him, playing him to get as much info about the acting biz as they could. He had left the club the woman had found him in over fifteen minutes ago.

Her name was Raquel. Other than that, Dennis didn't have a clue. He kind of liked the strong, silent type of woman, though, because it gave him more opportunity to talk about his favorite subject: himself.

He guessed that she was about his age, early twenties, though he tried to look a little older. She was wasp-waisted and carried firm, high cleavage. Her tight dress displayed the whole package at its best. When she'd taken his arm back in the club and led him out, he hadn't minded being seen with her.

From the jewelry and the car, Dennis figured she was rich. Or at least married to rich. That, he didn't mind at all. If he couldn't find a way to convince her to help produce the made-for-TV movie being marketed to the USA network, at least they'd have a good time without worrying about the future. He still couldn't tell the difference between cheap champagne and the more expensive varieties, but he liked telling people that he drank it.

Dennis turned to her, trying to catch her eye in the rearview mirror because he thought that just seeing his eyes might be kind of romantic for her. Hell, he counted smiling in a rearview mirror as foreplay.

Only the damn mirror seemed to be set wrong. All he could get a glimpse of was the back of the damn car. He looked at her hard enough to draw her attention.

Raquel gave him the benefit of a full glance, sweeping him from head to the material spread tightly across his crotch. "What do you have down there, little man?" Her voice was a cross between a purr and a challenge.

"Oh, that's my heat-seeker," Dennis answered.

"I'll bet." Raquel slipped a manicured hand up his thigh.

Dennis didn't move, giving her one of his cockiest smiles, the one that had gotten him so much attention as the resident bad boy on two soap operas here in New York before he decided to try his luck out in LA. He felt her hand cup his groin, then squeeze with enough pressure to be just short of hurting. Dennis moaned, giving her the full effect.

The woman pulled her hand away and down-shifted, pulling onto yet another side street. She turned to face him and smiled. "Have I made you curious?" she asked in that ultracool accent she had.

"What?" he asked, playing her game. He loved hearing her talk. As soon as he found a bathroom off to himself, he was going to try her accent out, see if he couldn't get it right. Then he'd spring it on his agent. The accent was totally rad.

"About where we're going," she replied.

"Raquel," he said, using her name because he knew chicks dug it when a guy used their name in conversation, letting them know the guy had stepped in for a reality check and actually knew who he was with, "I figure as long as I'm with you, I'm in good company." He put a hand over his heart.

She just gave him that frosty grin, then turned onto another side street, angling away from the downtown traffic.

Dennis made a show of looking around. "So, where are we going?"

"It's a surprise," she told him.

He shrugged. "I like surprises." But he also didn't like the idea of being surprised in the neighborhood they were currently in. He wondered if the woman could tell he was nervous.

Certain that he had the woman in the bag, Dennis turned his attention to the neighborhood again, ready to start playing hard to get. As much money as she seemed to have, he was sure he'd have to remind her that she might not get everything she wanted, to make her *really* want it.

The neighborhood looked run-down, filled with warehouses and factories. A burning stench coiled through the air, permeated by chemical stink. The headlights of the Mercedes cut a burning swath through the shadows ringing the squat gray buildings. A number of refrigerator trucks sat silent, waiting for morning at loading docks.

Raquel powered the Mercedes forward, bringing it to a screeching stop at the rear of a cinderblock building that might have been new around the turn of the century. At the very least, Dennis decided as he glanced at the chipped facade, the damn place was definitely pre-Woodstock, something that he wasn't.

The woman switched off the ignition and popped the door latch. She paused, looking back at him. "Coming?"

"Hell," Dennis replied, "I ain't even breathing hard yet." Still, he glanced around the squat building, spotting a couple dozen workers loading refrigerated trucks with boxes of product. The weak yellow light spilled from the warehouse over the waiting trailers.

Raquel walked away, her hips twitching suggestively.

For a moment Dennis considered pushing down the door locks and staying in the car. A mobile phone waited in its cradle. If the scene got entirely too whacked, he could always yellow-cab it out and get back to the bar. It wasn't too late. Then he looked back at the woman and watched her hips twitching some more.

He popped the latch and jogged after her. So maybe those martial-arts lessons he'd been taking would come in handy. Getting laid was getting laid, and being a little scared only added to a dynamite adrenaline flow.

"What the fuck are we doing here?" he asked when he caught up with her.

Raquel smiled at him but didn't answer. She walked up the ramp leading to a loading door and went on through.

Dennis stayed at her side. Okay, maybe her mysterious act seriously screwed over his mysterious act, because she had him hooked now. Still, she had chosen him back at the bar, not the other way around.

She led him through the bowels of the plant. None of the workers even gave her a second look. Dennis guessed maybe her husband owned the company, which would explain why she was so familiar with it. As he glanced in different rooms of the plant, the whine of saws echoed all around him. And in each of the rooms were huge, bloody animal carcasses. The workers cut on them diligently with electric carving knives, hewing slabs of meat from the bodies. Other workers used push brooms to clean the floors, shoving blood into the drains set into the floor.

Raquel took another turn and almost lost him. He hesitated a moment at the corner, and got a glimpse through an open door of a hook-and-chain pulley system inside, carrying a series of long black bags into the back of a waiting truck. For a heartbeat Dennis thought they looked like body bags. He had become intimate with body bags while playing the part of a coroner team on a recent straight-to-video release.

Then a guy in orange coveralls stepped in front of the door and blocked the view. Hackles rose at the back of Dennis's neck, and he turned away and scanned the warehouse, looking for Raquel.

She stood in front of a steel door, pressing a button on an intercom. Even over the whine of carving knives and the clank of the steel chains supporting the carcasses, Dennis thought the voice coming over the intercom sounded strange. There was a cadence to it that sounded hauntingly familiar, reminding him of the Latin service at Catholic churches he'd spent some time in as a kid.

Raquel answered back, but Dennis couldn't hear her. He approached, ducking around a guy wheeling through the corridor on a yellow Caterpillar forklift. The forklift driver looked pale, like he hadn't seen the sun in months, and the man stared at him with the deadest eyes Dennis could remember outside of Charles Bronson or Lee Van Cleef.

"What did you say?" Dennis asked, coming up to the woman. He was really nervous now, ready to call off the whole evening.

Abruptly, the woman turned to him, grabbing his jacket in both hands and pulling his mouth hungrily to hers. Her kiss was searing passion, and as he felt her body move against his, already seek-ing out that old instinctive rhythm, he knew he wasn't going to pass up a chance with her.

The steel door behind her opened, letting out dim, glittering light and a throbbing crescendo of brutal rock music.

"Wow," Dennis said. "What the hell is going on in there?" He peered over the woman's shoulder, seeing the writhing shadows inside.

"Party," Raquel answered. "Want to come?"

Dennis gave her one of his high-wattage grins. "Sure. I want to go to the party, too. Think you can handle both?"

Raquel's eyes gleamed as she pulled him in through the door, guiding him down the narrow stairway toward the dance floor. At the bottom, a hulking doorman who looked like he could have worked in the WWF kept watch over the entrance. His chiseled face looked anything but happy.

Dennis blew the guy off immediately. If the hulk had any real power to prevent him from being there, he would have already used it. Being with Raquel was obviously a free pass to this hidden wonderland of erotic delights. He had no illusions about what probably went on here. He had cruised after-hours clubs before. Drugs, drink, and dirty sex. It was truly his kind of place.

The sound system was awesome, the deep basso throbbing of the band stopping just short of torment. Lights glittered and flashed overhead, cool neons that barely lit up anything.

What really killed him were the floor and the walls, though, covered in white tiles, with chrome runoff gutters and drains that told him this had probably once been a killing room for the meat-packing company. He shook his head in amazement. Hanging around the acting crowd, he had seen some weird shit. But this really maxed out the concept.

The only thing that seemed to be missing was a bar. Dennis looked for it but couldn't find one. All he needed was a drink, maybe two, and his nerves would be settled just fine.

A strobe light flickered over the dozens of leather and latex bodies writhing on the dance floor as Raquel pulled him out there. Everyone seemed to be into tattoos and body-piercings. Above the dance floor, a DJ with twin head-mounted spotlights called the shots and laid down the riffs from twin decks, grooving to the music himself.

Without warning, Raquel's course led Dennis into a smooth-looking man in a business suit who seemed young enough to appreciate the decor and the atmosphere. His hooded eyes flickered with amusement and anger. Both emotions smoldered and quickly died away, and he strode deeper into the dancers.

"That's Deacon Frost," Raquel said. "He owns the club."

Dennis swallowed hard, feeling like he had the day the judge had given him a suspended sentence for his most recent DUI. Fucking guy had eyes on him that would have peeled paint.

Raquel pulled on him again, and he went with her.

"Some place," Dennis shouted to be heard over the din.

"I like it," Raquel said. "Dance with me." She pushed at him with surprising strength, getting him moving. She pulled him close, got his body swaying with hers.

Dennis let himself be pulled into her black, black eyes. He was feeling lucky, his earlier misapprehensions having left him. He moved in closer, grinding himself against her thigh. She didn't flinch away.

Suddenly he felt a tongue flick against his ear. He turned, finding a beautiful woman standing there. She was tall as he was, and slender, blond, with an unruly style in her short-cut hair, but coming across as deliberate trash. She pirouetted for him, giving him a view of the complete package, obviously knowing she could turn the head of everything male in the room with her skimpy outfit.

"My friend, Mercury," Raquel said. "Hope you don't mind?"

Dennis grinned, looking at the woman. "Not me. I always thought three was company."

Mercury grinned, moving in behind Dennis. She rubbed her pelvis against his hip, getting him into motion against Raquel again. "Music hasn't stopped," she said. "They're playing our song."

"I guess so," Dennis agreed.

This time when Mercury licked his ear, he saw the silver post on the underside of her tongue, startling against the deep purple flesh. When she drew her tongue back into her mouth, the metal clicked against her teeth. She ran her hands over his back, touching him lightly enough to threaten to drive him entirely crazy.

"Feel like sharing?" Mercury asked.

Dennis couldn't tell if she asked him or Raquel. "Not Sharon," he said, making a joke of it. "Dennis."

Mercury smiled and kept moving against him.

By now, Dennis was covered with perspiration. His senses swam as he tried to take it all in. The music somehow became even faster, even more overpowering. Around them some of the dancers started shedding their clothes, kissing and pressing bare flesh against each other.

It was wilder than anything he'd seen lately. Sure, there had been a couple orgies at other actors' and actresses' houses, but he'd known he was going to get into that before he got there. He was new to the club. For all they knew, he could be a vice cop. He considered that for a moment, thinking he should just walk up to some of the people around him, say, I'm not a vice cop, but I've played one on TV, see what kind of reaction he'd get.

But he kept dancing, feeling the seduction of feminine flesh pressing in against him from both women. He knew he wasn't going to be able to take much more of this without some kind of relief. From the way both women were breathing deep and looking at him, he knew the same was true for them as well.

He shouted to be heard over the music. "I need a drink!"

Raquel smiled at him, as if understanding the primitive needs that fired him. She did not, however, move away from him.

Something warm and wet struck Dennis's hand. It felt like spit, at body temperature and syrupy, sticky. For a moment, he thought someone had actually spit on him. Instant fear of AIDS or some other deadly disease flared through him. He glanced at his hand.

For one insane split second he thought the red liquid splattered across the back of his hand and his fingers was blood. But where the hell had it come from? He looked up at the ceiling.

More wet drops hit his face, landing on his lips. He tasted sticky warm salt. Then he closed his mouth tight, wanting to spit, gagging on the reflex as he fought to control it.

The music suddenly hit a crescendo. Then a torrent of blood poured down from the ceiling.

Horrified, Dennis shifted his gaze to Raquel's face. Her features were covered in the red liquid. She only smiled, flicking her tongue across her lips, then lapping it up eagerly.

Dennis stopped dancing. His heart sped up uncontrollably, pumping his system full of adrenaline.

Red droplets continued falling across the dance crowd, and they went on gyrating like they didn't have a care in the world. Dennis figured that a drain above had broken, leaking blood from one of the other killing floors in the meatpacking plant. Then he noticed the sprinkler heads, and realized the downpour had been deliberate.

Raquel turned her face up to the ceiling, holding her hands palms up at her sides, as if she were caught in a warm summer shower.

Then more people stopped what they were doing and turned their faces up to the falling red rain as well. The music continued, the backbeat knifing through the stillness of the dancers.

As Dennis watched, sick fear whirling in the pit of his stomach, the clubgoers opened their mouths and drank down the crimson liquid. He couldn't believe it, and turned his attention back to Raquel.

She gazed at him, but something appeared wrong with her face. It changed shape, morphing, becoming preternatural. She snarled at him, showing elongated canines. Then she spoke, with the same accent as before, but her voice had dropped a handful of octaves below where it had been. "What's wrong, baby?"

Dennis screamed before he knew it. He pushed out hard, with his hands flat against the woman. Surprisingly, she stood her ground while he went rebounding away. He turned, and almost ran right into Mercury, who was grinning with her own set of fangs now. In fact, as he gazed around the clubgoers—looking for 911 from anyone he could get it from—he noticed that *everyone* else in the club was now sporting a set of fangs set in animal faces.

"Come on, baby," Mercury said, her eyes blazing with an unholy light. "Ready for me to eat you all up?"

Dennis broke free of the two women and shoved his way through the crowd. A huge fist appeared in front of him as he ran for the stairway. It caught him full in the face, shoving him back, knocking him to the floor.

Dazed, he watched as the clubgoers surrounded him. Some of them hissed in anticipation, claws at the ends of their hands now instead of fingers. A young guy effortlessly picked him up from the floor. With a shove, he was sent spinning away. The other clubgoers turned it into a game, shoving Dennis from one to another.

It all blurred for him as his senses overloaded. The strobe lights playing over the crowd flashed into his eyes, and the music remained deafening. Before he knew it, he was back in Raquel's arms. She still didn't look human. And in her arms was the last place he wanted to be.

With a gentle heave that belied the incredible strength she possessed, she sent him spinning away.

Dennis tried to remain on his feet, but he couldn't. Raquel had been too strong. He went down, falling hard. He wrapped his hands over his head as he cried out in fear, and waited tensely for their fangs to sink into him. Never had he figured himself for a Tarantino finish.

He took a breath then. And another. Surprised that no one had attacked him, he looked up and found himself nose to boot toe with someone's feet. He also noticed that the blood rain had stopped, though it had left his hair sticky.

He looked up farther, craning his neck back, till he found the owner of the black boots.

The man stood alone in the midst of the vampires, like an island of jagged rock thrusting up from a cruel and cold sea. He dressed all in black, some kind of military getup with pockets and bandoliers, over which he wore a black-leather longcoat. His ebony skin seemed to absorb the strobe lights, and the black-lensed wraparound sunglasses he wore gave nothing away. His features showed only cruel contempt as he gazed at the vampires.

"Is that him?" someone asked.

Another voice said, "Jesus, that's him!"

"Blade!" a female vampire screamed, and there was arousal mixed in with the fear. "It's the Day-Walker!"

Dennis waited, shaking, not knowing what was going on. He didn't see how the hell the man dressed in black could cause a roomful of vampires to freeze.

Then someone moved.

And all hell broke loose in the club.

CHAPTER

2

Blade whipped the longcoat back and off, his gloved hands searching out the matte-black and silver-finished MACH pistol in the hip holster. He brought the weapon up and leveled it at the undead siren who'd lured the new meat into the club.

The female vampire came at him faster than anything human ever could, her razored fingernails lashing out at his eyes. Her mouth was open in a scream.

Only he moved faster. The MACH blasted out a drumbeat of death. The garlic-tipped silver dumdums smashed into the creature's face, exploding on contact, dropping her in her tracks. The body incinerated into a swirling cloud of black ash that sifted across his boots.

Blade turned, tracking all the vampires in the

room. His life was measured in the heartbeats as he maintained control of the situation. The pistol bucked against his palm as he stood his ground above the man cringing on the floor. The Hunter didn't hesitate, firing at every target. From his earlier reconnaissance, he knew the man before him was the only human in the room. The special bullets tore through vampire flesh, shredding undead lives—ashes to ashes that filled the air.

The MACH blew back empty, but the numbers of the clubgoers had drastically—and literally—dropped. He shoved the pistol back into its holster. Besides the MACH and the six-point adjustable body armor, he carried an assault rifle strapped over his shoulder, muzzle down; a customized cut-down shotgun sheathed on his leg that fired silver stakes, a bandolier of silver stakes across his chest; and an Indian-style katar punching dagger. A sword hung in a sheath down his back, the hilt within easy reach.

With the roll of gunfire silenced for a moment, the vampires grew braver. He knew they would. It amused him to see them regrouping like the predators they were, thinking they could take him down. Probably most of the bloodsuckers in the room had only heard of him, never been around any of the firefights he'd engineered.

He swung the assault rifle up. His thumb grazed the arming button for the spotter scope mounted on top of the weapon. It wasn't the usual ruby laser preferred by many police and military units as a deterrent to continued aggressive behavior. The light emitted from the spotter scope was ultraviolet, the best part of the sun in Blade's opinion.

He recognized the blond female vampire who had been with the man lured into the vampire club. The name clicked into place effortlessly, pulled from the mental data base he had compiled over the years of his hunt: Mercury, and the creature was definitely a threat.

Mercury avoided Blade, rushing with inhuman speed toward a doorway at the back of the club.

The assault rifle chopped a ragged line through the white tiles of the wall, staying just behind the fleeing vampire till she vanished.

Blade cursed silently, realizing he'd cycled the weapon dry.

Encouraged by his miss, and because he seemed to be out of bullets, the other vampires surged in. They hissed, their faces morphed into demonic convulsions.

Blade swept the UV spotter light over them. Even empty at the moment, the assault rifle wasn't useless. Everywhere the UV light touched the vampires, it burned them. He played it across their faces, where it would be the most frightening, and reached for another clip.

The vampires broke ranks, drawing back immediately when their skin started smoking from the UV light's corrosive caress. Eyeballs popped in their sockets.

Blade dropped the empty magazine from the assault rifle and shoved the full one into the receiver. He leveled the rifle and squeezed the trigger in rapid three-round bursts that took out vampire after vampire. The bullets were special wooden fragmentation rounds, and in most cases the killing didn't stop with the first victim. The DJ died in a blaze of glory, the lights on his head extinguishing in fountains of sparks.

Blade stepped over the man cowering on the floor, seeking out his targets with skill and precision. No one got close to him.

A handful of vampires tried to make a run for it up the stairway to the door leading back out to the meatpacking plant. The strobe light revealed their fear as they clawed at each other in their struggle to get to safety. Incinerating bodies clogged the stairway, and Blade concentrated on the group that had gotten stuck there.

The assault rifle jammed without warning. The wooden fragmentation bullets weren't ideal for cycling through the weapon at such a frenetic rate. He knew he would catch hell about it from Whistler later, but for the moment, he let the rifle drop to the floor.

Reaching back behind him, he grabbed the sword in a two-handed grip and pulled it free of the sheath.

Schinggg!

Three feet of acid-etched titanium alloy floated naturally into position before him, sharp enough to cleave a shadow in half. He had taken his name from the weapon, and with it, there wasn't a threat he wouldn't stand against.

Two vampires rushed him, claws outstretched.

Blade met them, sliding into a martial-arts kata, the sword flashing in his hands as he let his natural skills take over. He carried the sword high, hands tilted back to put the point down. At the last minute he stepped aside, avoiding the vampires. He whipped the sword around in a blinding arc, cutting at their waists, stepping through the blow and knowing they wouldn't be a threat any longer.

The keen edge slid through undead vampire flesh. One of the creatures died in pieces, while the other died nearly so. All of those pieces incinerated, turning to ash before they hit the floor. At the other end of the club, the final vampire Blade saw in the room made a break for the door through which Mercury had disappeared.

Setting himself, the Hunter hurled a silver throwing knife toward the fleeing vampire. It flipped end over end till it caught up with the creature, hitting it and impaling it through the heart against the white-tiled wall with a loud thunk.

For a moment the vampire fought against the knife, struggling like a butterfly pinned to a specimen board. When the creature went limp a moment later, it combusted and turned to ash.

Blade crossed the room. The music ended abruptly as the final song crashed through the audio system. He fisted the knife hilt and pulled the weapon free of the wall. Nothing appeared to be moving in the club except the man on the floor.

Blade looked out on the carnage and felt a grim satisfaction. The strike had gone well, perhaps better than he'd planned. But the number of vampires who had gathered there surprised him. Frost was getting brave, the Hunter thought, allowing his disciples to get even wilder in their predatory play.

As he walked back across the room, he sensed something rising up behind him. None of his natural senses told him of the coming attack. It all came from the combat skills he'd honed fighting this particular enemy for so many years.

Blade whirled, bringing the sword across and down.

The big vampire creeping up on him from behind moved with agile suppleness away from the blade.

Before Blade could pull himself back into proper form the vampire slammed into him, knocking him back thirty feet.

Blade tumbled over tables and chairs, unable to stop his headlong sprawl until he smashed up against the rear wall of the club so hard that tiles fell from the wall and the ceiling. He tried to push himself to his feet and reach for his sword, but his body ached all over from the impact, and the vampire was on him too quickly.

The creature was feral-faced, hardly recognizable. He had biker-length red hair and a matching beard that made him look even more demonic. He held a long knife in one hand and reared his head back and howled in insane glee, repeatedly smashing the knife into Blade's chest. The vampire's greater size and weight momentarily gave him the physical advantage.

The armor stopped the knife point from penetrating, but the impacts still struck with bruising force. Gathering himself, the Hunter shoved the vampire back, finally recognizing the creature.

"Quinn," Blade said quietly. A small, cruel smile curved his lips. He set himself into a martial-arts stance as the vampire came back at him. He avoided the knife by weaving to the side, then unleashed a series of punches that smashed into the vampire's morphed face with meaty pops. None of them would have a lasting effect on the creature, but it served to keep Quinn off-balance. Getting the rhythm and the weight behind him, Blade hit the vampire full in the face.

The vampire slid across the length of the room, fetching up hard against the opposite wall. A human heartbeat later, Quinn pushed himself to his feet, getting ready to charge again.

Blade slid the customized shotgun from the sheath on his leg. His motions, as always, remained conservative and calm. He flicked the release catch and brought it up. Without a wasted movement, Blade lined up his shot, squeezed the trigger, and put a silver stake through the vampire's shoulder.

The stake slid through Quinn's flesh with an audible slick hiss, catching the creature in midleap. The force of the projectile shoved him back against the wall. Still moving, the stake punched through the shoulder and nailed the vampire to the wall.

Quinn growled and reached up with his other hand for the silver stake.

Walking toward his opponent, Blade immediately fired a second time.

The second stake struck Quinn in the other shoulder, jerking the creature back. Pinned by the silver shafts, Quinn hung on the wall as the Hunter approached.

Blade smiled, and knew the expression carried nothing joyful about it. It was pure show for Quinn, something the vampire could take back to his leader when he regenerated. Vampires as old and as strong as Quinn were damned hard to kill, and he didn't have the time to finish the job now.

He sheathed the shotgun. Lifting the sword between them, rubbing it in how helpless Quinn was, Blade shook his head. "I'm getting a little tired of hacking you into pieces." He sheathed the sword down his back.

"Fuck you, Blade," Quinn snarled. "You just got lucky this time—"

Blade ignored the tirade. All the elder vampires he'd killed at leisure had something to say at the end. It came with a long life. Already dead once, they seemed unable or unwilling to comprehend that it could happen again. He unclipped an incendiary grenade from his combat harness and slipped the pin. "Thought I'd try fire for a change."

Quinn cursed loud and long, with an appreciable amount of color.

Blade was impressed. But he shook the grenade's spoon loose all the same. "If you make it through again, say hi to Frost for me. Let him know I'm coming." He tossed the incendiary grenade at the vampire, watching it roll just short of the creature's feet.

Quinn started screaming as Blade turned and walked away. The vampire was still screaming when the grenade went off with a *whoomph!* of exploding fuel mixture.

Blade felt the heat rush across his back like a thousand fleeing mice. It was almost hot enough to blister. He turned, pushing the wraparound sunglasses up with a forefinger.

Quinn ignited, burning immediately. The vampire howled as the flames consumed him.

Blade turned his attention back to the rest of the room, making sure nothing lived. Or still *un*lived. He shifted his gaze to the man huddled in the corner. Even from a few feet away, the Hunter's sensitive nostrils could detect the distinct odor of ammonia coming from the man. He walked over to him.

The man cringed back in wide-eyed fear. "Please don't—"

Blade ignored the plaintive cry, grabbing the man by the jaw. He tilted his head upward and rotated it from side to side. He didn't see any bite marks. Evidently the guy was luckier than he ever knew. He had survived the evening alive and untainted.

The sound of police sirens echoed down the stairway. Blade turned, gazing at the door as he heard footsteps.

Getting caught by the police wasn't part of the plan.

CHAPTER

3

Dennis Tohler looked up into the black-lensed gaze of the armor-clad man holding his head and saw his entire short life flash across those unforgiving twin screens. The man's fingers felt cold and strong as steel. Dennis had the impression the man could probably squash his face like an eggshell simply by closing that hand.

He couldn't believe he had pissed himself. And all he could do now was sit there in wet pants while the guy in black decided whether he wanted to rip his face off.

The sound of the police sirens was music to his ears. The cold, steely grip on his face relaxed. The man turned and walked away without a word, pausing only to recover his abandoned assault rifle and leather longcoat. Then he was gone, out the same door some of the other partygoers had escaped.

The burning vampire continued to howl in pain.

Dennis stared at it. Flames wrapped completely around the man's body. Anyone else, any-*thing* else, would already have been dead, either from the wounds or the lack of oxygen. Dennis had learned that while in the soaps, when his character threatened one of the show's heroines, telling her she would be lucky if she died of asphyxiation rather than burning.

The police broke down the door, spilling into the room the way they did on all the episodes of *Cops*, yelling and screaming at whoever might have been in the room, taking charge of the situation. Uniforms and guns were everywhere.

"Put your hands on your goddamned head!" an officer with a crew cut ordered.

Dennis put his hands on his head. "Don't shoot! I didn't do anything! Don't shoot!"

"Don't move!" the officer ordered.

"I'm not moving, I'm not moving!"

"Facedown on the floor, hands behind your back!" The officer kept his shotgun leveled.

"I'm lying down, just don't fucking shoot!" Dennis fell forward on his chest, keeping his hands tucked behind his back. He turned his head so he wouldn't breathe in the black ash scattered across the room. Christ, it would be about right that he survived a nest of vampires only to be blown away by those who were supposed to protect and serve.

Somebody clamped handcuffs around his wrists, locking them down tight. Dennis breathed easier. This routine was more familiar than anything else that had happened to him tonight.

"Anybody else still breathing?" the officer demanded.

"No," someone called back. "You got the only perp on-site."

The flaming vampire's howls continued.

Dennis watched in horror as the creature tried to yank free of the silver stakes pinning him to the wall. He hadn't thought he could survive. But it was only anything human that wouldn't have. These were vampires. And the cops didn't have a clue. He turned his head, looking up at the officer above him. "You gotta—"

"Shut up," the man said, shoving the shotgun into his face.

Dennis shut up.

"Get the paramedics in here!" someone yelled. "This poor bastard on the wall is still alive!"

Dennis watched in silence as white-suited paramedics ran down the stairway carrying bright red fire extinguishers. They hosed the vampire off with a cloud of roiling white CO_2 mist, not stopping till all the flames were quenched.

When they were finished, the vampire hung limp from the stakes through his shoulders and looked like a macabre snowman that had been burned around the edges.

One of the paramedics stumbled back, gagging as he dropped the fire extinguisher. "Christ, what a mess!"

Dennis found himself surrounded by police, thinking it looked like he was on the reunion set of *Hill Street Blues*. He looked around, taking in the piles of ash and the blood-drenched walls. There weren't any bodies left. Except for the one hanging on the wall. And Dennis was getting a really bad feeling about that body because he hadn't turned to ash as well.

The officer with the crew cut and the big shotgun pinned Dennis with his gaze. "What happened here?" He nodded at the vampire on the wall. "Who did this?"

Dennis tried to answer, his actor's soul reacting to all the attention he was getting. But he couldn't come up with one damn line.

Blade climbed up to an access grating in the street and got out. He moved the heavy grating back into place effortlessly, the scraping noise covered by the sounds of police cars, fire trucks, and emergency vehicles continuing to arrive at the scene.

He stood in the nearby alley across from the meatpacking plant, cloaked in the shadows. He still felt anxious despite the way things had gone. His training and the special senses he'd developed, which had helped keep him alive this long, told him it wasn't over.

Flexing his body as he watched, he checked

himself to make sure that Quinn's attack had only resulted in some sore muscles and bruises, nothing that would hamper him. It always took time to find the vampires and set up a means to execute them. The attacks were much shorter than the recon and research that went into an operation. Attending to those details always gave him too much time to think, too much time on his hands.

Whistler kept himself focused through his grief. Blade had only his anger, and he had to keep it in delicate balance. Anger all too often lacked real direction, shifted fronts without any kind of notification. It took real effort to make it work for him instead of against him.

He watched in silence, certain that no one would even know he was there unless he wanted them to. He pulled the longcoat back on, concealing his weapons again. The assault rifle was cleared and ready for action again, and the MACH was fully charged.

After a while, the paramedics brought out Quinn's body. The creature's corpse lay under a white sheet. Smoke still curled above it as the overheated flesh cooled.

The police had put up a barrier of sawhorses and yellow tape, but a few of the more adventurous reporters who by now had arrived at the scene surged forward to get some footage and pictures of the "victim."

Blade smiled, thinking how many of those reporters would be surprised at how the pictures and video footage turned out. Vampires had never been photogenic.

The paramedics put the gurney in the back of the ambulance, deliberately keeping the doors open a little longer to allow the media the opportunity to photograph the body. Everything hinged on sensationalism these days, and the public did its bit to provide some.

Finally, the doors to the ambulance closed, and it moved through the tangle of vehicles and people.

Blade watched the ambulance pass, then put his hands in the pockets of the longcoat and turned his steps toward the street, walking down the sidewalk. No one noticed him, as he lost himself in the circus of thrill seekers the police were attempting to control.

CHAPTER

4

"**G**ot a charred cadaver for you. Still warm, too."

Curtis Webb, forensic pathologist at the Metro Hospital, looked up as his assistant wheeled the bagged corpse into the autopsy room. Webb, his boyish good looks drawn in a look of atypical seriousness, wore his pale maroon scrubs like a badge of office. His brown hair was parted neatly on the right, cut every two weeks because he liked looking at the same man in the mirror every day without having to wonder if he needed a haircut. He was in his late twenties, and had already earned a high position at Metro.

He paused in the middle of taking down pre-liminary information on the hit-and-run victim that had moved up on his schedule. She had been well over the public-intoxication standard, proba-bly making the case for the driver that the woman had stepped out in front of the car. If the driver hadn't fled the scene. Now there was a hunt for that driver, and police detectives needed the information only he could give them. He dropped another paint chip he had removed from her right cheek into the glass evidence vial he'd already marked.

"What have you got?" he asked.

"Definite murder with intent," the assistant said, locking down the brakes on the gurney's wheels.

"Killings at this time of night are not an unusual occurrence," Webb said. But the distinct, sweet smell of burned flesh interested him all the same. He took pride in his work. "What makes this one so special that they're bumping the roadkill I'm already working on?"

"Guy who did it," the assistant said, "is still on the loose. Homicide detectives want whatever you can get as soon as you can get it."

Webb still played hard to get, reading the assistant's need for his moment of glory. He denied it, keeping the man in check. No one worked the autopsy room on Dr. Curtis Webb's shift without knowing that Dr. Curtis Webb ran that damn room while he was there. He liked it the way it was now: polished and gleaming, everything in its place.

"Did they round up the usual suspects?" Webb asked. "The mother? The father? The lover?" He replaced a used scalpel on the tray and reached up to adjust the microphone suspended from the ceiling in front of him. "Most murders do occur around the home."

The assistant was rawboned and rough. His hair was cut short and tinted a virulent green. Earrings ran in a row on both sides of his head, and piercings glinted in one eyebrow and his lower lip. "Yeah, well this ain't your regular murder. Detectives are wanting the information quick as they can get it because they're thinking the guy might try to pull it off again."

"Try what again?"

The assistant shook his head. "Uh-uh. You get to take a look. Get it cold. Just like me. Came close to hurling this time. One of those commode-hugging, morning-after feelings." He slapped his flat stomach.

And that enticed Webb even more. Nothing had ever made Mickey Toland throw up. "They think this might be a serial?" he asked. He had worked serial murders before, and loved the way the press flocked around him when they found out he was on the case.

Toland grinned. "That's the whisper I got."

"Well, I guess I should take a peek, then." Webb crossed the room and unzipped the body bag. The stink of burned meat hit him at once. No charcoal cookout ever had that particular scent.

The body lay inside the bag, burned so badly the weakened stomach tissue had burst sometime during the transit and worked at eviscerating the corpse. The face didn't even look human, more like some kind of animal. The limbs were contorted from the agony that had preceded death.

"Jesus, that's rank," Webb said. He prodded at the chunks of burned tissue with forceps from the equipment tray. Crusty bits of it pulled loose easily. He laid them inside the bag next to the body. "What's his story?"

"Paramedic I talked to said he was still screaming when they found him. Looks like some joker had stapled him to a wall."

Webb glanced up past the coiled mass of burned intestines and exploded juices and blood. He saw the gleaming silver stakes in the dead man's shoulders. "Pretty."

"I gotta get back," Toland said. "Reorganize a few bodies. Enjoy." He left the room.

Webb turned to his work, becoming increasingly interested. Violent death held such an attraction.

Karen Jansen studied the slide through the microscope, feeling Curtis Webb's eyes roving all over her and trying not to lose her temper. Whenever she argued with him, it only opened the door to more conversation. And that was the last thing she wanted from him tonight. Well, next to the last thing anyway.

The slide had been treated with Wright stain, so it left a blue color for the doughnut-shaped pink of the red blood cells to show up against the blue specks of platelets. The white blood cells were larger and fewer, paler blue.

"How's it going?" Webb asked, handing her one of the cups of coffee he carried.

"You took this off a DOA?" Karen asked. She was five-eight and trim, kept in shape through good genes and aerobics. Her skin was milk chocolate against Webb's tanning-booth color. She wore her black hair to her shoulders, and it had a lot of body when she took the time to work at it.

"Yeah," Webb answered after a moment.

The slow response told Karen that he was in the process of trying to look down her blouse as she bent over the microscope. She leaned back, not letting herself address him till she had counted to five. Twice. Then she looked at him. "This isn't making any sense."

Webb nodded. "That's what I was getting, and why I brought a sample to you."

Karen smothered a yawn as she looked around the hematology lab. Papers lay in disarray on the countertops. She knew that aggravated Webb, but she knew where every piece of paper was. Working method was only one of the differences they found they had—too late. She pushed back from the microscope, indicating Webb should study the slide while she talked. "Look at this blood smear."

Webb crossed the room, deliberately standing almost too close to her. He fitted his eye to the microscope.

Karen delivered the information as she would to one of the medical groups she lectured to, reminding him that blood was *her* field and she knew it as well as he did his. "The red blood cells are *biconvex*, which is theoretically impossible. They're hypochromic, there's virtually no hemoglobin in them." She shook her head, not believing she had fallen for one of Webb's ploys to get her attention. But he'd seemed so sincere when he had phoned a few minutes ago.

Webb nodded. "Look at the POLYs, they're binucleated."

"They should be *mononucleated*." Karen wondered how Webb had spoofed the blood test. Even during her graduate days, she'd never seen anything like this. So strange it had to be fake; yet so real it had to be, well, *real*.

Webb lifted the sheet of paper he held, revealing it to be a computer printout. "Did you check the chem panel? Blood-sugar level is three times the norm, phosphorous and uric acid are off the scales."

Karen took a deep breath through her nose and let it out through her mouth. She had a headache all of a sudden, and knew who was responsible. "All right, Curtis, very clever. I don't know how you worked this up, but it's *three* in the morning, and I'm *really* not in the mood." And that was another thing that had ultimately divided them despite the chemistry that was there only a few months ago: his own warped sense of humor.

Webb looked indignant, favoring her with one of the practiced glares that usually worked so well with nurses and interns. "This isn't a joke. I've got the body sitting in the morgue right now."

Karen didn't buy into the act, no matter how good it was. Self-righteousness was an art form where Curtis Webb was concerned. She returned his gaze full measure, crossing her arms over her breasts because she knew Webb had a habit of unconsciously gazing at them when he talked to her. "I thought you promised to give me some distance?"

Exasperation showed in Webb's body language, and that wasn't something Karen had seen a lot of. Unless it was in a full-blown Oscar contender. "What are you talking about?" he demanded. "I just want you to take a look at this."

Karen was surprised at the sincerity in his voice. She rolled her eyes to let him know in advance that she wasn't buying into any of it. She sighed, letting him hear that, too. "Okay, all right, show me the body. But I don't want to hear a *word* about *us*."

Webb shrugged like it was no big deal. "Done. We've had that conversation."

She took up the research notebook she'd been writing in before he had arrived and deliberately made no effort to clean up her desk area. When Webb didn't comment on that, she became even more intrigued.

•   •   •

Karen watched Webb work over the body on the autopsy table. Her breath puffed lightly against the mask she wore over her nose and mouth. One thing she did still like about Webb was watching him operate. He had deft, sure hands, and an air of confidence that broke just short of egotistical, the way a good curveball broke over the corner of the plate. He was good, and he knew it.

He stood on the other side of the autopsy table, the corpse spread between them like some insane feast. He had already marked the preliminary exploratory Y-incision for males across the dead man's chest, reaching from shoulder to shoulder. But he had yet to start cutting.

The silver stakes embedded in the dead man's shoulders had shocked Karen, as had the burns. Webb hadn't mentioned anything about them. Of course, he wouldn't. In his line of work, it just wasn't that interesting. It made Karen glad that she worked where she did, away from all the hurt and violence that otherwise normal, rational people could do to each other.

"You haven't started on the internal organs?" she asked.

"Just the blood sample from the pericardial sac." Webb leaned closer, studying the corpse's face. "That's weird."

Karen looked up from the burned flesh, grateful for the distraction. The Vick's VapoRub she used to block the stench only blunted the odor. "What?"

Webb appeared uncertain. "Hmm, I thought his injuries were more extreme than this."

Karen pulled out a pen flash and flicked it on. Mesmerized by the contorted face of the dead man, she shone it into the corpse's open mouth. Slipping a probe from one of her smock pockets, she poked at the dead man's gums. "The maxilla looks a little deformed, and there are some odd muscle structures around the canines, the hard palate."

Webb picked up a scalpel and leaned over his subject's face. "I'm going to open the trachea and check for smoke inhalation." The gleaming edge slid into the burned flesh easily. The crack of the fire-hardened skin seemed to fill the room.

Karen shivered in spite of herself.

Webb glanced up at her, real concern in his eyes. "You going to be okay?"

"I'm going to be just fine," she said in a voice thicker than she wanted.

"I know it's been a while since you were around for anything like this."

She cut him off, bringing the conversation back to the professional level she had decided to operate on. "Get on with it."

"Tell me something," Webb said, probing with the scalpel, "*honestly*, you ever have second thoughts about us?"

Karen was angry that he'd brought the subject up after promising not to. But at least it took her mind off the bloody corpse. However, she also didn't want to fight. "Sometimes." She gave him that, hoping he would stay mollified and leave it alone. Because she had thought about them, and wished things could have been different. But they weren't.

Webb, however, wasn't inclined to leave things alone. He looked up from the corpse and gave her a grin she could see even under his mask.

"But then I remember what an asshole you were," Karen went on.

Webb shook his head, negating what she'd said. "Come on, cut me a little slack here. I'm trying. *Really*. You wanted time to cool off, you've had it."

She bit back an angry retort. She was on the verge of walking out and leaving him with his corpse, but wanted to draw the line again, too. And at the same time, she didn't want to hurt him. At times he was so much like a little kid. That was partly what had drawn her to him. "Look, I'm sorry, Curtis, but it's over. Why can't you understand that?" She had more to say, but what occurred during the next few seconds drove it right out of her mind.

Without warning, the corpse surged up from the autopsy table. The dead man wrapped his long fingers around Webb's neck. The corpse's mouth opened, revealing the long incisors that gleamed pearly white in the strong light available in the room. Then the corpse bit down, sinking them into Webb's neck. And blood seemed to spurt everywhere.

Karen pushed herself back, stumbling, trying to force a scream for help from her paralyzed lungs.

Webb tried to fight, tried to escape. But the corpse handled him as easily as if Webb were a child. The massive hand snapped Webb's neck. As the doctor's musculature relaxed in death, the corpse flopped his head back farther, allowing easier access to the neck. The dead man drank thirstily, sounding like a vacuum cleaner as he sucked in the blood.

Karen reached for the door behind her, finding it with real effort. The scream still wouldn't come. She watched the dead man rise from the table, tossing Webb's body to one side.

The dead man grinned at her, raking back blood-soaked lips to bare gleaming viper fangs in his charred beard. His throat lay open from the scalpel, healing as she watched, the flesh knitting back together. He gave a guttural growl as he pushed himself off the table and came at her.

CHAPTER

5

Karen burst through the swinging doors into the corridor. Hospital staff filled the hallway ahead of her. As she ran, she tried to remember how to speak. Even over the din of voices, she heard the dead man running behind her, his bare feet slapping against the tiled floor.

The boom of the doors when the ambulatory corpse passed through sounded like thunder.

Karen shoved aside an empty gurney, then pulled it around as a defense. She knew instantly she shouldn't have done that, because it gave her another look at the dead man. Her mind whirled, grasping for explanations—no matter how far-fetched. The dead man wasn't dead from the burns and the wounds because he'd been on PCP or crack or any of the other drugs for sale out on the street that pushed the human body past the point of death. *OhmigodCurtisisdead*! Consciousness had returned on the autopsy table, perhaps triggered by the new pain or the strong lights registering against the back of the brain even through closed eyes. *Snappedhisnecklikeacheapwineglass*! He wasn't dead, and he was coming straight for her, still growling.

No one came to help her. Even the orderlies she'd watched handle prisoners brought in by the police—dementia-crazed alcoholics, drug users scooped up from the street, and adrenaline-laced body builders working out a steroid craze—gave ground before the hideous apparition lunging at her across the gurney.

The dead man's hand closed around her throat, choking off her air with bruising force. The gurney went down in a collapsed tangle of warped metal.

Karen put both hands on the dead man's wrist and tried to get away. Pressure points she remembered from self-defense class didn't work. She kicked the man, trying to catch him in the groin.

The dead man only grinned, exposing those impossibly long fangs again. "Too weak," he said in a voice that sounded as if it had been squeezed out from between two flat rocks.

Karen swung at the end of his arm, her feet inches off the floor. He was so strong.

Snappedhisnecklikeacheapwineglass! Out of the corner of her eye she saw the panicked crowd of orderlies and nurses drawing back. Nobody wanted any part of the dead man.

Then she saw the night duty nurse on the phone.

Karen couldn't remember the woman's name but knew whom the woman would be calling. Police officers stayed around the hospital with one case or another nearly all day in this section of the city.

She continued struggling, watching as the dead man's face seemed to open and become all mouth and fangs. His features blurred in her fading vision. Then she couldn't see his face anymore because he'd buried his fangs in the side of her neck, drinking deeply from her carotid artery.

The cold, burning sensation that ran through her torn throat headed straight for her spinal cord. She felt it spread, bringing with it an instant paralysis.

The dead man nursed at her neck. She heard the slobbering sounds he made and knew he was sucking down her blood the same way he had with Webb's. And she couldn't even fight back, could only hang there helpless from that impossibly strong grip.

The guttural growls shifted to sounds of pleasure, of conquest.

Karen felt the blood rushing through her mind, but it was weaker than she'd ever felt it. And it grew steadily weaker as she felt faint.

At first, when she saw the black-gloved hand reaching over the dead man's shoulder, she thought she was hallucinating. Then the fingers knotted in the corpse's burned hair, gaining leverage as the hand yanked the head back.

The dead man pulled his fangs from Karen's

neck and looked up at the man dressed all in black. The corpse released his hold then, letting Karen drop bonelessly to the floor.

She tried to move, but the paralysis still gripped her. She could only watch helplessly as the dead man squared off against his attacker.

"Well, well, just as I figured," the man in black said softly.

"Blade," the vampire said. His face pulled back in a rictus of a smile. "Welcome to the feast."

"Came back to finish you off," Blade said.

Karen watched the black-gloved hands, almost too fast for the eye to follow, as Blade powered short jabs into Quinn and drove the monster away. She wanted to scream out a warning, tell the man in black that the dead man was too impossibly strong, that he would need more than just fast hands to kill the creature. It surprised her when she realized thinking of the dead man as a creature somehow seemed more natural.

Quinn staggered under Blade's attack, alternately trying to swing at him and cover up. "Get out of my way, you freak!"

"Ride's over," Blade said. "My mistake in letting you live this long." He delivered a spinning back kick, driving the bigger man away.

Karen couldn't believe Blade actually appeared to be winning. Some movement returned to her. Weakly, she put a hand to her neck, thinking she needed to have pressure to stop the wound from bleeding because she could feel blood coursing warmly down her neck. Mesmerized by the savagery she'd been victim to, she pulled her hand away and gazed fearfully at the blood staining her hand. There was so much of it. She struggled to control the sudden hysteria that gripped her, finally able to force her hand back onto the wound, knowing she should never have looked. She took her first real breath since the dead man had locked his hand around her throat. It burned, but brought more feeling back, including the incredible pain.

Roaring loudly, Quinn reached for a portable electrocardiogram unit sitting on a wheeled table. Incredibly, the vampire lifted and threw it easily.

Blade moved fluidly, dodging the machine and ripping a sword free of a scabbard on his back. The gleaming edge whispered through the air, then flashed at Quinn.

The big creature moved quicker than Karen would have thought possible, but didn't completely get away. The sword severed his arm, dropping it free below the elbow. But before it could hit the floor, the hand and forearm exploded into a cloud of black ash.

With Quinn off-balance, Blade moved on the vampire. Karen saw the pitiless expression on Blade's face and wondered what his eyes looked like behind those black-lensed sunglasses. Would they be narrow and hard, or would they be open, as if this was business as usual? He was the only person in the hallway who hadn't seemed surprised to see the dead man drinking her blood.

Blade shifted points of balance, getting ready to swing the sword again. Quinn appeared helpless.

Then the sound of shots filled the hallway. When Karen heard the shots, she expected to see policemen firing on the dead man. She was surprised to see Blade take a half step back like he had been hit instead.

Blade spun, looking back down the hallway past Karen. "What the fuck are you doing?"

Karen managed to turn her head. At the other end of the hall, two security guards stood with their weapons drawn. My God, she thought, they had been the ones who had fired, not trained police officers. How could they have made such a mistake? She tried to find her voice, to tell them they were shooting at the wrong man. Or *had* shot the wrong man. She remembered the way Blade had rocked back.

Then movement behind Karen yanked her attention away from the security guards and Blade. Her mind screamed at her to move, that the dead man was coming for her again.

When she looked, though, she saw the dead man running flat out for the window at the end of the hallway. As soon as he got within range, he hurled himself forward, smashing the glass into a thousand gleaming shards as he went through.

Karen knew they were four floors up from street level, over the emergency-room exit. There was no way the dead man would survive the fall.

Was there?

CHAPTER

6

Quinn flew through the air. He stared down at the street four stories below, then noticed that he hung for a moment over a parked ambulance. He fell, flailing with his single remaining arm and not quite able to get his balance.

Quinn wanted to laugh because the vampire knew he had escaped. The fall wasn't going to kill him, and neither was Blade. Though it had been surprising to see the Hunter at the hospital. Quinn had to get back to Frost, tell Frost that the Day-Walker was here, that he had somehow found them again, and the killing would start anew.

The creature wrapped his arm over his face to protect it as he crashed through the top of the ambulance. Not that the face needed protecting. As long as the vampire had plenty of blood, he could grow himself a new one. Same as he would regrow the arm Blade had taken tonight. Only the young vampires at the club had died again.

Metal screeched and tore as Quinn hammered through the vehicle's roof, hitting a gurney and smashing it flatter than it had been, winding up next to an old woman strapped to it. She stared at Quinn in apoplectic fear, eyes wide over the oxygen mask fogging up with her labored breathing. The paramedic with her cowered away, dazed.

Quinn gazed at her, for a moment thinking about taking her blood as well. But the special radar he had been gifted with the night he'd risen from the dead as a vampire told him there wasn't much energy left in the tired old crimson that flowed sluggishly through her veins and arteries. The creature smelled the coming death on her.

Even strapped to the gurney as she was, she managed to cringe away from him.

The vampire pushed himself up on his remaining arm and growled at her, feeling the savage glee as she struggled against her bonds. Sheep had reason to be afraid of the wolf.

Quinn turned and kicked the back doors of the ambulance open with ease now that his full strength was returning. It wrenched and tore the hinges, leaving the two doors hanging haphazardly. His two *donors* had possessed healthy blood that he was glad to have taken.

The vampire started to climb out the back of the ambulance, knowing that the law-enforcement teams would begin the hunt. And Blade would be there somewhere around them.

Quinn vaulted from the back of the ambulance and ran into the night. The new blood flowed within, moving to repair all the damage that had been done to his body. He was alive, and it would be Blade who died the final death. Frost would see to that. Frost was working on getting more power, and was going to be stronger than Blade had ever counted on.

The Old Secrets were going to be found once more.

Blade stared at the empty window that Quinn had leaped through. A few steps and he knew he would be stepping in the vampire's shadow again. Quinn couldn't get away. Blade's back still hurt from being shot, guaranteeing a bruise, but the Kevlar armor had stopped the bullet.

A mewling sound came from behind him.

Blade turned, the sword still heavy in his hand. He gazed down at the woman bleeding her life away on the floor. He knew what she had coming, and he blamed himself for it. Quinn was an old vampire, a strong vampire. His bite was *way* worse than his bark.

The nurses and orderlies moved toward the security guards. Evidently the hospital staff knew most of them. They also served to block the guards from Blade.

"Please," the woman said in a thin whisper. "Someone help me."

Blade gazed at her, keeping his level of involvement nonexistent. She was just a civilian who had gotten caught in the war. Civilians died all the time. He was fighting to keep all of them from dying. It came down to a choice: get Quinn or try to help the woman. He figured he had a better chance of nailing Quinn.

Without warning, the old memory ghosted out of the past and touched the Hunter, chilling him to the bone. His mother's voice hung in his ears, a plea thirty years gone that hadn't saved her. Blade remembered her voice, remembered the smell of all the blood, and remembered all the pain they'd both gone through.

"Put the gun down, buddy!" one of the security guards ordered, trying to push through the hospital staff.

"Not him!" one of the nurses yelled hysterically. "He was only trying to help! It was the other one!"

Blade sheathed the sword and crossed over to the woman, watching her eyes widen as she focused on him. She shook her head, definitely not enamored of the idea of going with him.

A small knot of policemen arrived, filling the corridor. "Get down now!" someone yelled. "Now!" A pistol blasted.

Blade bent down and scooped the woman up effortlessly as he watched the hospital staff go to cover on the ground or behind the desk. The policemen would have shooting room in seconds. But they saw him with the woman and hesitated. In that moment, the Hunter crossed the corridor back to the broken window. He peered out, evaluating his escape routes.

The best, the one the woman seemed most likely to survive, was the rooftop of the parking building adjacent to the hospital. Thirty feet lay between him and that building.

The woman pushed at him, trying to break free. She was weak. Even had she been at full strength, she couldn't have broken free, and Blade knew it.

The policemen opened fire behind him. The bullets thudded into the hospital walls, shattering picture frames, potted plants, and ripping into a nearby couch. And they hit Blade, only to be stopped by the Kevlar lining in the longcoat.

Setting himself, hearing the woman begin to scream because she realized what he was going to do—or at least thought she did—Blade threw her.

CHAPTER

7

The woman sailed through the window. Blade watched in satisfaction as she arced without spinning and came down on the rooftop of the adjacent building.

When she came down, though, she hit hard, landing on her shoulder and instantly clutching it in pain. She tried weakly to get to her feet.

Blade watched her in silent appreciation. She had a lot of courage. Then he lost admiration for her because he knew she had become a ticking bomb, potentially dangerous even to him. He stepped into the window frame, hammered by bullets from behind as screams laced with the sounds of gunfire, and leaped.

He almost made the thirty feet to the other building. It was one thing to use his body weight to throw something that far, but another to heave that same body weight across the distance. Knowing he was falling short, he lunged in midair, stretching out the length of his body, barely able to wrap the fingers of one hand over the rooftop's edge. He slammed into the building hard enough to hurt himself, even under the protective gear. The rough brick scoured his cheek as he reached up with his other hand. When he had the grip he needed, he pulled himself up.

Bullets drilled into the parking building as the police officers filling the hospital windows fired at him.

From the ledge, Blade saw other police cars arriving, squealing to tire-eating stops in front of the emergency-room entrance. Quinn was nowhere to be seen.

Having hauled himself up, Blade stayed low, rolling across the rooftop to crouch next to the woman. She looked up at him, tears streaming down her face as she held her injured arm. "My shoulder—dislocated."

Blade glanced at her injured arm and saw that the shoulder had been dislocated in the fall. Putting one hand on her shoulder and another on her elbow, moving too quickly to allow her to respond, he brutally popped the shoulder back into place.

She passed out.

He felt bad about that, a little, but decided he didn't have the luxury. There were things a lot worse that could happen to the woman after being bitten by Quinn. He picked her up, holding her tight against him.

He jogged across the rooftop, breathing easily, her weight not slowing him down in the slightest. His mind worked quickly, juggling all the variables the scene at the hospital had brought into play. Whistler had taught him that focus, and it had saved Blade's life when he thought he'd left humanity far behind.

The rooftop access door was locked when he reached it. He placed a hand on the corner and set himself, catching the flash of movement from the periphery of his vision as a police sniper with a rifle settled into one of the hospital's windows. He yanked on the steel door and it groaned, rivets popping, as the hinges tore loose. The first rifle bullet slammed into the door as he ducked inside.

His car was nearby, and normally he would have left it behind and come back for it later. But where a guy in a black longcoat walking down the street might be ignored, a guy in a black longcoat carrying a woman under one arm definitely wouldn't be. Not even in this city.

He took the stairs down, fast-stepping through two landings to the second floor, where he'd left his car.

Dim bulbs illuminated the parking garage, casting gray shadows around the stained white cinder block. Graffiti lined some of the walls, and the stink of piss and vomit hung in the air.

The woman settled down in his arms, regaining partial consciousness and crying silently. He felt her body jerking in his grip, and it touched him in a way he'd never experienced. Emotions were things he'd viewed for a long time from a distance, things he worked to stay away from. Whistler had saved him from the madness of despair and taught him that those feelings were a vortex that could suck him down and make him lose the thin edge of control.

Blade knew that the only way he could survive in the world was to become the void that was the epitome of martial arts. Whatever the woman made him feel, it was only borrowed emotion, and in another moment or two he would distance himself from it again, put it back on the shelf.

He didn't have the luxury of emotion.

The car stood next to a yellow-striped support post. Dark gray, the 1969 Dodge Charger was the definition of a high-performance, heavy-metal muscle machine. The weak light seemed to be absorbed in the custom paint.

He opened the passenger door and put the woman down. Closing the door, he went around in front, moving quickly now because he knew the police would be trying to cordon off the area.

The woman watched him, her wet eyes focused on his sunglasses. When he was over halfway around, she tried the door latch, intending to escape.

Blade knew it was useless. The inner latch had been disconnected. When he put someone or

something in that seat, they didn't get out unless
he allowed it. He dropped behind the steering
wheel and keyed the ignition. The engine caught
immediately, sending a shiver throughout the
whole car as the throaty roar filled the parking
garage.

He shoved the gearshift into first and left rubber on the concrete floor. He *enjoyed* driving the
car, enjoyed the power and the way it handled.
Whistler may have preached about the evils of
emotion, but he hadn't said a damn thing about
not liking cars.

He threaded the muscle car through the parking garage, arriving at the main entrance in short
order on squealing tires. The parking attendant
lounged in his seat with his face buried in a comic
book, only looking up when he realized the car
wasn't slowing down. The attendant was in his
early twenties, dressed in a black T-shirt with a
caped and costumed hero on it. His jaw dropped
as the Charger slammed through the wooden
blocking arm. Pieces went back over the car.

Blade pulled the wheel hard, then pressed the
accelerator to the floor. The Charger lunged forward like a great cat, straightening out as the huge
power plant sprang to full life. Gunshots sounded
behind him. He glanced in the rearview mirror,
spotting the handful of police officers out in the
street in front of the emergency-room entrance.

He took the first right he came to, leaving the
hospital behind.

CHAPTER

8

O nce he was clear of the hospital zones and certain the Charger hadn't been made by one of the police officers on the scene, Blade slowed to just below the speed limit. Meanwhile, the woman's breathing deepened and she slept, giving in again to the pain.

The Hunter glanced at the woman as the lights from the downtown district played over her. She was pretty, even with the blood from her wound streaking the expensive blouse and the lab smock.

He left the radio off, listening to her steady breathing because that was more calming to him than anything else he could imagine. Now that the initial rush of adrenaline was starting to die down, he felt his concentration wavering. He knew that movement, or the preparation for movement, was his focus, the strongest of the threads that kept him together. His weakest times, when those cold fingers of uncertainty twisted through his heart, were in the moments immediately after a battle.

The woman's breathing deepened still more. He breathed with her, mimicking the calm pattern, feeling his focal point shift. He drove automatically, sorting through the cityscape with practiced economy. Knowing the terrain was the most basic element of any protracted engagement. Whistler had taught him well.

He experienced a split second of anxiety as a police car pulled up behind him and turned on its lights. He glanced at it in the rearview mirror and searched for running room in the lane with oncoming traffic.

Then the police car pulled away, swooping in to the curb where a guy was trying to hold on to two women in scanty clothing and shock hairdos. Evidently the guy was an undercover cop and had called for backup. The working girls hadn't appreciated getting arrested.

Blade watched them only a second longer, putting his foot on the accelerator and cruising by the line of cars starting to slow down to watch the sideshow. He practiced pacing his breathing with the woman's again, getting back into the serenity it promised.

The downtown district funneled directly into the warehouse district, where the city had been birthed and fleshed out, constructed in the huge monsters of factories, then built out around it. And every bit of the new city growth sapped the strength and will from the warehouse district, leaving only degenerated neighborhoods behind.

He made the final turn, still breathing with the unconscious woman, and drove down the two-lane street leading to the mammoth industrial facility ahead. The Charger rolled across a desolate railway track, powering past the freight train clacking by in the opposite direction.

Cyclone fencing topped with razor wire cordoned off the facility from the rest of the area. Floodlights stood silent sentry on top of poles and the fencing, casting what seemed a cool light. But Blade knew that all of the bulbs were ultraviolet. They were there to keep out the rough trade. There were also security cameras staggered around it with overlapping viewing fields. Maybe the bloodsuckers couldn't be photographed or videotaped easily, but they often used humans who could be.

Blade halted the car, his foot resting lightly on the brake. He rested in what felt like a light trance, hypnotized by the sound of the woman's breathing. It made him feel more peaceful than at any time in his life. It was an incredible discovery to make. Whistler had taught him the benefits of breathing, how to control it to get the maximum use of his muscles and effort, and how to use it to wait when there was nothing that could be done.

But he'd forgotten how restful simply breathing could be. His mind rolled back, reaching for a distant memory that offered comparison. Then the pain and fear that were associated with it kicked in as well.

He came out of the trance with a start and a choked gasp. His heart hammered inside his chest. Angry at himself, focusing on that old standby emotion that had taken him through so much of his life, he glanced at the unconscious woman and cursed the weakness she'd brought out in him. There was little chance of him saving her. And he wasn't a savior anyway; he was a hunter. Saviors had bright futures; hunters lived for the moment, for the kill.

He punched the remote secured to the sun visor.

In front of him, the gate ratcheted back into its housing. He paused, waiting till the electronic spikes built into the street at the entranceway also retracted, then he rolled in. The gate closed, and the spikes extended automatically behind him.

The remote also opened the bay doors of the building in front of him. Tall and squat, it resembled a watchtower from an old castle. And it was closely akin in purpose. He drove through the doors, extinguishing the headlights and the dashboard panel. Even in the womblike darkness he knew the way. He followed the concrete loading ramp down, twisting into the bowels of the building. A heavy iron door lifted in front of him.

He rolled on through and parked with precision. When the iron door behind him descended and locked into place, UV lights flickered on with thunderous humming, revealing the outlines of a massive industrial elevator. The humming grew louder, then the elevator bucked and started up. The UV lights remained on.

The industrial elevator stopped with a booming clang, and the rear doors opened. Putting the Charger in reverse, Blade turned to peer over the seat and rolled backward into the next room, where more light was provided by high-intensity UV lamps.

Whistler's workshop, set up in the old iron-works, looked like a cross between an auto junk-yard and an armory. Equipment was strewn throughout the large room, including mills, ancient furnaces, gutted vehicles, and an ad hoc surgical theater. All of it was jury-rigged to operate close to peak efficiency. Whistler wouldn't have things any other way. All of it looked brutal: dynamic need fused with low tech and polished by a sheen of oil.

Blade killed the Charger's engine and climbed out. He rounded the car, breathing deep, centered again, aware that his breathing pattern was different than the woman's. He could hear her even over the grind of a large industrial lathe turning over in the corner.

Removing the woman from the car, Blade turned and gazed at the slim, wiry silhouette working at the lathe. He knew Whistler was aware that he'd returned, knew that Whistler was aware he'd brought someone back. And Blade knew that Whistler was pissed because Blade had violated one of the firmest rules the older man had laid down in their relationship.

Blade raised his voice. "Whistler!"

The lathe continued grinding away, sparks jumping from the worked metal. Partially bound by the band securing the protective goggles to his bearded face, Whistler's long gray hair whipped around across the broad shoulders. He wore a sleeveless black tunic top and jeans tucked into motorcycle boots. A metal brace encased his right leg.

"Whistler!" Blade let some of the anger out in his voice. It was all the warning he needed to give, and it remained to be seen if the older man was going to take it as a challenge.

Whistler put the shaping tool down and switched the lathe off. He took time to hang the goggles neatly, then ran his hands through his hair, letting out a deep breath that could be heard over the lathe's brake kicking in. Then he took down the cane that had been a part of his life for many, many years.

He turned and hobbled out of the shadows. Gimlet-eyed, his face lined with wrinkles above the beard, his half sneer as bitter as green persimmons, he looked old.

Blade knew other people had made that mistake. Abraham Whistler had given up being a man long ago and chosen to become instead an unyielding force. The white-gold wedding ring on his left hand was a constant reminder of that commitment.

When he spoke, his voice was rough, heavy, and the sarcasm as strong as boiling carbolic acid. "We bringing home strays now?"

Had he let them, Blade knew the man's words would have hurt. The only person in the world that the Hunter let himself care about stood in front of him. Yet the woman hanging in his arms was mute testimony that he'd risked them both. Was *still* risking them. "She's been bitten," he stated flatly.

And Whistler would have known that anyway. He had seen plenty of vampire victims over the years of his personal crusade. The sound of the woman's breathing, the gray tone to her skin, all of those signs would have told him even if the wound on her neck hadn't been so apparent.

"Should have killed her, then," Whistler said.

"I know." Blade faced him, returning that pitiless gaze full measure, not wanting to admit that he couldn't even explain to himself why he had bothered to take the woman. "But I didn't."

For a moment the silence held between them, a tension that hadn't been in their lives before. Blade regretted it, wished he'd chased after Quinn instead, maybe even died if that proved to be a safe alternative, rather than risking his friendship with Whistler. But the confusion of the moment had only given him this choice.

Finally, Whistler turned and headed over to the operating theater. "You watch her close," he said in a matter-of-fact tone. "She starts to turn, you finish her off." On the other side of the hospital table, he faced Blade. "*Or I will.*"

And Blade didn't doubt that for a moment.

CHAPTER

9

Blade gently put the woman down on the operating table, then stepped back. Whistler knew more about medical problems than he did. He stood by, silently waiting.

Whistler switched on the overhead light, bathing the woman in the bright, unforgiving glare. He studied her in silence, his face giving nothing away.

The woman didn't look good. That much Blade knew. She was sheathed in sweat, and her milk-chocolate complexion looked ashen from blood loss. Quinn had been thirsty. Wounded vampires always were; regeneration required a hell of a payback.

Whistler snapped on a pair of green disposable surgical gloves. Taking an antiseptic swab, he probed the wound in the woman's neck. A lot of the capillary damage emanated from the punctures, and the tissue already looked slightly gangrenous. A bruised imprint of Quinn's hand stood out against her throat.

"Localized necrosis," Whistler said.

"Where does that leave us?" Blade asked.

Whistler glanced at him. "You. Not me."

Blade nodded slightly, accepting the judgment. "Me."

Whistler looked back down at the woman. "She's borderline. Another hour, and she'd be well into the Change."

Then she still had a chance. Blade accepted it with the stoicism that Whistler had given him, and which the old man had evidenced when he'd first seen the woman. Had there been no chance, Whistler would have put a silver stake through her heart. And Blade knew he would have let him.

"It was Quinn," Blade said.

Whistler glanced up, the first stirrings of interest on his lined face. "Frost's little errand boy? Did you get a lead on him?"

Blade shook his head.

"Too bad," Whistler said. "What happened?"

Blade told the story without inflection. Whistler already knew about Raquel, knew that Blade intended to follow the creature. The club at the meatpacking plant was a surprise.

"You took a risk walking into that," Whistler said.

Blade shook his head. "Not really. They were

mostly young vampires like Raquel. Still flaunting the difference, still involved in their own perception of immortality. Mercury got away. The rest died easy."

"Except for Quinn."

"Yeah."

"So you followed him to the hospital?" Whistler reached for a vial on the shelf nearby. Like everything else in the work space, the shelf was filled to overflowing. But the places that needed to be clean were clean. That was Whistler.

"Thought he might come back. I tried to find him, but I had trouble getting through hospital security."

"And by the time you got there, the woman had been bitten."

Blade nodded.

"You feel responsible for her being in this shape?" Whistler waved at the woman on the table.

She looked small and vulnerable in the unyielding light.

"No," Blade answered.

"You sure?"

Blade looked at his mentor. "Being sorry doesn't kill vampires, does it?"

"Never has."

Blade nodded. "Then I guess you know where I stand on this. If she makes it, she makes it. If she doesn't, we stake her and move on."

Whistler didn't push him. He cracked open

the smelling-salts capsule he'd taken from the vial and waved it under the woman's nose.

As the strong odor filled her nostrils, she started to stir. Blade watched her in silence, keeping his distance.

She moaned in pain, her eyes beneath her heavy lids tracking Whistler as he reached for a massive syringe filled with a caustic-looking green fluid. She focused on the syringe, grabbed a quick breath, and tried to get up from the table. But the actions were human, not feral.

"Hold her," Whistler ordered.

Blade grabbed her wrists, effortlessly pinning the top half of her body to the table while Whistler held her legs. Then the old man leaned in with the needle, his face totally unreadable.

Blade understood the woman's fear. She didn't have a clue whether they were there to help her or harm her, and Whistler wasn't making it any easier. Truthfully, he didn't know if they were there to help or harm her either. It depended on how far the disease running rampant throughout her system had spread. Either way, he had plans for her he was sure she wouldn't approve of.

Karen struggled against the two men holding her down. At first, when she'd regained consciousness with the strong odor of smelling salts in her nose, she thought she might have gone to sleep in the lab again, and Webb had sneaked in to hit her with the smelling salts as a joke. He'd done that before, repeating it well past the point of irritation. They both knew she pulled long, hard hours in the lab working on her research.

But Curtis didn't do that anymore, she realized, and on top of that, he was undoubtedly dead. Images of the dead man attacking Webb, ripping out his throat and sucking his blood, had haunted her dreams.

Her own throat hurt, and the wound in her neck burned with cold fire. She cursed the two men holding her, struggling against them as much as she could. It wasn't much, and it was nowhere near enough.

With practiced ease, the old man tapped the gigantic hypodermic with his forefinger, making sure the air was gone from the needle. He leaned forward again, reading her name tag. "Dr. Karen Jansen." His pale eyes, like chips of granite set in ice, moved to hers. "Listen close. I'm going to inject you with allium sativum—garlic. This is going to hurt. *A lot.*"

Without another word, the man did exactly that. The needle pushed into the wound in her neck. The pressure from the injection built immediately, flooding into the soft tissues of her throat. A shot that big, she thought, should have been given in a major muscle group.

Then the true pain hit her. It crackled and sizzled across every synapse in her brain, shorting out all other senses, but leaving her in the most intense agony she'd ever felt. If someone had told her she'd just been injected with boiling sulfuric acid, she wouldn't have been surprised.

She shrieked, felt her body going into uncontrolled paroxysms, as if she was having a full grandmal seizure. Smoke curled up at the corner of her eye. It took the length of her second scream for her to realize the smoke was coming from the wound on her neck. Some of the cold burning inside her throat began to fade, though.

She clutched at Blade's arm, digging her nails in, trying to make him share the pain. He looked back at her through those emotionless black lenses, saying nothing.

"If she makes it through the night," the other man was saying as he walked away, "she might have a chance."

The world went dark. It took her a couple seconds to realize that she'd closed her eyes. She blinked them back open, trying to focus on images that had grown indistinct.

She noticed that Blade had leaned in closer. But there was no indication of what he was thinking on his face. Then night closed in without warning and took her away from everything.

CHAPTER

10

Gaetano Dragonetti studied the photographs in front of him with increasing displeasure. He was old, older even than he looked. And he knew he looked *very* old. His hands had withered over the passage of centuries, turning into claws. But he didn't mind that; he had power, and power made up for a great many of what other beings might term shortcomings. Parchment skin stretched over skull-like features. He wore his thin blond hair pulled back, coated with gel to keep it in place. His suit was Italian, a craving that he carried over from his days when he'd been more venal. It was no craving now because he was past caring about such trivial things as appearance, but it gave others who were responsible for attending to his appearance direction.

The photographs only showed two figures, one

a cowering man sitting in a corner of the club, and the other a hated warrior dressed in black.

Dragonetti tossed the photographs aside. Then he turned to the long conference table and stared out over the eleven faces assembled before him. Carafes filled with blood sat within easy reach of every vampire there. Men and women, in a rainbow of colors, all vampire lords in their own right, waited on him to speak. That was power.

Pallintine was the one Dragonetti had known longest, but they had all shared wars and triumphs. The setbacks and defeats had been kept within acceptable losses. Pallintine was by nature a restless warrior, tall and broad and dark, a being who went against the odds when the prize was worth it.

Von Esper, a portly and studious-looking being who maintained dueling scars for the impact they made on people who dealt with him, worked in the shadows. Ashe, with his patrician Mediterranean countenance, had lived in ancient Rome, and he radiated a military demeanor at all times. Bava, wily and scurrilous, had brown skin almost as dark as the Hunter's, and had lived in Africa most of his unlife. The Fasutina sisters, identical redheaded twins who didn't look old enough to vote and wore revealing clothing, had been talking out in the hallway about a new assault rifle that would be released in the European market, where they did much of their business these days.

Dragonetti cleared his throat, capturing the

attention of all at the table. He spoke in the secret tongue, the ancient vampire language. "Blade, the Day-Walker," he spat. "Still pursuing his ridiculous crusade." He glanced at Pallintine because he knew the man kept track of such things as second nature. "How many died?"

"We don't have an exact count. Apparently he used a lot of silver. We're having difficulty—"

Purposefully, Dragonetti pulled his withered face into a scowl, letting the others know he was going to deal with the source of the problem, letting them know, too, if any of them were getting too sympathetic to Deacon Frost and his heresies, he was going to deal with that as well.

No one said anything.

Dragonetti dropped a bony forefinger on an intercom button on the tabletop. "Send in Frost." He leaned back in the chair, resting his elbows on the supports as he placed his fingers against each other.

They all waited in the silence Dragonetti deemed appropriate. This was his world. Minimalist though it was, the room reflected the clarity with which he chose to work. From this conference room, with a few well-placed phone calls, he could change the fate of nations should the right circumstances, or even the wrong ones, arise.

An underling crossed to the doors. He opened them and leaned outside. "Deacon Frost. You can come in now."

The sound of a lighter flicking came from the

hallway, followed by the scent of burning tobacco. It was Frost's way of passively rebelling.

Dragonetti waited, getting more angry as time passed.

Nearly a full minute passed before the boardroom doors opened on oiled hinges, and Deacon Frost stepped into the room. As an underlord in the vampire hierarchy, there was only one reason Frost would be summoned to the room. Everyone knew it.

Calmly and collectedly, Frost took a seat a few chairs down from the overlord. He maintained his silence.

Frost was of medium height. He looked much younger than he was, maintaining a late twentyish or early thirtyish appearance, which Dragonetti considered a waste of Frost's vampiric powers. He had high cheekbones that could make him look cruel if he wasn't smiling; and Frost rarely smiled. His dark hair reflected his unruly nature and made his pale face appear even paler. He did, however, wear his clothes well, though they looked too casual for his position.

Dragonetti broke the silence. "The Day-Walker continues to plague us."

Frost sounded totally unconcerned, even making his response in English instead of the ancient tongue they all were supposed to use while at the House of Erebus. "I'll take care of Blade."

Von Esper leaned in and made his words an accusation. "You insult the House of Erebus by addressing us in the humans' gutter tongue. Have you no respect for tradition?"

Frost lifted his head and blew a perfect, belligerent smoke ring. "Respect has to be earned." But he answered in the secret tongue.

The other eleven lords drew back, instantly looking at Dragonetti. Some of them might harbor secret sympathies for Frost and his rebellious style in these new times, but Dragonetti knew they would never expect their overlord to brook such behavior. Frost was so young he had only heard stories passed down about Dragonetti; he had never experienced Dragonetti's discipline firsthand.

Pallintine spoke first, picking up the challenge to relieve Dragonetti of taking a firm stance immediately if it was not necessary. The overlord knew he was always a good lieutenant, though he would never be a general.

"These nightclubs of yours are an embarrassment," Pallintine said. "As we've seen, they draw needless attention to our kind. You know our policy."

"*Your* policy, not *mine*." Frost smiled, his eyes flashing challenge.

Dragonetti growled in menacing displeasure. "Our livelihood depends on our ability to blend in, on our *discretion*."

"Well maybe it's time we forgot about discretion." Unbelievably, Frost got out of his seat and took steps forward, closing the distance between himself and Dragonetti without permission. It was an affront of the highest order, and the old vampire knew Frost was well aware of it. Frost continued speaking. "We should be ruling the humans, not running around making back-alley treaties with them. For fuck's sake, these people are *our food*, not our allies."

"You're out of line, Frost," Pallintine warned.

Frost turned to the man, raising a mocking eyebrow. "Am I? Maybe I'm just the first to say out loud what we've all been thinking."

Dragonetti cut him off. "We've existed this way for thousands of years. Who are you to challenge our ways? You're not even a pureblood—"

"Like it matters?" Frost asked.

"I was *born* a vampire!" Dragonetti slammed his withered fist down, splitting the table in spite of his fragile appearance. The nearby carafe of blood cracked, releasing a single trickle of crimson that oozed out onto the conference table. He rose, pointing at each of the other vampire lords. "As was every other member of this House. But *you*, Frost, you were merely *turned*."

Despite the inflammatory denigration, Frost stood his ground, then slowly looked at the others around the table. "We deserve better than this, Gaetano. The world belongs to *us*," he addressed them, "not the humans. You know that."

Dragonetti chose to ignore the affront till he could deal with it later. For the moment, though, Frost could still be put in his place. The overlord glanced at Pallintine. "Do we have any more business to discuss?"

A brittle, unforgiving winter quiet descended over the room, filling it. Dragonetti felt Frost's cold gaze on his face but continued to ignore it. Having his own sense of self-importance deflated was one of the most cutting things to Frost.

Pallintine glanced at Frost, revealing his own nervousness.

And Dragonetti knew then that Frost's power was greater than he'd believed it was. The realization was very unsettling.

"Well," Pallintine said, "there's the matter of our offshore accounts."

Frost's voice cut into the conversation with the grim finality of an executioner's ax. "Careful, old man," he said to Dragonetti. "You might wake up one day and find yourself extinct." Without another word, he turned around and exited the room, not giving the overlord a chance to make any response.

Dragonetti forced himself to remain. The room, his sense of power, didn't feel the same, and he was just starting to think maybe it would never feel the same again. The broken carafe continued to weep crimson. Fear touched him for the first time in centuries, and he was ashamed.

CHAPTER

11

Karen Jansen woke in darkness, in a room unlike any other she'd ever seen. Calling the room Spartan would have been an understatement. There was a bed, a suitcase that looked lived out of, a handful of books, and a lot of knives. But all the edged weapons were dwarfed by the huge sword hanging in a sheath from another knife embedded in the wall. A monk would have been more extravagantly housed.

Looking at the sword brought up the question of safety. The sword looked like it was the most dangerous weapon in the room. She knew she'd never handle it with the same ease the man in black had shown, but it might be something. After all, if they'd had good intentions for her, they wouldn't have taken her prisoner. She'd have woken up in a hospital.

She sat up on the bed cautiously, listening to the warning throb in her head and pacing herself accordingly. Lifting a hand to her throat, she discovered that the wound there had been dressed. Touching it still hurt.

Crossing to the wall, she took the sword's weight for a moment, not believing how heavy it was. As soon as she touched it, though, it started ticking like a bomb, and the hilt began rotating. Nervous, she took her hand back. In the next second, a series of razored blades sprang from the hilt. She gasped in surprise, but managed to keep from screaming. If she'd kept her hand on the hilt, she knew those blades would have cut her hand to ribbons.

In another few seconds, the blades withdrew into the sword hilt again. She moved away from the sword, away from all the weapons.

The dark curtains over the room's only window kept the afternoon sun outside at bay, but she knew it was daylight. Brightness reflected off a plastic surface on the small nightstand beside the bed.

She leaned forward to look, curious. A tattered and bloody driver's license lay there. The picture showed a young black woman, probably even younger than herself. She was smiling. Her first name read *Vanessa*, but the long-dried bloodstains blurred the surname.

She left the license on the table and got up slowly. When she could stand without feeling vertigo, she tried a step toward the door. Satisfied with the result, she continued walking, expecting to find the door locked. Surely, the two men who'd kidnapped her wouldn't leave it open so she could just walk out. But she couldn't just sit on the bed and do nothing.

She was surprised when the doorknob turned, and even more surprised when the door opened smoothly and without a sound.

Karen gazed down the long hallway that stretched before her. Mechanical sounds came from the large room at the other end. She stared hard at the opening, trying to fit it in with the little she remembered from the night before.

Where were her captors? Why hadn't they at least felt it necessary to tie her up? Dammit, if they'd at least had the decency to tie her up, she wouldn't be taking her life in her hands by creeping around thinking she might escape.

For a moment she hesitated. Maybe they thought she was smart enough to figure out for herself that she had nowhere to go.

And even at that, she hadn't escaped, only walked out of the room. The whole building could be locked up tighter than Fort Knox.

Steeling herself, she started down the corridor, toward the opening at the end. Halfway down, she heard voices from the large room. She recognized them. One was Blade's, and the other belonged to the old man who'd given her the injection. She paused, listening.

"How many did you take out?" Whistler asked.

"Couple dozen," Blade replied.

"Christ! What'd you do to this shotgun anyway? This is a hand-tooled weapon. It's going to take me days to get it back in shape."

She turned the corner, staying hidden, totally unprepared for what she saw through the tangled maze of machinery ahead of her.

Blade sat in a surgical restraint chair near the small operating theater she remembered. He was being strapped in, naked from the waist up. His lean, muscular body was slick with sweat, as if he was burning up with fever. The old man finished with the last leg restraint, then pushed himself up, favoring the leg with the metal brace on it. He stepped back, eyes locked on Blade's.

"I'm ready," Blade said.

"I must be getting soft in my old age, letting you bring home a stray like that," Whistler said. "It was damn stupid of you. We might've lucked out, though. I checked her background. Turns out she's a hematologist. She might be useful to us."

If she hadn't been so damn scared, Karen knew she would have been totally incensed about the cavalier attitude Whistler exhibited concerning her worth or nonworth. She remained still, not making a sound, hardly daring to breathe.

"I doubt it," Blade responded.

Whistler lifted a notebook. Karen recognized it at once as her research notebook. "I'm serious. I took a look at that notebook of hers. She's onto something."

Immediately, she wondered how the hell the old man had made any sense of her notes, much less the type of research she was doing. God, she thought, things just get weirder.

The old man walked to a table almost within Karen's reach. She watched as he prepared a solution from white powder and other liquids. When they were mixed together, the solution turned red. He reached back for a CO_2-powered pistol injector and filled the reservoir with the red fluid. Nothing showed on his face, but to Karen he appeared hesitant.

"I had to increase the dose," the old man said. "You're building up a resistance to the serum."

Blade sounded impatient, tired. "Just do it, old man."

The old man nodded, then fitted Blade with a bite guard. Karen watched, her heart beating hard enough to make the wound in her neck throb in sympathy. She couldn't just stand there, she thought, and let whatever was going to take place happen. But she did.

CHAPTER

12

The old man pressed the injector against Blade's carotid artery. The *whip-snick* of the charge being blown into Blade's bloodstream sounded loud to Karen. She wondered about the serum, what it was and what it was supposed to do. And the old man's announcement that Blade was building up a tolerance to it definitely sounded ominous.

Her own thoughts surprised her. How the hell could she be feeling sympathetic toward people who kidnapped her?

Blade began shaking violently, straining against his bonds. Somehow he remained silent through whatever agony he was feeling, but his teeth ground through the bite guard. Veins stood out on his neck.

The old man held his hand through it all, never letting go, being Blade's anchor back to a world without pain.

Karen felt the kinship between them then, knew the bonds that held them to each other were strong. She remembered Blade throwing her through the air, then making that incredible jump himself. He was strong enough to crush the old man's hand, but somehow he maintained enough control over his body even in his agony that he didn't. And the old man had to know how badly the younger man could hurt him, but he gripped Blade's hand anyway.

Karen watched, forgetting to breathe herself.

Then the agony left Blade's body. He slumped forward in the chair, held up by the straps. Exhaustion etched every line of his body. He took a deep, shuddering breath. He started to say something, then stopped, looking up without warning.

The man's black-lensed gaze brushed Karen's, locking on her eyes like a white corpuscle attacking an invading virus inside the bloodstream. She drew back at once, cursing herself for being foolish enough to stay there. She looked for an exit, spotted a doorway to the right, and pushed herself at it, staggering from the effects of her wound, the sick vertigo suddenly spinning inside her head again.

Marshaling her reserves, she ran for the doorway. When she got there, the way was blocked by a solid steel door. Throwing herself in another direction, she ran at another door farther down. A security gate covered this one.

Before she could pull away from it, she heard footsteps behind her. Breathing in ragged gulps, she turned and saw Blade standing behind her, the sword at the ready in his strong hands.

Blade seized the woman by one wrist. He held his sword in the other. He still felt weak from the injection of serum Whistler had given him, but was easily strong enough to catch her and keep her from falling.

She pulled away, and he let her go, wanting her to know that he meant no harm.

At least, he meant no harm as long as she didn't show effects of the Change in progress. If she did, he meant to take her head.

She hesitated, obviously at a loss. "I'm sorry, I—"

"Wandered off the beaten path, Doctor?" the old man asked, entering the room from a second doorway.

The woman looked at the old man, shrinking from him and Blade.

"You have yourself a nice nap?" he went on. "You were out for most of the day."

The woman shook her head. "Who are you people?"

"My name is Abraham Whistler." He nodded at Blade. "You've already met Blade."

She looked at them both, then gave up and headed back to the room they'd left her in.

Blade watched her go.

"Spunky," Whistler said.

"Yeah," Blade agreed. "Gonna be an asset later tonight."

"Going to be risky, though," Whistler mused. "For both of you."

"Only choice we've got. And if the Change is going to take her, I need to use her while I still can."

CHAPTER

13

Blade pulled on the body armor from the Dodge Charger's trunk, suiting up for the nightly hunt. Now that he'd found the vampires' nest there could be no let-up. Time would only allow them to dig in tighter, cover their tracks better.

Karen Jansen leaned against a packing crate only a short distance away. She had showered sometime during the day. Blade's sensitive nostrils could smell the soap on her. But she had no choice except to put her own clothing back on. It looked like she'd made the attempt to wash the bloodstains out of her blouse and lab smock as well, because they had faded considerably.

Blade slid his gun belt around his hips, locking it into place, then knotting the thigh tie-down. The headache from the serum had persisted all day, finally easing up when the night arrived over the city. He always felt stronger at night.

"So," Karen asked, "am I a prisoner here?"

Blade knew she'd been drawn to the workshop by the sound of activity. Whistler had made a picnic basket from food stores on hand and carried it back to her earlier. Neither of them had talked to her since. Everybody involved seemed more comfortable with that.

"Not at all," Whistler said as he walked up. "We just had to take certain precautions before we let you go." He wiped grease from his hands with a red towel that had seen better days. He shook a cigarette out of a pack he kept under the shoulder of his shirt and lit it. Then he lifted the dispenser nozzle for the gasoline and started fueling the Dodge Charger. "We hunt them, you see, moving from one city to the next, tracking their migrations."

"Hunt what?" Karen demanded.

Whistler answered without pause. "Vampires. The homines nocturna. They're hard to kill. They tend to regenerate."

Blade worked the action of the MACH, making sure everything moved perfectly. He listened to the conversation but kept his distance. The fact that the woman was going to be leaving tonight had preyed upon his mind more than he'd expected it to. He pulled the trigger on an empty chamber, and the dry pop echoed over the work space.

Karen jumped and glared daggers at him.

"My God, I'm supposed to believe—"

Blade cut in, growing more irritated at her and himself. "You saw Mr. Crispy at the hospital." He watched her face, seeing in her eyes that she might not be willing to believe, but there was some serious doubt messing with her belief architecture at the moment.

She shifted her attention back to Whistler. "So what do you use then? Stakes? Crosses?"

Blade watched the exchange with amusement. For a smart lady, Karen Jansen seemed determined to deny everything that had happened to her the previous night. It was better that she wasn't around, he decided, because that kind of attitude would get on his nerves. And when it got her dead, he didn't want to be anywhere near. Whistler had taught him a long time ago that only those who wanted to be saved could be saved. He hadn't taken up this fight to be some kind of vampire-hunting Don Quixote.

Whistler shrugged, answering Karen's question. "Crosses don't do squat. Some of the legends are true, though. Vampires *are* severely allergic to silver. Feed them garlic, and they'll go into anaphylactic shock."

Scooping up the customized CAR-15 assault rifle from the trunk, Blade snapped on the UV spotter light. It worked, but he changed the battery all the same. When he needed the light, he needed it badly.

Whistler pulled the nozzle from the Charger's

gas tank and put it away, continuing to answer the woman's question. "And, of course, there's always sunlight, ultraviolet rays." He turned his attention to Blade. "Got this sucker up and running; give her a try tonight."

Karen shook her head. "And you honestly expect me to believe all this?"

Blade couldn't take any more of her denial. Once she got home, she could practice it all she wanted to, bury her head in the sand like a damned ostrich. But this place was his and Whistler's, and he didn't want that kind of nonthinking anywhere near him. He turned and walked away, getting his mind set for the night. Things would move very quickly.

The *things* he hunted always did.

With less than an hour before sunset, Blade was ready to roll. He walked to the Charger, ignoring the glare he got from Karen. "Let's go," he growled. "You want to live to see another day, you'd better be out of the city by nightfall."

"I can't leave here," she protested. "I have a life here, a career."

"You've been *exposed* to them." Blade glanced at Whistler, not wanting to look at her anymore. "One way or another, somebody's going to take you out." He felt her eyes on him, the way he could sense it when anyone looked at him too hard or too long.

Whistler waved a hand toward the windows and the darkening sky high overhead, directing his words at Karen. "There's a war going on out there. Blade, myself, a few others—we've tried to keep it from spilling over onto the streets. Sometimes people like yourself get caught in the cross fire." He shrugged. "Not much you can do except warn people."

"I have blood samples," Karen protested. "I can go to the police."

"They *own* the police," Blade replied.

"That's ridiculous!" Karen snapped. "No one's that powerful."

Whistler sighed and shook his head. "They're everywhere. Chances are, you've seen them and not even known it. On the subway. In a bar."

Impatient, Blade triggered the hidden stud in his sword hilt to deactivate the built-in booby trap, then sheathed it. He started toward the Charger, gesturing for Karen. "Get in. I'm taking you home." He got a glance of the stunned expression on her face.

"That's it?" she asked. "You guys just patch me up and send me on my way?"

Whistler tossed a small metal canister to Karen. She caught it. "Vampire mace. Silver nitrate, essence of garlic."

Karen stood at the passenger door, gazing incredulously from one of the men to the other, then back again, as though she couldn't believe what she was hearing now any more than she could seriously discuss vampires.

Whistler scratched at his beard, as if thinking hard. "Yeah," he said, "there is one other thing."

Blade listened to his mentor's voice, knowing Whistler was going to give it to her cold now.

"I'd buy myself a gun if I were you," Whistler said. "If you start becoming sensitive to the daylight, if you start becoming thirsty regardless of how much you've had to drink—then I suggest you take that gun and use it on yourself. Better that than the alternative."

Blade turned away from the look of horror that filled the woman's face. He slid in behind the wheel and keyed the ignition, waiting till she joined him in the car.

Karen gazed out over the dusk-clad cityscape spread before her, amazed at how the oncoming night seemed a continuation of the previous one. And yet it seemed that she'd never seen this city before in her life.

Blade drove, using the car's muscle and speed to get them through the streets quickly. He was like a cruise missile, homing in on his target.

Her mind reeling, Karen finally voiced the question that had been on her mind since they left the safe house in the warehouse district. "So you're saying I may have been . . . ?" She let the rest of it trail away, hesitant to voice the possibility aloud.

Blade only nodded, not even bothering to look

at her. "You're infected. The venom's still inside you. There's a chance you could still turn."

"And then what?" Karen felt like a stone wall had gone up between them.

He was silent for a time. Just when she was going to ask the question again, he answered. "Then I'd have to take you out, just like any other bloodsucker."

Karen had no doubt that he meant it. As they changed directions, following the street, the fat red-gold sun hanging low in the purple western sky suddenly shot through the windshield and stabbed into her eyes.

She was acutely aware that despite how normal it was for someone to pull down a sun visor against the direct glare, Blade could read something else entirely from the movement. She looked over at him.

And found him staring right at her, whatever he was thinking masked behind those black lenses.

CHAPTER

14

Deacon Frost sat at a high-tech steel and glass desk that was littered with computer equipment. The room was dark around him, only the sickly glow of the monitor throwing off any light. He wore a headset, listening to the blitzkrieg of heavy metal from the CD player.

Stacks of books and scriptures surrounded him. The library had grown impossibly large over the years despite efforts to digitize everything, swelling to fill even the large rooms that had once been available. More information came in all the time.

Personally, he felt it should have all been scanned into computers ten or fifteen years ago and saved as electronic data, and the books gotten rid of. Except for those tomes that were of a sizable monetary value and didn't give away too many of their secrets.

There were several others, however, who did not agree with his assessment of the situation. That wasn't surprising. He was a forward thinker surrounded by creatures that still apparently longed for the Dark Ages. For Christ's sake, paperback editions would have been better than books that weighed fifteen or twenty pounds apiece.

Frost studied the digitized image of a book page he'd taken from an ancient manuscript. The decrypting software he was using in an attempt to decipher the page held an open legend in the lower left corner. The software was straining, working, but barely. The headway he was making was abominably slow. Of course, that it was able to work at all on the dead language was a miracle. Frost had chosen to take that as a sign.

"What are you doing here?"

Frost paused, looking up from his work, and saw Gaetano Dragonetti step from the shadows. He made no attempt to answer the question.

"You've been warned before," Dragonetti challenged. "These writings are restricted to pure-bloods—you wouldn't even understand them. Whatever secrets they hold have been lost. It's a dead language, Frost. There's no use trying to translate it."

Frost didn't even attempt to humor the old vampire. He had granted Dragonetti a chance to save face this morning, at the expense of his own, but here in the library things would be different.

Dragonetti drew closer, studying the monitor, but Frost could see the lack of confidence in the older vampire. "I can't begin to imagine what a Philistine like yourself would want with them," Dragonetti said.

Frost returned the stare. The computer represented one of the swords he had to hold over the old vampires' heads. He was smarter about this world than they were, more aware of the possibilities today's technology offered.

Most of the economic decisions regarding new investments, new business, and creating tax shelters as well as money laundering facilities had come from the younger breed of vampires like him. They were a threat to the old hierarchy.

"Dammit, Frost," Dragonetti exploded, "I'm talking to you!" He lunged forward, trying to rip the headphones from the younger vampire's ears.

Frost grabbed the man's wrist, stopping it short and holding it tight. He smiled sarcastically. "Keep your voice down, Gaetano. We're in a library. You don't need to shout, I can hear you."

Dragonetti ripped his hand free, quivering with pent-up rage. "What are you up to, Frost?"

"Wouldn't you like to know?"

"These childish games of yours are beginning to tire me."

Frost pushed himself up from the chair, staring full into the older vampire's burning gaze. "What are you going to do, *pureblood*? What, exactly, are you going to do?"

Unable to maintain the challenging eye contact, Dragonetti turned away. Then, before Frost knew it was coming, the old vampire whirled around and slapped him hard enough to nearly knock the younger vampire from his feet.

The pain exploded in Frost's head. He let his anger loose, not wanting to restrain himself anymore. But when he looked for Dragonetti, he found that the old vampire had already disappeared into the shadows.

Frost chose not to go after Dragonetti. He touched the side of his face and worked his jaw tenderly. He reminded himself to be patient, that the day of reckoning was coming soon enough. Dragonetti knew it, too. That was why the old vampire was pressing his luck now. Not much time remained.

Peering through the darkness, Frost saw the huge shape quivering in fear. Pearl had heard and seen everything, not even showing the good manners—or sense—to leave. Frost ignored Pearl as well, turning his attention again to the computer monitor. Blade was in the city now, and the other vampires would be concentrating on him instead of what Frost was doing.

Considering the background Blade had and what had been deciphered about the ancient manuscript so far, Frost considered it all ironic. He felt good, and he enjoyed the feeling.

CHAPTER

15

Karen watched the street corner in front of her building coming up. For a moment she didn't think Blade would stop in time to make it, but he worked the clutch and brake, swooping into the empty space at the curb with room to spare.

She hesitated, looking at him. The stone face he showed her gave away nothing. She kept her tone cool when she addressed him. "I suppose I should thank you, but I really don't feel like it."

He didn't respond to that. What he told her was, "Remember what we said. Keep your eyes open. They're *everywhere*."

"But it's daytime." She felt irritated. Damn him and Whistler for acting so serious about something that couldn't possibly be true. It was one thing for her to be afraid at night, but they weren't going to take her days away from her, too.

Blade regarded her silently with his black-lensed gaze.

Karen climbed out of the car, thinking about the neighbors she'd lived among for the last few years. Her apartment building was in a nice part of the city, but it wasn't as security-conscious as many of them. So far, it hadn't had to be.

She felt at a loss, thinking about Blade going away. No one would be at her apartment. She was already dreading the waiting loneliness. The only solace would be a phone call to her mother or sister, and that would be cold comfort at best.

She kept recalling what she'd seen that morning, how Whistler had held Blade's hand while whatever serum had been administered coursed through his body. She looked at Blade again, but he was already facing the street ahead, both arms resting on the steering wheel, boxing himself off from conversation.

When she stepped way from the car, Blade put the accelerator down and roared away, the Charger slipping through the traffic like a big gray tiger.

Karen watched the vehicle till it vanished, wondering if she would see him again. Then she wondered why she'd thought something as dumb as that. One thing she was sure of was: She never did want to see him again.

She turned and went into the apartment building. Her neighbors took on whole new aspects as she considered Blade's final words to her. She heard them again, in a whispered rush: *They're everywhere!*

She used her key to enter the building, crossed the lobby to the elevator, and pressed the button. A young couple joined her, looking like they'd stepped out of a fashion magazine. That made Karen feel even worse about her own appearance. She wanted a bath, a chance to fix her hair, and clothes that she hadn't been wearing for two days.

As she waited, the indicator light beginning its inexorable crawl down to the lobby, she felt the seconds tick away slowly. She glanced at the couple again, hoping she wouldn't get caught looking, but after everything she'd been through, it bothered her that she didn't remember them as her neighbors. Of course, it was foolish to think she'd know everyone in the building. She noticed that both had matching tattoos on the back of their necks. The doors opened with a musical *ping* of noise, and she entered.

The couple got on with her and didn't speak a word. That bothered Karen more than she wanted to admit. She almost started a conversation just to break the tension she was feeling. But that would have been giving in to Blade and his whole paranoia.

Still, she had to ask herself if she'd really be able to tell if the couple weren't human. She thought she could feel their eyes on her, and she knew then that her imagination was getting the best of her. She made herself glance at the man.

"How are you?" he asked, smiling politely.

Covering the movement with her nod, Karen slipped the container of vampire mace from her pocket. "I'm fine, thanks." And conversation was over. They were human, she told herself. They had to be.

The elevator stopped on Karen's floor, and the doors opened. She got out and headed left, toward her apartment. Still, she couldn't resist a quick glance behind her.

The tattooed couple got out behind her, following her. Suddenly, Karen's heart felt like it was going to burst inside her chest. The deserted emptiness of the hallway hit her like a physical blow. The sun had almost gone down, and she could see only long shadows at both ends of the hallway. She realized how far she was from her apartment and a phone. She lengthened her stride and walked with more haste.

The sound of footsteps behind her grew closer, faster.

Unable to stand it anymore, she whirled around to face the couple, the vampire mace clutched tightly in her hand.

Only—no one was there. The hallway was empty.

She'd imagined it. She sighed in relief, finishing up cursing Blade and Whistler.

At her apartment, she fumbled for her key at the door. Her breathing sounded loud in her ears, drowning out the sounds of sitcoms and their laugh tracks coming from the other apartments.

Keying the lock, she let herself in, leaving the door open behind her in case she had to make a hasty retreat. Everything looked normal, though. The television was off, but the radio was on, as she'd left it. A stack of towels she had folded but not put away remained on the couch. An empty coffee cup sat on top of the medical journal she'd fallen asleep reading the last night she spent in the apartment.

Everything *was* normal.

She took a deep breath and promised not to overreact anymore. Blade and Whistler had seriously creeped her out, that was all. She was sane, and everything was normal.

Except that the wound in her throat had started throbbing again. A tiny voice in the back of her mind asked if the wound's sudden pain had anything to do with the arrival of nightfall.

She took another few steps into the room, listening to the heavy silence all around her in spite of the radio. The pain in her throat seemed to pick up tempo. Memories of Curtis Webb getting killed in front of her suddenly surfaced in her mind. Then all at once she knew there was no damn way she could stay in the apartment, in this building, or even on this block. Maybe not even in the city.

Blade was right. She wasn't safe. And she had no business being by herself. Maybe the only menace she was actually saving herself from was him.

But he was the embodiment of a threat. She crossed the room to the phone and dialed 911. She shivered, listening to the terror in her heartbeat as she heard the phone ring. She shivered, thinking it was a damn emergency phone line and why the hell didn't somebody just—

"Emergency, Operator 789," the practiced voice on the other end said. "State the nature of your emergency, caller."

Karen tried to speak but couldn't get her voice to come out. What was she going to say? That she was possibly being stalked by vampires? Oh Christ, no telling what kind of help was going to be sent with that announcement. They might show up on her doorstep with a straitjacket and a big-game tranquilizer rifle.

She slammed the phone down in its cradle, hyperventilating and feeling totally, horribly helpless. She breathed in through her mouth, trying to take in enough oxygen to calm herself, then went to her bedroom and pulled a suitcase from the closet. Throwing it on the bed, she started tossing clothes onto it; she'd worry about getting them *in* the suitcase later.

First and foremost, she had to get away, had to leave the building. If the vampires came looking, they'd know where to find her. And Blade had dropped her off there. She might as well have handed out engraved invitations. Once she was packed, she'd call her sister, see about staying there for a few nights. Gail would wonder why she wasn't staying home, but she could say that the whole episode in the hospital had left her feeling rattled.

That sounded rational, didn't it? God, actually it was the first thing that had since last night, and that was definitely scary.

Something moved beside her. She glanced up, tracking the motion, then seeing her own reflection in the vanity mirror beside the bed.

The white bandage stood out starkly against her dark throat. She looked at it, wondering why she couldn't see the throbbing that she felt beneath it. She touched it lightly, doing some exploratory searching.

The click out in the entryway sounded like a gunshot in the stillness of the apartment.

Karen's mouth went dry as she turned toward the door. She took the vampire mace from her pocket and crept toward the living room. She was five stories up; she couldn't simply dive out a window a phenomenal distance to another rooftop the way Blade had.

She rounded the corner with the mace held before her, heart pounding. The wound in her throat echoed her heart. Even expecting something, she froze, unable to move, seeing the man in front of her, only inches away.

"What are you doing here?" Karen demanded
when she got her voice back.

The man in front of her looked young, barely
into his twenties. He was blond and blue-eyed,
with a slightly rounded face that looked like it had
just been scrubbed clean. The lines of his police
uniform were neat and precise. He'd jumped back
when he had nearly walked into her, obviously surprised to find her there.

"I'm sorry, I—" The police officer pulled back
another step, two, holding his hands up placat-
ingly. "I didn't mean to scare you. The door was
open, I was worried about you."

Karen relaxed a bit. The uniform was helpful,
and his obvious nervousness at the situation was
real. She lowered the mace, and he gave her a
weak grin.

"You're Karen Jansen?" he asked.

Karen nodded, reading the name badge on the man's breast: Officer Krieger. She stepped back, but she didn't let her guard down.

Krieger looked at her neck, raising his eyebrows at the bandages. "Are you all right?"

"I'm okay," Karen replied. "I guess I'm a little freaked out. But that doesn't explain what you're doing here now." She maintained an edge of suspicion somewhat jealously.

"I was in the neighborhood," Krieger explained. "I ride patrol through here on the four-to-midnight shift. The dispatch officer called me, said 911 got a hang-up call from your address, and wanted me to check it out." He shrugged. "You're listed as a probable kidnap victim. The PD's interested. And I just wanted to make sure you were here, or find out who was pranking on the phone."

"Okay." Karen released a long breath, feeling the tension leaving her body. The explanation made sense. "Actually, I'm glad you're here."

"Glad to be of service," Krieger said. He looked around the room, his hand dropping to the pistol at his side. "Is anyone else here? Is that what you're worried about?"

"No," Karen said tiredly. "Nobody's here but you and me." She walked back into the bedroom for the suitcase. "Listen, do you have any idea what happened to the other doctor I was with last night?" She thought there could be only one answer to that question, but she had to ask it. She tried vaguely to recall who was left of Webb's family, hoping she couldn't remember or even find out because, otherwise, she knew she'd feel the need to at least call them.

"Curtis Webb? Oh, he's dead." Krieger's reply was matter-of-fact, nearly cold.

Karen looked up at the man, almost angry enough to tell him he lacked a lot in the tact department.

"But I wouldn't worry about that if I were you," Krieger went on.

The adrenaline rushed through Karen, making her wary. "Why?"

Krieger smiled, but the expression was not that of the easygoing young man who had stood in front of her an eye blink before. He drew his pistol so fast Karen didn't even see it rip free of leather. He said, "Because you're dead, too."

Karen moved faster than she thought she ever had before, bringing the canister of vampire mace up and unleashing a small cloud of mist into Krieger's face. He must have been reluctant to start firing if he didn't have to, because he stumbled back, blinded and cursing.

The police officer rubbed the heel of his palm against his eyes, managing to back away instinctively and block her path to the door.

Karen waited tensely, wondering if that was how a vampire died by garlic mace. From the movies she'd seen as a girl, she expected Krieger's face to light up like a blazing comet.

Instead, he seemed little more than discomforted. He calmed down quickly. "I thought that was pepper spray, or maybe perfume." He sniffed his fingers, not taking his eyes off her. "Garlic?"

Karen spoke before she knew she was talking. "He said it would work against vampires." But maybe she wasn't talking to Krieger, maybe she was only complaining to herself.

Krieger smiled again, then rushed forward and forced Karen against the wall, pinning her body with his weight as he shoved the pistol barrel roughly against her temple. "Vampires?" he repeated. "Who said I was a va—?"

"Nobody."

Karen had no difficulty recognizing the cool voice that had answered Krieger's question.

CHAPTER

17

Blade reached for Krieger's gunhand, clamping down on it and yanking it away from Karen Jansen's head easily. His forefinger found the weapon's safety and immediately flicked it on. He squeezed hard, then kicked out, sweeping Krieger's feet straight out from under him.

The police officer dropped hard in front of Blade, pain whitening his face. He breathed in through his mouth in panicked breaths, gasping. The Hunter felt no remorse at all for the damage he'd inflicted. If he hadn't cared enough about Karen Jansen to not want to kill the man in her apartment, it would have already been done.

"Get over here." Blade dragged the man to his feet and looked at Karen. "He's a familiar." Then, before Krieger could make a sound, the Hunter smashed a blow into Krieger's face, breaking off the scream before it started. "A vampire wanna-be." He hit the police officer again, knocking him to the floor. "If he's loyal enough, if he *proves* himself, then maybe his master'll turn him."

Krieger still moved, but his nervous system seemed disjointed. He had no more crawling ability than even a newborn.

Blade picked the man up and flung him across the room. The anger was on him now, and he went with it, hoping it would burn out his unaccustomed feelings. "How 'bout it, Krieger?" Blade asked. "You a good little bloodhound? You gonna tell us what your master's been up to?"

Across the room, Krieger tried to rise, stretched a hand toward the door.

Crossing the room, Blade kicked him, driving the air from Krieger's lungs again. And he kept on kicking, enjoying the anger because it was the only truly human emotion he could permit himself. Need, desire, passion—all were off-limits, by Whistler's decree as well as the Hunter's own knowledge of himself.

He stopped kicking when the man slumped to the carpeted floor more unconscious than conscious. Blade looked up at Karen then and saw her shocked expression. That single, simple expression distanced them. Blade felt it, and tasted the sweet and bitter dregs that accompanied the knowledge. Distance meant they were both safe from his memory of how her breathing had calmed him, had made him feel more at peace than he had in years. And distance meant he was again that much further from what he most wanted to be.

"You okay?" he asked her.

Then her thoughts came together. The Hunter could see it in her eyes. "Wait a minute," she said. "Hold on here—you used me as bait?"

"Get over it," Blade advised. And he was angry at himself, too, because her words hurt more than he'd expected. Sure he'd used her. Hell, he used everything he could get his hands on to fight the vampires. It was that kind of war, and there was no stronger enemy. He slammed Krieger's face into a table, crashing through.

"Hey!" Karen protested. "Is that really necessary?"

Blade picked Krieger up again, fitting him into a headlock this time. He turned the man's head, inspecting the neck, the skin behind the ear. "See this mark?" He pointed the tattoo out to her.

Karen moved closer, but still remained out of reach.

He told himself the reaction didn't matter. But it bothered him that he'd thought that before; it wasn't acceptable. "That's a glyph," he said, pushing the thought aside. "Kind of like a vampire cattle brand. That means Officer Krieger here is someone's property. Any other vampire tries to bleed this little hooker, they'll have to answer to Krieger's owner." He peered more closely at the glyph, surprised but only somewhat, since he'd halfway expected what he found. "How 'bout that?

Deacon Frost. We've been tracking that one for a long time."

Blade dropped the man and methodically stripped him of his wallet and watch. He emptied the cash from the wallet and put it in his pocket. After a quick glance assured him the watch was worth taking, he dropped it into his pocket, too.

Karen sounded amazed when she spoke. "Great. So now you're robbing him. You gonna rob me, too?"

Blade ignored the sarcasm and stood. "How do you think we finance our operation? We're not exactly the March of Dimes." He hauled the half-conscious Krieger over his shoulder and started for the door.

Karen appeared to hesitate, but his hearing told him she was following in his wake. He cursed, knowing she was going to be more trouble than she was worth.

CHAPTER

18

Blade kept Krieger moving, holding the man in a martial arts come-along grip that promised broken bones if he tried to get away or resist. The Hunter was alive to the darkness surrounding them in the parking lot, letting all his senses bring information to him. The siren call of the night was all around him, but he didn't give in to the dark-hearted seductiveness.

Karen followed behind them, alternately falling behind, then catching up in quick running steps. Passersby ignored them, seasoned by the violence they regularly saw to know not to get involved. Even if the muggee was a cop.

The police car was conspicuously parked at the curb. Blade shoved the man facedown across the hood, keeping the captured arm levered up high behind Krieger. He knew if they were seen like that, a man dressed all in black bending a uniformed cop over the hood of a police cruiser, they'd get instant attention, so he worked fast.

Blade searched through Krieger's pockets, finding his keys. "Let's go," he growled at the police officer, pulling him to the rear of the car. He opened the trunk, and, as it rose, the light inside flashed on to reveal the contents.

The Hunter didn't know the name of the sophisticated medical cooling unit in the back of the car, but he knew it was used for transporting donated organs to transplant sites. He opened it and coolant vapor hissed out, spreading a gentle gray fog over the trunk's interior. Inside the unit were neatly stacked plastic bags of blood. "Looks like our friend was blood-running."

"Hillburn Clinic," Karen said, forgetting her fear as she stepped forward and read the label on the unit. She ran her fingers along the stainless-steel surface as if she needed the contact to know that it really was inside the trunk of the police car. "I know this place. It's a blood bank."

"Owned by vampires," Blade replied. "There's one in every major city. And they always deliver." He turned his gaze on Krieger. "Where were you headed?"

The police officer's lips were split, puffy over chipped teeth. "I don't know what you're—"

Blade pulled the man's face into the trunk of the car, hard enough to bounce Krieger's head like a rubber ball. "Do it again if I need to."

"Hey, take it easy," Karen said.

Blade ignored her, dragging Krieger back into position to slam him again. "I'm not going to ask you again, Krieger. Where were you taking this?"

Krieger's nose lay crookedly across his face. "Mphuck yourself."

"Go fuck myself? Go fuck myself?" Blade backhanded the man across the face.

Krieger spun away, dropping to the ground in obvious pain.

Satisfaction touched the Hunter, but he welded it to the anger. He drew the MACH pistol.

"What are you doing?" Karen demanded.

Blade didn't spare her a glance, his attention riveted solely on the target in front of him. "Preventive medicine." He lifted the pistol.

"No!" Karen stepped in front of him, getting in the way of the shot. Her eyes were on him, searching him for mercy, something he was all out of.

"Move," he told her.

"You can't do this," she told him. "He's human. It's *murder*."

Blade shook his head. She was wrong, didn't know the full scope of things. It was hard to know the right and wrong of things as they were without having been where he was, where Abraham Whistler had been. "It's *war*," he growled at her. "Now get the fuck out of my way!"

Before he knew what was happening, Karen grabbed his arm and wrestled with him, trying to push his gun hand away. He flicked on the safety automatically, not wanting to hurt her inadvertently. He also couldn't use his full strength against her for the same reason. Over her shoulder he saw Krieger make a break for it.

The man ran for all he was worth, pumping his arms and legs as he cut across the street. A car screeched, narrowly avoiding him.

Getting a grip on Karen, Blade shoved her aside and lifted the MACH. His forefinger slid across the safety, releasing it, then coiled inside the trigger guard. He caressed the trigger, watching the muzzle flash flare out around the end of the pistol.

The bullet scored the brickwork just above Krieger's head. Before Blade could line the pistol up again, Krieger turned the corner and disappeared.

The sound of the shot hung in the air, echoing between the buildings. Blade knew there was no time to hunt the man down. Other police would be in the area at once after they discovered that a fellow officer had gone missing, shot at while fleeing for his life. Even though he didn't see them now, the Hunter knew eyes watched them. He wheeled on Karen, his anger dangerously near the point of no return now. "Goddammit!"

Karen stared him down, not backing away from his wrath. "You were going to kill him. What was I supposed to do? Shut my eyes and pretend I didn't see what I saw?"

Blade made a final effort to control the rage

building within him, but it was no use. Frustration chipped away at the foundation of the emotion, turning all the safeguards he had in place into loose debris.

His control slipped, and the cold darkness waiting inside him took advantage of his weakness.

Karen took an involuntary step back when she saw Blade's face. White fire glimmered in his eyes—a reflection of something so inhuman it chilled her to the bone. She had never felt closer to death, not even when the dead man had attacked her the night before in the hospital, Curtis Webb's blood still all over him.

Blade holstered the MACH, his face cool again, as featureless as the black-lensed sunglasses. "You better wake up. What you've *seen* so far is *nothing*. The world you live in's just the sugar-coated topping. There's another world beneath it, *the real world*—and if you want to survive in it, you'd better learn to pull the trigger."

Karen heard his words, delivered flat and harsh, and she also heard the ring of truth and sincerity in them. Still, he had no right to treat her like she was stupid.

She believed him now. *They* really were everywhere around them. *Vampires.* And, from the way the wound on her neck was throbbing, there was every chance that she could turn out to become one of *them*.

The Hunter turned to go.

She grabbed his arm and, with the strength of her fear, managed to turn him back, though he was far stronger than she. "Wait a minute! I'm coming with you!"

Blade shook his head, but he didn't knock her hand away. "You're useless."

Karen stepped around him, putting her face close to his, letting him feel her anger. "Hey, if what you've been saying is true, if there's a chance I could turn into one of them, then I've got no choice, do I?

He got into his car, stepping around her effortlessly and sliding behind the steering wheel with practiced ease.

Karen let herself into the passenger seat, somewhat surprised when he didn't try to stop her. "I *have* to work with you," she continued. "I need to learn everything I can about them. It's the only way I'll be able to find a cure for myself."

"There is no cure," he told her flatly, and keyed the ignition.

"Don't be so sure." Karen felt the big engine vibrate the car as it fired to life. She leaned back into the seat, surprised that he wasn't kicking her out. She took a deep breath and hoped she really knew what she was doing. Right or wrong, it came down to live or die.

CHAPTER

19

Blade stayed in the shadows as he surveyed the entrance to Karen Jensen's apartment building. The lady herself still occupied the Charger's passenger seat, though he didn't know why exactly that was still taking place. There remained a good chance that she would turn, becoming a vampire herself. Hell, tonight might even be the night. Just in case, he kept his hand near the silver-bladed katar punching-dagger tucked in his boot.

The remains of Chinese takeout littered the console and the dash. Every now and again, one of them would discover a taste for something left over. Conversation, not surprisingly, was minimal. The only thing they had in common, neither of them really wanted to talk about.

The moon had risen hours ago, draping the city in silver-kissed shadows, softening the city skyline. And the predators were out in force. All of them. Blade was attuned to them. There were only two kinds of creatures in the world: the hunted and the hunters.

"He's not going to come back," Karen said finally. "We've been here a couple hours. No one's *that* stupid."

Blade almost responded. Having the woman in the car, in the middle of his operation, made him feel uneasy. Especially after she'd been bitten. It was like inviting bad karma in.

Before he could say anything, though, Krieger sneaked back through the shadows, crossing the street and making for the police cruiser abandoned in front of the building. Evidently no one had called the police in, or Krieger had managed to circumvent any possible 911 calls.

Either way, it didn't matter to Blade. The Hunter grinned evilly. "Looks like he's pretty fucking stupid."

Krieger climbed into the police cruiser and peeled out of the parking space.

Blade keyed his own ignition, sweeping empty and nearly empty cartons of takeout food into a plastic garbage bag from the glove compartment. When he and Whistler put an operation together, between them they prepared for pretty much anything and everything.

Slipping the gearshift into first, Blade pulled onto Krieger's backtrail. He reached under the dashboard and clicked on the Scan-Lock cellphone scanner mounted there. Numbers flashed across the LCD screen as it searched for the strongest signal, which Blade hoped would be Krieger's.

He listened to two bits of conversation, both pedestrian in nature, then heard a dial tone fill the speaker. The Scan-Lock always picked up the nearest, strongest signal. He drove, waiting, listening to the number being dialed.

The automated voice sounded muffled over the scanner. "You've reached a number that is no longer in service. Please consult your operator and try again."

Krieger spoke loudly over the recording: "It's Krieger, PIN 16009."

A man's voice came on the line, smooth and calm, but the resonant quality in it told Blade that it had been filtered. "Yes?"

Blade leaned back in the seat, following the police car through the late-night traffic with ease. He saw Karen glance at him, her eyes widening at how easy he made it look. He pushed away any thoughts that she might somehow come to see things his way. She'd lived her sheltered life too long, built illusions that were too strong. She hadn't seen firsthand all the horror the creatures were truly capable of.

The police car continued to hurtle through the night-darkened streets.

The Charger paced it easily, a big beast just hitting its stride.

"Get me Pearl!" Krieger shouted.

"Pearl is feeding," the calm voice replied.

"Look," Krieger went on, "I've got a delivery from Frost here, and I just had a run-in with Blade. We've got to clear out the clinic on Hillburn."

"Got another bad news flash for you, boys," Blade said quietly as he switched lanes. "The night's still young."

CHAPTER

20

Blade drove the Dodge Charger through the back streets of Little Tokyo, following his prey back to the nest. The area was familiar to him, and he thought perhaps he'd even walked along these streets while meeting his own needs.

Krieger pulled the police car into a secured parking area serving a building constructed of black stone, which was settled heavily between a pawnshop and a small office building. He abandoned the vehicle in the middle of the parking lot, waving at one of the valets.

The only sign on the building was a neon purple scroll above the street entrance. A flashing kanji that matched the glyph tattooed on the back of Krieger's neck pulsed on the scroll.

Krieger took the cooler unit from the police car's trunk and went inside.

Blade parked the Charger at the public parking area across the small street. The other slots were empty, silent testimony that any vehicles left there were considered fair game to the gangs that prowled through the area. He killed the engine, sat waiting quietly for a time, trying to build a map of the building inside his head. But he knew there was no way to do that properly. The vampires would have done whatever they wanted with the structure—without permits and the hassle of public officials. It was more a nest than the club at the meatpacking plant had been. This place showed evidence of having been inhabited for a long time.

"Looks like we hit pay dirt," he told Karen. "This place is crawling with them. See that graffiti?" He pointed at the graffiti-covered wall to the right. Whorls and loops and lines all combined to look like postmodern hieroglyphics. "Those aren't gang tags; those are vampire markings. It means there's a safe house nearby. A place they can go if dawn is coming."

He got out of the car and walked over to the graffiti-covered wall, studying it. Karen stood beside him, looking at the tags with obvious interest.

He pointed at the secured parking area next to the black-stone building. He could make out the name of the place on the sign: The Black Pearl. "See the valets over there? They're vampires. So is the doorman." He still felt the need to explain it to her, to interpret how he saw the world, and what his part in it was. He listened to the calm way she breathed now in spite of the tension of the moment.

"How can you tell?" she asked.

"The way they move, the way they smell." Blade scanned the area, pointing out a few more likely candidates that he wasn't completely sure about. But he wanted her to get the feel of looking for them, and to understand how easily the vampires could be overlooked if they wanted to be. "The whore on the corner is one, too." He studied the men vying for the whore's attention as the female vampire played hard to get, unable to keep the evil smile from his face. "Those johns are in for a surprise."

"Why don't you go warn them?"

Blade looked at her. "I can't save them all. Best way I know how to do that is hunt down the bastards I can find and kill them." And that pretty much summed up the night's agenda. He reached into the backseat and retrieved his sword and a worn leather satchel. He pulled a sliding rack out from under the backseat, took out the twelve-gauge shotgun sitting there, and started putting rounds into the scattergun's breech, gazing at the target site again.

"I can't believe there are so many of them," Karen said softly. "This is a nightmare." Her fingers strayed to the bandage on her neck.

It was a reminder that they didn't know whether the Change was going to affect her or not. Blade put the thought out of his mind, not daring to hope, and said, "There are worse things out here than vampires."

She looked the challenge at him. "Like what?"

He racked the shotgun, slipping a shell into the breech with smooth, practiced ease. "Like me." He opened the door. "Let's go."

Blade pushed away from the Charger, letting the shotgun disappear automatically under the folds of his longcoat. He started across the street between the light traffic, the lights playing over him for an instant. There was no mistaking his destination; they'd know he was coming. He heard Karen running to catch up to him.

When she was beside him, he said, "All right, listen up. Vampire Anatomy 101. Crosses and running water don't do dick, so forget what you've seen in the movies." He held up his gloved free hand, counting off on his fingers. "You use the *stake*, *silver*, or *sunlight*. Got it?"

She nodded, but the tightness around her eyes revealed she wasn't as accepting as she tried to act.

In the shadows along the sidewalk in front of the black building, Blade took out a small Glock pistol and held it up. "Know how to use one of these?"

Karen took the Glock from him, running her fingers and eyes all over it. Despite her willingness to handle it, he knew she was unfamiliar with it. "No," she finally admitted, her tone telling him that she was not happy with having to tell him that.

Blade took the gun back and snorted derisively, making sure both of them kept their distance now. It was her choice to walk into the building; his mistake to let her. He wasn't going to be able to cover her completely inside. There were too many variables.

"Safety's off, round's already chambered." He used his thumb to drop the magazine for a moment, showing her it was full. "Silver hollowpoints filled with garlic. You aim for the heart or the head, anything else is suicide. They're hard to stop." He gave the weapon back to her.

Karen knew enough to hide the pistol against her body. She brushed the hair out of her eyes.

"When it gets nasty in there," Blade said, "and it will, do your damnedest to stay out of my way." His words were cold, chipped ice, letting her know how it was.

She took it, though, and that bothered him more than if she had exploded in anger. He was being hard on her, and she already had enough to deal with.

Blade wheeled around the corner leading to the recessed entrance. He took a couple quick breaths to pump his system up, getting his focus and stepping outside the few uncertainties floating around in the back of his mind. No one was at the entrance except the large bald doorman, who could have been a Sumo wrestler in the tailored suit.

The doorman spoke in Japanese, not expecting Blade to understand it. "I'm sorry, sir, do you have an invitation?"

Knowledge of the language was only one of the surprises Blade had for the creature. "*Hai*." He slipped a silver stake from the armor and moved on the vampire, shoving it deep into his chest. "And I'm gonna engrave it."

Karen held her breath as Blade shoved the dying vampire doorman through the entranceway of The Black Pearl. The hinges ripped out of the wooden moorings with shrill cries. The doorman turned to ash before he hit the floor, swirling up and being sucked back out the door. Karen thought she was going to scream, and barely managed to stop herself.

Stepping through the entrance, Blade scanned the room, holding Karen back protectively. She looked over his shoulder, not believing what she saw. It made her tighten her grip on the pistol.

The business inside was set up as an all-hours strip club/casino combo. Dim light barely broke through the heavy clouds of cigarette smoke filling the room. Music blasted away at a deafening intensity from the speakers, a crashing heavy-metal storm front at ground zero.

Go boards and pachinko machines were set up in the back; Karen recognized them from outings she'd gone on with Curtis Webb. Webb's restless nature had taken them a number of places she'd never been before. Japanese men in black suits played with a consuming intensity, evidently taking a break from the *zaibatsu* district. Heavy business required heavy play to let down.

The waitresses were petite enough to pass as children, delicate little women who looked like they'd been stamped out with a cookie cutter. They wore what appeared to be traditional black-and-white school uniforms, the skirts a little too high to meet regulations.

Scantily clad and oiled strippers worked the circular pit tables, surrounded by howling men playing grab-ass. And money hit the tables with the regularity of oak leaves in the fall.

A manga-girl hip-hop duo worked the main stage, twisting their heads so their ponytails flew in all directions. They sang in little-girl-doll voices, and the backbeat was a heavy-metal riff that could have done double duty as a wrecking ball. They showed a lot of leg beneath the short skirts, and a lot more besides. Their white panties barely hid their modesty.

"The clientele aren't vampires," Blade said. "The operation is set up to drain a cash flow, not blood. Different resource, but the same victims. The economic needs being met help finance the vampires' holdings." He moved forward, heading past the bathrooms to the right.

Karen followed, spotting Krieger ahead of them and wondering if she'd be able to use the pistol to defend herself and Blade if she had to. Blade spotted the man, too, and pursued immediately. Then she realized Krieger wasn't carrying the cooling unit anymore.

Another broad Japanese male worked behind the bar, staring intently at them. Blade kept going, and the Japanese bartender moved to intercept them.

Karen's stomach clenched up tight as a fist as she watched Blade move on the larger creature, thinking Blade was about to get crushed.

"Hey," the guard said in English, reaching behind the counter for what had to be some kind of weapon.

Karen pulled the pistol up, ready to shoot if she had to. She didn't know if it was to prevent anything happening to Blade because she wanted to protect him, or if she just didn't care for the idea of being left alone in the club.

Blade moved before either she or the guard could act. Vaulting over the counter, Blade kicked the vampire in the face and knocked him back against a pyramid of bottles. Before the bartender could recover, Blade staked him, letting him turn to a pile of ash on the black-tiled floor. Blade went on ahead to the hallway, following him into the huge kitchen area beyond.

Krieger stood alone in the kitchen. He whirled around, then started looking for a place to run. But the only way out was through Blade. Krieger rushed forward, surprising Karen with his desperation. She stepped back involuntarily as Blade moved fluidly. Krieger threw a punch. Blade caught the fist in his hand and controlled the blow so fast that Karen almost couldn't see the move. In an eye blink, Blade had Krieger's arm levered up behind his back, using the hold to slam the man face first into the nearby shelving unit on the wall.

Karen winced, drawing back from the violence, regretting the easy way it came to Blade. Her instinct was to leave the room, but she made herself stay. She had no choice but to remain with the Hunter; her future seemed tied to his for the moment. If he had one. Attacking a nest of vampires by himself wasn't exactly what she would call a prescription for probable survival.

The shelving came down all around Krieger. The man cried out in pain, flailing, trying to get back up. Blade reached down, knotted his hand in the man's hair, and yanked his head up.

Krieger screamed in pain.

"Where's the entrance?" Blade demanded.

Krieger strained to keep the pressure off his hair, but Blade didn't let up, yanking on the handful of hair more forcefully. "I can't. They'll kill me!"

Karen was confused. Clearly, there wasn't another door in the room.

In the darkness of the room, Blade's eyes glowed with white fire.

For a moment, Karen thought he was about to lose his control again. She took a step forward, raising the gun in her fist, not knowing what she was going to do.

"I've got news for you, friend," Blade said. *"You're already dead."*

Krieger's weak attempt at courage and lying shattered, taking his composure with it. He shivered. "Oh God, shit! It's through the freezer!"

Obviously not believing the man, Blade slammed Krieger's face into the wall again.

"I swear, I swear!" Krieger shouted, panicked and pleading. "It's actually in the freezer!"

Blade dragged the man through the loose pile of shelving and canned goods, stopping in front of the freezer. He turned and saw Karen almost holding the gun on him. "Covering me?" he asked. "Or protecting him?" His words were a sneer, a verbal slap in the face.

Karen felt their sting. She wanted to argue with him, tell him that it wasn't easy making the change from a normal, sane person with everyday problems to some kind of vigilante hunting creatures she'd believed only existed in fiction.

He moved on before she had time. Going to the freezer, Blade pulled the door open.

It took a second for the freezer light to flicker on. Then, through the cold, white-gray haze of vapor fog that came boiling out of the room, the dim outlines of a stairway leading down to an elevator took shape.

Karen stared at the doors, suddenly entranced by the arcane possibilities presented by the discovery of the hidden elevator. In the corner of her eye she saw Krieger moving on his own in Blade's inexorable grip, and was grateful that the man didn't appear to be hurt too badly, because she didn't want to be part of that.

Blade drew the assault rifle from his back and placed it against Krieger's forehead. "Give Frost a message for me. Tell him it's open season on all suckheads."

Krieger trembled, eyes opening and closing rapidly like he couldn't decide what to do with them, whether to watch death coming or not.

Then Blade pulled the assault rifle back and nodded for Krieger to leave.

Krieger bolted at once and didn't look back, stumbling and bouncing off the walls of the narrow hallway leading back to the bar's main room. Spectators had gathered there, but no one appeared interested enough to come after Blade.

Looking at Blade, Karen said, "I'm impressed. An hour ago you would have killed him."

Blade's voice was colder than the mist coiling from the big freezer. "I have. He just doesn't know it. I want Frost to know I'm coming." He kept the weapon in his hand as he motioned Karen toward the hidden elevator. "After you."

Somewhat reluctantly, Karen stepped into the

small cage, grateful there were no recriminations about her ability to keep watch over his back. Or questions about whose side she was on.

Blade stepped into the cage with her, then pressed the only button on the control panel in front of them. He kept his gaze and his thoughts to himself as the doors closed and they went down.

Karen couldn't even guess what they were about to walk into, but her skin was prickled from more than just the cold inside the freezer.

CHAPTER

22

Blade kept himself centered as the elevator dropped, physically and emotionally. He breathed, taking it in deep, as Whistler had taught him, holding it for just a moment, then blowing it out in a silent rush. He holstered the assault rifle and took up the shotgun from under the folds of his long-coat. The twelve-gauge had more sheer knock-down power even than the CAR–15.

A tone chimed as the elevator came to a stop. The doors hissed open, revealing rows and stacks and shelves of books, documents, and papers.

Blade held the shotgun in both hands as he took point and moved out of the elevator cage. "Stay close," he told the woman.

Karen was at his heels.

The stacks created a maze across the huge floor. If it had been empty, it would have been a cavern beneath the city. The dim lighting hardly penetrated the shadowy darkness at all. And it was so cold that his breath and the woman's came out in frosty gray plumes.

"What is this place?" Karen whispered.

Blade didn't worry about cautioning her not to talk. She was human; the vampires down here would sense her long before they heard her. "Some kind of archive. This must be where they keep their records." He couldn't help thinking how Whistler would have had a field day down here. The old man was positively a researchaholic.

Karen glanced at the stacks doubtfully. "Isn't this all a little high-tech? I thought vampires were more into cobwebs and coffins."

In spite of the situation and the doubt he had about her, Blade smiled a little. "You've been watching too much TV. They've got their claws sunk into everything—finance, real estate, politics. They own half of downtown. Frost is their ticket to the twenty-first century." He took a CD-ROM disk from the shelves. The spine was labeled in glyphs that he couldn't read.

A distant whisper reached his keen ears, someone talking, trying desperately not to be overheard.

Blade returned the disk to the shelves and cautioned Karen to be quiet. He let the shotgun lead the way through the stacks, closing in on the whisper like he was running on radar.

●   ●   ●

Deacon Frost walked through the crowd thronging the rooftop pool inside his penthouse apartment in Edgewood Towers. The building was located on the periphery of the city, close to the urban sprawl that he found so intoxicating, with its patina of decay and violence. He dressed casually in evening wear. After all, his day was only beginning.

Turquoise tile lined the bottom of the lighted pool, making it seem a giant jewel set in the rooftop. The lights embedded in the pool walls lit the water up clearly.

Mercury danced in the moonlight flooding through the shuttered windows, swaying with abandon to a hypnotic beat, her blond hair spun white gold. As Frost watched her from above the deep end of the pool, he felt desire for her build. It wasn't often that he felt passion, but with the moon burning down bright and memory of Dragonetti's affront still fresh in his mind, perhaps, he thought, he felt like a conquest.

And, too, there'd been the recent success with the ancient manuscript. Pearl had proven unusually resourceful.

Usually those needs were best served by a human female. A *scared* human female who had no idea what sort of creature she had let next to her until it was much too late.

Occasionally, though, less and less these days as the years passed by much faster, Frost found himself drawn to one of his own. He liked the idea of Mercury, knowing that she could fight back when the time came, perhaps even as fiercely as he. Her own strengths, treacheries, and passions made their infrequent couplings exciting.

And then there was the woman who regularly shared his bed, who attended his every need. He'd turned her himself, made her his very own. She loved him with an intensity that was infrequently seen among vampires.

Quinn sat across the table from Frost. The big man chatted with a young nubile wanna-be he'd been bringing to the ongoing party occasionally the last few weeks. As he spoke, he picked unconsciously at the new flesh growing on his face and at the stub of his maimed arm. The lost limb was regenerating quickly as a result of the extra feedings he'd been taking.

"Hey," Quinn said to the young woman next to him, speaking loudly enough that Frost could hear him, "you wanna meet Frost? I can make that happen; I'm tight with him." He looked up at Frost, acting cool. "Deacon, Deacon—I'd like you to meet Shelly here."

Frost deliberately circled around the pool away from them. Quinn knew how he hated to be used for anyone else's successes.

"Oh, he's not in the mood right now," Quinn told the woman.

As he moved through the crowd, there were others who operated out of the same motivation as Quinn. Everyone wanting to use him as a touchstone for fame. He made small talk, disposing of them quickly, raking his hot gaze over the human females that interested him, making sure they knew it.

Officer Krieger approached him through the crowd, cradling his ruined hand in his good arm, his battered face downcast as he continued to look at the ground. The Black Pearl was less than five minutes away if a man was in a hurry. Krieger obviously was. One of the other familiars at the club had called Frost with the news of Blade's arrival there.

Frost moved away from the man, making him follow like a dog at heel. The vampire lord didn't ask any questions and didn't offer any observations. Conversations dropped away as the partygoers became aware of Krieger.

The police officer broke the silence that had hung on for the last few minutes. Frost had known he would. Humans didn't have the benefit of a long life in which to view the passage of time properly. Nor did they fully appreciate how short that life could become.

"I know you're disappointed," the police officer said.

"Am I that transparent?" Frost asked.

"Blade was waiting for me," Krieger insisted. "Look, I had no idea he'd be there. You have to believe me. The whole thing was a setup, you see? He used her as bait, right—"

"And you were stupid enough to take it, is that

what you're trying to say, Krieger?" Disgust for the human filled Frost within the first few sentences out of the man's mouth.

Soundlessly, Mercury moved up behind Krieger. He became aware of her, but tried to pretend he wasn't afraid of her.

"All right, okay, going to Pearl's was a mistake," Krieger said desperately. "I realize that, dumb-fucking-me. But we can still get the girl, it's no prob—"

Before the man could get a word out of his mouth, Frost uncoiled like a snapped spring. Morphing his hand into a talon-filled claw, he ripped it through Krieger's throat. He caught the dying man by his necktie and hauled him up.

The partygoers watched in stunned amazement. Some of them had never seen a vampire kill before. None of them reacted badly. They all wanted to be what Frost was.

"Wild," Quinn said appreciatively, grinning widely.

Frost offered his kill to Mercury. She bent over the dying man, drinking deeply from the bloody fountain spurting from his throat. Then she put a hand on Frost's arm and leaned in for a kiss.

Frost bent to her, took her lips in a thirsty crush. The savagery unleashed in him sang an ancient song that he was still learning about. He knew he had power at those times. Now even Mercury felt the strength in him.

Her eyes were ablaze with passion as well

when she pulled back from him. A smile was on her face as she flicked her tongue over her lips. She savored the flavor of the blood, then frowned in disappointment. "O negative. Figures."

Frost nodded, joining her in her disappointment. Krieger's quivering dead body was only a vessel that held an ordinary drink when they were both thirsty for much more. He released the corpse, letting it drop. The police officer's body dropped through the cool blue water, turning it murky with his blood. His badge twinkled like buried treasure.

"Forget the girl," he told Mercury and Quinn. "That was a long shot anyway. I want Blade."

Mercury smiled conspiratorially, thinking she understood. "I know you do."

Frost shifted his gaze to Quinn, making the assignment with his eyes. "And I want him alive."

The eager smile dropped from Quinn's bearded face. "Wha—why?"

Frost only smiled. There were things no one else needed to know. He loved putting on a show.

CHAPTER

23

The whisper in the vampire archives grew steadily louder in Blade's ears. He rounded the corner, crossing the threshold of a vestibule that seemed to lead, incredibly, to a bedchamber. Even as long as he'd been hunting vampires and thinking that he'd seen it all, what he knew he was about to see was something he thought he'd never get used to.

The bedchamber had rice-paper shoji screens as walls to separate the room and tatami mats covering the floor. Scented candles glowed within the final room, illuminating a monstrously obese shadow through the translucent paper walls.

Blade kept his voice at a whisper, referring to the man they were about to encounter. "His name's Pearl. He's their curator. You won't believe this motherfucker."

The shadow spoke in a tremulous, birdlike voice, but the speaker littered its conversation with harsh words that Blade couldn't understand. The language, however, confirmed that the creature on the other side of the rice-paper wall was a vampire.

"I understand, Deacon," the tremulous voice said, "but the prophecy of LaMagra is ancient."

Blade put the shotgun away and drew his sword, knowing that if the vampire was one of the Old Ones, the edged weapon would put more fear in him than the twelve-gauge.

"I understand, Deacon. I understand, but the prophecy of the Blood God is ancient. It took time." The massive shadow froze, letting the Hunter know the creature's keen hearing had picked up the sound. "Krieger," the vampire asked, "is that you?"

Hooking his fingers in the nearest shoji screen, Blade slid it open and stepped through. As he studied the man revealed in candlelight before him, Karen gasped behind him.

Blade didn't blame her for being shocked. He was, too, even though he'd heard stories about the vampire from Whistler. The creature before them weighed easily nine hundred pounds and was of Asian origin. He sat on the biggest ass the Hunter had ever seen, lounging fearfully on the pillowed rice mats and wearing a communications headset that connected him to a videophone before him. He had a buttermilk complexion, his skin so tight

and engorged from recent feeding that he was actually *sweating* blood. Blade had never seen anything
like it.

Monitors and keyboards surrounded the creature on counterbalanced arms like the outer edges of a nest. They gave the appearance of a giant mechanical spider waiting to serve its master's every need. With the setup, the corpulent vampire could easily access any of the machines.

"Oh my God," Karen said.

Blade shifted his gaze, seeing what she'd seen. Beside the fat vampire, a recently drained plastic blood bag with the Hillburn Clinic logo on it had been discarded like a banana peel or a candy wrapper. Everything inside was already gone.

The fat vampire's head swiveled around to face the Hunter. He spoke hurriedly over the videophone, eyes widening in absolute fear. "He's here!"

Blade recognized the face at the other end of the videophone connection at once as belonging to Deacon Frost. "Congratulations, Blade," Frost said.

"Hello, Frost," Blade said.

With a speed belying such huge bulk, the fat Asian vampire lunged for the trackball at the end of an arm. He fumbled for the DELETE button.

Blade shifted, swinging the sword around. He sank the sword point into the first inch of the fat vampire's neck, freezing the creature in place. He glanced at the monitors, seeing the single page of glyphs covering the screens. He didn't have a clue what it was, but the vampire's actions let him know it was considered important.

Deacon Frost grinned into the videophone, oozing confidence he certainly didn't have at the moment. Blade should never have found the Black Pearl. Finding the vampire archives was something the Hunter had never done before. "I hear you've been looking for me. I'm flattered."

Blade stared back coldly from the videophone, the small shake of his head blurring slightly because the video feed couldn't generate pictures quickly enough over the analog systems of the phone line to make them smooth. "Don't be. You're another notch on my sword hilt, nothing else."

Frost settled into a chair in front of the videophone. In spite of the situation, in spite of the breach of security Blade's presence at the archives represented, Frost enjoyed the game of cat and mouse between them. Blade was a worthy opponent, and there were no politics involved between them the way there was with Dragonetti. It was nighttime now, and the city was within Frost's grasp, filled with his agents. Blade had to know that. Going up against the forces Frost could summon was a death wish.

But then, Frost conceded, that *was* Blade: a death wish walking.

Pearl spoke, his high-pitched voice sounding almost comical even with the fear threading through him. "He's going to kill me, Frost! You need me! He—"

Frost interrupted the vampire. "You're history, Pearl. Have the good grace to die with some dignity." Frost punched off the channel, losing the smile at once. "Fuck!" The vampire opened up another channel and punched in Quinn's cellphone number. Blade was at the archives, and Frost knew for a fact that Quinn could get there before the Hunter could leave.

The Hunter would be captured within the hour.

CHAPTER

24

The sound of the dial tone filled the bedroom, harsh and insistent. Blade turned the videophone off.

"Frost!" the fat Asian vampire blubbered. "You ruthless son of a bitch."

"Keep him covered," Blade ordered.

Karen lifted the pistol and aimed it directly at the fat vampire. Her hands shook, but she didn't have a doubt that she would pull the trigger if the monster before her tried to move.

Blade tossed the worn leather satchel on his shoulder to the bed. He opened it, revealing a hand-held UV lamp hooked up to a nine-volt battery.

Pearl quivered in fear at the sight of the device, and the jiggling rolls of flesh almost made Karen sick. "What's that?" the vampire asked in his falsetto voice.

Blade's reply was harsh, clipped. "Ultraviolet lamp. We're going to play twenty questions. Depending on your answers, you might get yourself a tanning session." He tapped the nearby monitor.

Karen glanced at the monitor as well. The digitized image there looked like an old illustrated manuscript page that resembled ones she remembered from her lit classes in college.

"What's that?" Blade asked.

The fat vampire glanced nervously from Blade to the monitor, then back again. He licked his lips, drawing little beads of blood from his upper lip. Karen's stomach rolled, her finger almost pulling through the pistol trigger reflexively.

Blade flicked the UV lamp on. The cone of light bathed the fat vampire, causing the creature's face to smoke profusely.

Karen made herself watch. This was further proof that what Blade told her about vampires actually *was* true. The back of her neck tightened, prickling. The pressure of her skin, pulling, also made her aware of the throbbing still going on in the wound in her throat. The resulting fear that coursed through her made her stronger than the sickness.

Blade flicked the light off.

Cringing and growling, Pearl drew back. Even after the few seconds of exposure, his face was as blistered as a severe second-degree burn victim's. Pearl had trouble speaking, gasping, "It's nothing, just a fragment of a Prophecy."

The way Pearl said it told Karen that it was Prophecy with a capital P. She glanced at Blade, wondering if the Hunter knew what the vampire was talking about. But his face remained expressionless.

"And which prophecy would that be?" Blade asked.

Pearl hesitated.

Blade didn't, flicking the lamp on a heartbeat after asking the question. He left it on longer this time.

"It contains a ritual to unleash LaMagra!" Pearl screamed in a pain-laced voice.

"Who's that?" Blade demanded.

"The Blood God comes!" Pearl yelled.

Hypnotized, numbed by the fear she felt for herself and the rage over Curtis Webb's death, Karen watched as Pearl thrashed and covered his face with his arms. Pearl's hands turned black almost immediately, the skin sizzling away to expose the finger bones underneath. She averted her head, unable to watch any more at the moment.

The snap of the lamp being turned off brought instant relief. Karen took a deep breath, struggling for control. The stench of burning flesh filled her nostrils despite the scented candles, bringing back memories of the other dead man from the night before. She turned back to the vampire.

Pearl snarled at Blade, who didn't appear

impressed by the vampire's performance or predicament. Quivering with poisonous rage and pain, Pearl exploded vehemently, speaking in a tongue Karen couldn't understand. "The Sleeper awakens! The Blood Tide comes! And you can't do a thing about it, Day-Walker!"

Blade leaned in closer to the vampire, eye-to-eye with the shaking monster. "Is that so?"

Blistered face convulsing, Karen recognized the fear in Pearl's eyes, knowing the vampire realized he'd said way more than he should have.

"Well," Pearl said, stumbling over his own words, "that's what Frost says." The vampire cast a sidelong glance away from Blade, his eyes fixing on an armored door almost hidden in the shadows.

"Uh-huh." Blade appeared noncommittal. "Well you don't mind if I just borrow that, do you?" He reached out and tapped the CD-ROM drive, ejecting the tray. He took the CD out and dropped it into a nearby jewel case, which he then pocketed in his jacket.

The computer screen faded to gray snow. A message came up only a little later. DEVICE NOT READY. ABORT? CANCEL? RETRY?

Blade straightened, handing the UV setup to Karen. "If he moves, *cook him*."

Karen took the UV lamp, uncomfortable with how much the Hunter seemed willing to trust her. She watched him walk to the armored door, and saw that it opened to a vault built into the wall.

Blade crossed the room and sized up the locking mechanism on the armored door.

Pearl appeared close to panic. "There's nothing in there! It's just a storeroom!"

Blade took an aerosol can from his longcoat and fitted a nozzle to it. He sprayed deliberately, saturating the hinges and the channels between the door and the wall. In seconds the chemicals combined and started to sizzle. Karen recognized that a chemical reaction was taking place, but didn't know what to expect.

"Then you won't mind if I take a look," the Hunter said.

"No!" Pearl screamed. The vampire lunged from the bed, pulling at the computers and hardware mounted on the counterbalanced arms.

Thinking about how Curtis Webb had been killed, and her own uncertain future because of creatures like the one before her, Karen switched the UV lamp on. And left it on. The exposure blacked Pearl to a crisp in heartbeats. Karen didn't even think about turning it off.

The bloated corpse of the vampire hit the tatami mats in front of her. Smoke curled up from the quivering mass of charred meat that remained.

Karen left the light on till she was certain the thing was dead. Then she switched it off. She glanced up at Blade defensively, thinking he might be mad at her for killing his interrogation subject.

Instead, a smile twisted his lips beneath the sunglasses.

Karen shrugged, not believing he didn't have at least something to say. "He moved."

Even if Blade had said something, the blast that went off behind him would have covered it. Karen ducked away, feeling the rush of super-heated air blow by her. When she turned back around, Blade was walking into the open room beyond the demolished door. She followed, know-ing the other people in the building had to have taken notice of the sound caused by that much destruction.

Papers fluttered through the air, some of them burning completely before they hit the ground while others only smoldered. Glass-encased docu-ments lined the wall, but some of the glass panes were shattered and starred, reflecting that they were specially reinforced.

Blade stepped forward, examining the pages.

Karen joined him, studying the glyphs and the illustrations. "These are just like the page on the computer. What is this?"

"A *gold mine*," Blade answered. "These are pages from the *Book of Erebus*."

"I don't know what that is," Karen said. All of the drawings were macabre, darkly evil. She was getting an emotional reaction from just looking at them.

"The vampire Bible. It's got everything in it, their entire history." Blade's voice turned musing, the first time Karen had heard him think out loud. "LaMagra must be one of their legends."

"Why is Frost so interested in LaMagra?" Karen asked.

Blade shrugged, shaking his head as he scanned the illustrated pages. The pages reflected in the lenses of his sunglasses. "Why is Frost so interested in vampire history?" But the question seemed directed more toward himself than her.

Before Karen could even venture a guess or another question, she watched Blade tense, going into hunting mode.

"Quiet," he said. Then he was moving, tracking something or someone. His movements and his attention were totally focused.

Karen spun, far behind Blade when it came to movement, but getting there. She watched him reach out to grab a small figure by the shoulder. When he turned her around, Karen saw the little girl first, then the vampiric features second.

The female vampire snickered, flicking her talons at Blade's face. He whirled out of reach and twisted back the way they'd come, staring along their backtrail. Karen realized they'd been tricked almost as soon as he did.

The way back to the vault contained a handful of figures, with others standing farther behind them, blocking the only exit.

A svelte blonde stood next to the vampire Karen recognized as the previous night's corpse. His burns and cuts had healed dramatically. Even the missing arm had partially regrown. The skeletal framework was there, supporting masses of cartilage, sinew, and muscle, only barely covered by flesh that appeared red and raw.

"*Hola, amigo*," the creature said, grinning. "Remember me?" He licked his fangs as its eyes moved to Karen. "How ya doing, Doc?"

CHAPTER

25

The little vampire girl attacked again, snarling and hissing as she raked her talons at Blade. He threw her to the side, smashing her through a small counter.

Still in motion, the Hunter fisted the pistol grip of the shotgun as he dragged it from beneath the folds of his longcoat. Quinn closed on him before he could get it all the way up, knocking him back against the glass panels covering the *Book of Erebus*. Glass smashed as the wind left Blade's lungs in a rush.

He struggled to push himself back up, watching as Karen Jansen tried to run. But there was nowhere to go. She grabbed a rack of books and brought them tumbling down across one of her pursuers. Before Karen could move again, Mercury had her claws unsheathed and around Karen's neck.

Blade's blood chilled as he thought of what the vampires would do to Karen. Christ, he'd known better than to bring her here. If she got killed, it would be his fault.

The vampires came at him en masse then, swarming over him like pack predators. He slipped one hand to his collar and jammed the micro ear-coil radio receiver into place. "Whistler," he said.

"I'm on my way, kid," the old man radioed back. "Give me a sec."

Blade didn't bother to tell Whistler that might be more time than he had.

At Quinn's direction, the vampires hauled him to his feet, pinning him against the vault wall by sheer numbers.

Quinn shoved his face forward, a leering grin under his glowing eyes. "You took my arm, Blade. But that's okay." He held up his twisted mockery of a limb, new tissues glistening in the light provided in the vault. "I'm growing a new one." The vampire peeled a burn-ward gauze glove from its maimed hand, then flexed the fingers. The bones rattled against each other with gliding snaps. "Nice, huh? Think I'll ever play the piano again?" He shrugged. "You can slice him, you can dice him, and the man just keeps on coming." Quinn laughed maniacally at his own humor.

Blade struggled against the vampires holding him, trying to get an arm free, trying to get at Quinn. But he couldn't.

One of the younger male vampires, dressed in black Goth-style clothing, picked Blade's sword up from the floor. "Check it out, I've got his pig-sticker." He waved the sword around enthusiastically, fencing against a shadow opponent.

Despite the situation, Blade grinned in anticipation.

Without warning, the hidden blades in the sword hilt sprang out, lopping off fingers and cutting up the creature's hand. The young vampire howled in pain and disbelief, crying over his injured hand.

"Crease," Quinn said, "you're a fuck-up." The vampire slipped the gauze glove back on over his own regenerating limb as he returned his attention to Blade. "Well, you're just full of surprises, aren't you, chief?"

"Got a habit of causing people to go to pieces," Blade replied.

Quinn stepped in and began unloading with its good fist into Blade's face, smashing the Hunter's head back against the wall with incredible power.

Centering himself mentally, Blade pushed himself through the pain, past the pain. He was there/not there, his body disassociated from his mind. He let his head loll forward, not using any of his muscle groups.

Quinn worked at it until the vampire was winded, his face dark with suffused blood he'd borrowed from whatever donors he had found since the previous night. The creature closed his good hand under Blade's face, lifting it to stare into the Hunter's eyes. "Stay with me, sweetness, I'm not through with you yet."

Blade looked past the man, not registering Quinn's presence.

Quinn pulled Blade's jacket open, revealing the bandolier of stakes across his chest. The vampire tugged one out, looking at it in open admiration. "Silver. Nice craftsmanship." Quinn looked over his shoulder at the other vampires. "Now here's a man who takes his job just a little too seriously, don't you think?"

The audience responded with a chorus of affirmations. Mercury grinned, still holding Karen in her clawed grip.

Quinn turned back to the Hunter. "Which reminds me, Blade, I think I owe you one." With incredible strength and speed, the vampire rammed the stake into Blade's shoulder, ramming it through the flesh and blood and into the wall behind him, pinning him.

The pain flooded the Hunter's synapses, breaking through the barrier he'd put up inside his head. Blade cried out and struggled again to free himself. But the vampires holding him didn't let up. He slumped back then, managing to get around even this pain.

Across from him, Karen looked away, not wanting to see his agony.

"Actually," Quinn said with a sadistic grin, "if

you want to get technical, I owe you *two*." He reached for another stake from the bandolier.

Blade made himself laugh, and the effort rolled like thunder through the enclosed vault space.

Quinn stepped back uneasily. "What's so funny, bright eyes?"

"I'm expecting some company," Blade replied. "You should get a bang out of it."

Quinn stared at the Hunter, finally noticing the micro ear-coil radio receiver in Blade's ear.

"Duck and cover," Whistler said over the radio.

Blade waited, not at all surprised when the sound of an explosion temporarily deafened them all. A huge section of the vault wall exploded inward, knocking Quinn and the rest of the vampires from their feet, tumbling Karen from Mercury's grip.

Whistler stood in the smoking hole where the wall once stood. He brandished his cane in one hand and an automatic rifle in the other. "Catch you fuckers at a bad time?" he asked.

CHAPTER

26

Balancing the rifle against his hip, Whistler opened fire on the vampires, driving them from Blade. Two of them turned to ash in quick succession as the garlic-laced silver bullets chewed through them.

Released by the vampires, Blade pulled himself free of the wall. The stake remained in his shoulder, buffeting him with white-hot pain. Crossing the distance between them, he backfisted Mercury, knocking the vampire down and away. Mercury scuttled out of sight immediately, as Whistler put a burst in the space the creature had just vacated. Blade reached down for Karen, helping her up from where Mercury had dropped her.

Autofire from Whistler's assault rifle rolled over them. "Gotta move!" the old man yelled, reflected muzzle flashes glinting fire in his pale hair. He yanked a backpack over his shoulder and threw it.

Blade spotted the LED readout flashing numbers in a descending sequence on the backpack, indicating a countdown to an explosion. Whistler was a man who always carried heavy destruction. The Hunter managed to grab one of the parchment pages from the floor at his feet and his sword, then ran for the hole blown in the wall, dragging Karen after him.

On the other side of the wall a subway tunnel ran parallel to the archives. Releasing Karen, he gripped the silver stake in his shoulder and yanked it out. He wiped it on his leg, then replaced it in the bandolier. The pain wasn't nearly so severe now that the silver was gone.

"How did you find us?" Karen asked Whistler. A cut over one of her eyebrows leaked blood.

Whistler answered her question, but his attention was divided between her and his watch. "We keep in radio contact." He tapped the tiny radio headset curled around his ear.

"You've been listening in the whole time?" She sounded incredulous, and pissed.

Blade watched Whistler, choosing to ignore both emotions.

"You think I'd let him run loose without a chaperon?" Whistler grinned, still looking at the watch.

Blade led the way to the end of the access tunnel, the others close behind him. He stepped out onto the subway tracks.

Thunder filled the tunnel, and Blade at first thought it was the sound of the backpack blowing up. When the light flared into his vision at the other end of the tunnel, however, he knew he was wrong. Even his incredible strength and balance almost weren't enough to move them from the subway tracks in time. The Hunter pulled Karen up against the wall on the other side of the tracks, protecting her as the subway train suddenly bore down on them. He reached down and unleathered the MACH, watching the subway train as it passed. Astonished faces whipped by at a dizzying speed.

When the train passed, he spotted the vampires boiling through the tunnel the three of them had just abandoned. Whistler clung to the wall to one side of the tunnel, breathing hard and favoring his leg in its brace. "Christ, I'm too old for this. Somebody get me a goddamn wheelchair."

"You bastards get after them!" Quinn roared. The vampire glanced around the tunnel, his vampiric vision taking away all the shadows. Whistler had killed a few of them, but there were enough left to kill the old man and capture Blade. Quinn tried not to think of what Deacon Frost was going to say about all the destruction to the archives.

Gaetano Dragonetti was going to be a bitch to deal with.

Quinn led the other vampires through the hole in the wall. Then the vampire saw the backpack lying in the center of the tunnel behind him, the LED numbers flickering red. Counting. *Counting down!* The creature dived for cover, watching as Mercury dived as well. He started to yell a warning to the others, who hadn't noticed the device. But the words were swallowed up in the thunderous *BOOM!* that followed.

The vampires closest to the backpack were engulfed in flames, becoming human-shaped flares that screamed in pain.

Quinn forced himself to his feet, running once again. Only this time the vampire was running into the subway tunnel, away from the massive fireball that billowed out toward it. The creature smelled charred skin, pushed along by the growing heat wave that was overtaking him.

At that instant, Blade heard the sound of an explosion ripping through the subway tunnel, louder than the noise of the passing subway train. Smoke mushroomed out through the hole as big chunks fell away from the wall. Several thudded harmlessly against the sides of the last subway car as it passed.

Blade figured the *zaibatsu* crowd playing games and watching the strippers on the above-ground floor would definitely be getting a wake-up call about the institution now. And when the police arrived to follow up on the calls from the subway officials, that wake-up call would get even louder.

Whistler whooped enthusiastically. "Oh yeah! There may be a few more gray hairs, but I can still bring the house down!" He glanced at the empty subway tunnel. "Let's go!"

Blade followed the man across the first set of tracks, noticing the other set farther over.

"Look!" Karen shouted, pointing behind them.

Blade turned, spotting a dozen vampires who hadn't been killed in the explosion surging into the tunnel like hungry wolves. Mercury and Quinn were in the lead. A glowing nimbus of light formed around them. It took Blade a second to figure out what the light source was before the vibrations through the track at his feet gave it away.

Karen turned, frozen in the middle of the tracks as a second train hurtled straight for her. Blade shifted his gaze to her, realizing that she wasn't moving fast enough.

The subway train raced forward, the brakeman blowing his horn in warning.

CHAPTER

27

Blade threw himself across the intervening distance toward Karen Jansen. He hit her at waist level with his wounded shoulder. The pain exploded inside his head like a napalm blast, almost burning out his senses. The force of his lunge carried them across the track just ahead of the approaching subway train. Everything around them was light and noise and rumbling movement.

Karen groaned in pain when she hit the ground, and Blade kept them rolling clear of the train. He looked up, only to see the leaders of the pack of vampires almost on top of them.

He helped Karen to her feet, barely holding it together. The wound in his shoulder was already starting to heal, but it had taken a tremendous toll on his system.

"Where's Whistler?" Karen asked.

"He can take care of himself." Blade pulled her toward him, watching the subway cars speeding by. When they were gone, he pulled her after him. "Jump!"

They leaped, reaching the central divider between the tracks. But Karen didn't have her balance completely and stumbled, falling forward toward the third rail of the track.

Blade helped her to regain her balance, then picked up movement in the periphery of his vision. Looking back, he spotted Quinn and the other vampires racing toward them. Their numbers had been supplemented by guards from the Black Pearl. Firing the MACH quickly, the Hunter managed to drive the vampires back for a moment.

More thunder filled the tunnel as another of the city's major subway lines ran through on schedule. The headlights ignited the tunnel, driving away all the shadows.

Blade grabbed Karen again and threw them into a rolling heap on the nearby platform, out of the train's way. Quinn made it across as well, but the next two vampires got smashed across the front of the speeding train engine like bugs on a windshield.

One of the vampires smashed through the windshield and crushed the motorman, who was too surprised to move. The falling tangle of bodies slammed against the deadman's handle and caused the train to gain speed.

Blade lifted the MACH again and tried to aim at Quinn. But the vampire moved too quickly, making an incredible leap onto the platform with Blade and Karen. Blade grabbed his opponent, not quite even with the vampire's strength, but hoping to make up the difference with his martial-arts skills. Quinn was too damn strong. They rolled and struggled, knocking Karen from the platform.

She tumbled into the gap between the platform and the grinding train wheels, and Blade's attention was diverted. The crushing, cutting steel wheels were only inches from her face.

Getting some leverage, Blade threw Quinn aside. He reached down to Karen to help her out, but before he could manage it, Quinn kicked him, causing near-paralyzing pain to surge through the Hunter's nervous system. Rolling to his feet, Blade drew his sword and swiped at Quinn's head.

Quinn ducked beneath the hurried swing and retaliated with a solid punch to Blade's wounded shoulder. Pain flooded through Blade's arm. The sword fell out of his hand, skittering across the concrete and dropping off the edge of the platform.

Karen dodged frantically to get out of the sword's way. The sword thudded into the ground at her feet, vibrating in place.

Blade chopped at Quinn, only managing to get in a few solid blows without getting the leverage he needed to get the vampire off him. Quinn snarled and spit in the Hunter's face, his breath foul with the scent of blood and death.

Going down under the vampire's renewed onslaught, taking more damage to his wounded shoulder, Blade saw Karen rip the sword free of the ground. But she didn't know how to disarm the booby-trapped hilt. He tried to call out a warning to her to drop the damn thing, but Quinn caught him in the face with a blow that rocked his head back. In the next instant, Quinn froze, roaring in pain.

The vampire stumbled back, gazing incredulously at the sword sticking out of his crotch. Blood streamed down his pants.

Karen backed away from the sword, releasing the hilt just in time to avoid the maiming booby trap.

Blade moved at once, grabbing Quinn's head and shoving it into the passing subway train. The vampire's face slammed against the cars, shredding flesh.

"They're still coming!"

Looking up at Karen's screamed warning, Blade saw brief kaleidoscopic images of Mercury pacing frantically on the far side of the train like stop-motion photography. Then he spotted Whistler, so far unnoticed by the vampires, ducking down into a maintenance access shaft.

Karen gazed at the gaps between the cars. "We're running out of train." The last car was already in sight. "Once it clears, they're going to be on top of us."

"I know," Blade replied over the rumbling roar. He let go of Quinn, and the vampire crumpled at his feet. Much as he wanted to, there was no time to deal with the creature if they were going to make any kind of escape. After he sheathed his sword, Blade grabbed Karen and pulled her to him. "Hold on to me!"

Karen glanced at the train, but amidst the tumult, it was a moment before it occurred to her that what he was planning was impossible. "Oh my God!"

Blade saw her eyes widen, and he understood her disbelief. The subway train was passing at sixty miles an hour. As the last car quickly approached, he saw Mercury and the other vampires moving closer.

Readying himself, dropping his arm over, then tightening his grip on Karen, Blade lunged forward. Lightning-quick and steel-strong, the fingers of his free hand closed on the safety rail on the back of the rear car as it flashed by. He screamed with the agony that ripped through his shoulder, spreading down his entire spinal column, but held on by sheer willpower, even after he felt the shoulder slide out of its socket. Then he pulled them both onto the coupling footplate.

Once Karen had her balance, Blade rammed his spiked shoulder against the emergency-exit door, trying in vain to knock the lock open.

"Blade!" Karen pointed behind the Hunter.

He turned and stared, not believing what he saw.

Quinn was running after the subway train, racing down the tracks. Incredibly, Quinn was gaining, closing fast. Then the creature threw himself forward from thirty feet out.

Blade, dazed from the pain, couldn't get out of the way in time.

Quinn's good hand wrapped around his ankle, and, pulled by the vampire's weight, the Hunter went off-balance and down at once. Quinn maintained his hold, weighing Blade down, tugging him back out of the subway-car door.

Karen, trying to help Blade, grabbed the back of his jacket and pulled.

Blade knew it was no use; Quinn was dragging them both off the car. He held on to the railing with one hand, feeling the stress through his dislocated shoulder, and flicked a hidden wrist-blade into view.

Quinn shouted at him, knowing what was coming, unable to release his grip in time.

Blade swung the wrist-blade awkwardly, but the edge was sharp enough to cleave through Quinn's wrist. The vampire fell to the tracks, tumbling head over heels. In seconds he disappeared into the darkness.

The amputated hand burst into sudden flames as it continued to clutch at Blade's ankle.

The Hunter cursed in disgust and kicked the flaming piece of flesh away from him. Then he turned back to the locking mechanism, where Karen was still frantically trying to get the door open.

"Mind your fingers," he said. When she stepped away, he slammed the wrist-blade into the lock, smashing it open. He let her enter the car first, glancing back to make sure they'd gotten away. Inside the subway car, his wounds took their toll on him. Dizzy and weak, he fell in the aisle. He tried to get up, but couldn't make it. He cursed again, hating the helpless feeling that filled him.

The subway car kept hurtling along its prescribed route, but the passengers vacated to the car ahead of them in record time.

Wearily, Blade looked up at Karen. Once Quinn had released his hold, she'd released hers. He looked into her eyes and saw revulsion and fear. Among the things she'd learned tonight was that he was as potentially bad as any of the things he pursued.

Blade knew that the decision about what to do next had to be hers. At the moment, he couldn't even help himself. With his exertions, the serum in his bloodstream had been depleted, and now the darker side of his nature was overtaking him.

It was all he could do to keep the dark Thirst that threatened to consume him from reaching out for her.

CHAPTER

28

Karen Jansen had made hard decisions in her life, over career choices, friends, romance, economics, and even life and death, when she was an intern in the ER. Most recently, as a consultant on blood order diseases and types of cancer, she'd told patients they were terminal, that they were never going to get any better.

Now, she looked at Blade, who was weakly managing to sit up. If she wanted simply to push him out the back door onto the tracks, she didn't think he could stop her. And once he was off the subway car, she felt certain the vampires chasing them would kill him.

She couldn't help thinking that maybe he'd lied to her. Maybe the only reason Krieger had come to her apartment was to get a chance at

Wesley Snipes stars as Blade, the tormented superhero who has dedicated his life to fighting the vampire clans that threaten humanity.

Kris Kristofferson is Blade's mentor, the vampire hunter Whistler. His high-tech science provides the ferocious arsenal of weapons that Blade uses to fight the vampires.

Dr. Karen Jansen (played by N'Bushe Wright) is infected with deadly vampire venom when Quinn attacks her in the hospital morgue.

Blade races across traffic in pursuit of his old enemy, Quinn.

Stephen Dorff is Blade's archnemesis, the dangerously ambitious vampire lord, Deacon Frost.

Blade is as deadly with his namesake sword as with his assault rifle, MACH pistol, and blinding UV laser—all specially designed to kill vampires.

Blade sends his adversary fleeing in a bloody confrontation in Chinatown.

Blade has the enormous physical strength of the vampire, but, because of his human blood, he can also withstand direct sunlight.

Dr. Karen Jansen reluctantly teams up with Blade in his fight against Deacon Frost and the vampire clans.

Whistler and Blade **share a uni**quely powerful bond: vampires have **killed** Whistler's wi**fe and da**ughters—Blade is the only family he has left.

Blade's motorcycle allows him to roam the streets at all hours of the day and night.

Blade prepares for the final, bloody showdown with Frost and his vampire army.

Blade, the "Day-Walker."

Blade. Maybe she was being used as bait by both sides: Blade's and the vampires'.

That thought made her confused about what she should do.

She stared at him, certain he knew what she was thinking. He was for damn sure more than human. A human couldn't have taken that stake in the arm, incurred the blood loss he had, then fought his way clear of the vampire nests. A human couldn't have grabbed on to the back of a subway train going sixty miles an hour, *and pulled her onto it at the same time*.

But did the evidence that he wasn't human mean that he was more than human? Or less?

It was a question she didn't feel comfortable asking. Her first instinct was to be rid of him. Only bad things could come from being around him. She'd seen some of them firsthand. People and *things* died around Blade.

He could also be absolutely infuriating, with his attitude and the blunt way he had about him. Even in the condition he was in, hurting as he was, obviously unable to do for himself, he wasn't asking for help. Those black-lensed glasses hid whatever he might be thinking from her.

She knew what *she* was thinking, though, and hoped she didn't live to regret it. After all, she told herself, whatever his faults, he was the man who has saved her life three times in the last two nights. And maybe, she realized, he was the only chance she had at continuing to live herself. She reached down for him, taking him under both arms.

He was weak, she saw, unable even to stand on his own. She pulled his arm across her shoulders, feeling the loose way it moved. "Your shoulder's dislocated," she said.

"Yeah. Noticed that."

She helped him into the subway car, swaying with his weight. The front of his jacket was covered with blood.

A half dozen passengers had crowded to the back of the next car to see what was going on in the car they had just deserted. As soon as they saw the blood covering Blade, they crowded to the front of the car. Then full immigration to the next car ahead began in earnest.

Blade sat on the floor, obviously in pain. He looked gray, his color drained dramatically.

Karen checked his wounds, hardly believing that with all the damage to his body, Blade was still conscious. She took hold of the elbow connected to the dislocated shoulder, put her other hand on his shoulder, and shoved, brutally popping it back into place.

Blade yelled and cursed, losing the wraparound sunglasses.

She saw his eyes for the first time. They were liquid brown, attractive eyes. But the whites around them were horribly threaded with red.

He fumbled in his longcoat pocket with his other hand, barely able to handle the small, CO_2-powered pistol injector he took out. He took filled ampoules from another pocket and shook one out. Trying to load the pistol injector with one hand proved impossible owing to all the wounds.

His voice was filled with frustration when he spoke. "I need help with this."

"I can do it." Karen took an ampoule and loaded it into the pistol injector.

Blade shrugged out of his jacket and bared his arm. He held it out to her.

She immediately noticed how much he was shaking. Like an addict needing a fresh hit. "What am I injecting you with?" she asked.

Blade's voice was weak, distant. His eyes focused on hers. She knew how vulnerable he was at that moment, and knew that he knew it, too. "Serum. It's a human hemoglobin substitute. My last dose is wearing off."

A thousand questions fired through Karen's head, foremost among them why Blade would need a human hemoglobin substitute. His body should make its own. And if it was blood he needed, it was more like a transfusion.

Then a cold dawning of realization flooded her mind. The damage he had taken, and survived, all the impossible feats of strength she'd seen; the war on the vampires . . . All of it went through her thoughts.

The fact remained, though, that he needed her help—and she had to depend on him.

She found a vein, then pressed the pistol injector against it and squeezed the trigger. The dose shot into his bloodstream with a harsh hiss.

The serum affected him at once, throwing him into convulsions. Blade fell backward, away from her. He put his hand on the wall behind him and tried to hold himself together during the attack.

Karen struggled to hold his hand, but his grip was like a vise. She barely saved her fingers from being crushed. Blade's feet drummed out a tattoo against the subway-car floor. His breathing sounded like a bellows pump, rasping even over the sound of wheels skidding across the tracks.

Gradually, the attack lessened. When it abated, he slumped over. He looked exhausted, flushed with sweat.

Karen couldn't keep her conjectures to herself, even though she knew she probably should. "You're one of them."

He kept his eyes averted from hers. When he spoke, his voice was filled with self-loathing, the first weakness she'd seen in him. "No. I'm something else."

CHAPTER

29

"He's a hybrid," Whistler said. "Half human, half-vampire."

Karen sat across from the old man at a table in the refurbished ironworks where Whistler and Blade had holed up for their siege on the vampire nest they'd uncovered in the city. Neon colors stained the painted plate-glass windows behind Whistler. The old man used a first-aid kit to clean the scrapes and bruises they both had. His touch, Karen found, was surprisingly gentle.

Blade had disappeared into one of the other rooms almost as soon as they returned. Karen had tried to go after him, but Whistler had known immediately that he didn't want company. Karen had taken the hint reluctantly.

"He knew you were going to tell me?" she asked.

Whistler grinned and shook his head. He blew on his coffee, then sipped it. "What the hell else were you and I going to talk about?"

Karen conceded the point. "Why didn't he stay?"

"Because of you."

"But I didn't say anything," she protested. And she hadn't. Even though she didn't understand everything that was happening, they'd been through a lot together in the last twenty-four hours. "He might need first aid, too." He hadn't looked good even after getting his last injection.

"This time tomorrow, all those wounds of his'll be healed. He still ages like a human, though. See, vampires age slower. That little punk, Frost? You wouldn't know it to look at him, but he's two hundred years old. Unfortunately, Blade also inherited their thirst."

"You're saying that I bother Blade?"

"Not you personally," Whistler said. "It's what you represent."

"And what do I represent?" Karen wondered if she should take offense.

The old man looked at her and shook his head. "Dr. Jansen, you're a good-looking woman. You smell nice, and you got this way about you that's just . . . womanly. I don't know how else to say it."

Karen decided to wait before reacting. Neither Blade nor his mentor seemed especially good at sugarcoating things, but they had both been brutally honest.

"What you represent is the real world. People

just doing regular things. Blade doesn't fit, and he knows it."

"He thinks he's too good for it?"

"Fuck," Whistler said, "if that's what you think, then even *I* ain't got any business talking to you." He pushed himself up from the table, favoring the crippled leg.

"Wait!" Karen said.

Whistler didn't make it easy, staring down hard at her.

"I'm sorry," she told him. "That's not what I'm thinking. I'm just trying to understand him."

Whistler's craggy, beard-stubbled face softened. "Good. Gives the two of you something in common. Because I can tell he doesn't quite know what to make of you, either. Blade isn't one for relationships, doesn't know much about making friends. And you being a woman—that's definitely going to throw a monkey wrench into his thinking. Hell, it already has." He sat back down. "Spent his whole life trying to figure out where he stands in all of this. You think you know something? Hell, you don't know the half of it."

"I'm trying," Karen said honestly. "How did he get to be a hybrid?" There must have been dozens of questions buzzing around inside her brain regarding that issue alone.

"Blade's mother was attacked by a vampire while she was pregnant. Ultimately, she died, but her unborn child lived. Unfortunately, he'd undergone certain genetic changes while in the womb."

Whistler reached for a pack of cigarettes and shook one out. He cracked a wooden match with his thumbnail and took a long drag. "I found Blade when he was thirteen. Vampirism doesn't manifest itself until puberty in those born to it. He'd been living on the streets, feeding off animals." He took a drag on the cigarette and let it out. "I took him for one of them at first, almost killed him, too. But then I realized what he *was*."

"How?"

"I've been hunting these creatures for years," Whistler explained. "I know what to look for. He didn't completely fit the profile."

"And you took him in?"

"Yeah." Whistler took his time scraping the ash from his cigarette into the silver tinfoil ashtray. "Blade's unique, you know. One in a billion. He can withstand garlic, silver, even sunlight. And he has their *strength*. But the Thirst came with it."

"I thought the serum was supposed to suppress that."

Whistler shook his head. "Time's running out. His body's starting to reject it. And so far, all my efforts to find a cure have ended in failure."

"What happens to Blade then?"

"The Thirst overcomes him, just like the others. It's not something he can control." Whistler stated it matter-of-factly, but she saw the pain in the old man's gray eyes.

•   •   •

Blade crouched in the corner of his room at the workshop. He focused on his breathing, willing the serum in his system to work and control the Thirst gnawing at the back of his mind.

The urge was sweetly seductive, pulling at him in dulcet tones.

Another series of shakes racked him. He held himself in check, feeling his body heal. If he allowed himself to drink blood, he instinctively knew he would heal even faster.

He wasn't going to allow that to happen.

He also knew Whistler and Karen were talking about him. Sweat bathed him, making him alternately cool and hot. He wondered what the woman would say after his mentor told her all of it. Then he supposed he would know soon enough.

The shakes hit him again, making his stomach and blood roil like a volcano blossoming with lava-heat.

"You sound like you've given up," Karen said.

Whistler looked away. "Time's working against us, Doc. I could work on a cure, or we can kill vampires. Can't do both."

"Maybe I can help." She was surprised at how readily the offer came to her lips. But that was what she'd trained to do: help.

"Like to think so," Whistler admitted. "But I've been over this problem from one end to the other. Not much I haven't considered."

She wondered briefly how to phrase her next statement, then decided to take a page from Blade and Whistler's book of etiquette. "No offense, Whistler, but you haven't exactly been working with state-of-the-art equipment. You might have missed something."

"I doubt it. I've been doing this a long time. Since before you were born."

Karen nodded, conceding the point for the moment. It was tough handling male egos, especially when it was something they cared about deeply. "Why *do* you hunt them?" She couldn't make herself say *vampires*, not in public.

"Habit, mostly. Just like this." He held up the cigarette, then stubbed it out in the tinfoil ashtray. Smoke curled up in front of him and he blew it away. "Had a family once. A wife, two daughters. Then a drifter came calling one evening. A vampire."

Karen recognized the name from the phone call in the archives. "He killed them?"

Whistler nodded, his pale eyes hard and distant. "Eventually. Toyed with them first. Tried to make me choose, you understand? Which order they would die in."

Swallowing the heavy lump that had suddenly formed in her throat, Karen asked, "How did you escape?"

Whistler smiled bitterly. "I *didn't*. The monster let me live." He reached down and slapped the leg brace. "Even gave me a souvenir to remember him by."

"And now you're using Blade to exact your revenge?"

Returning her gaze unflinchingly, Whistler said, "Nobody's using anyone. Blade hates them more than I do. We kill as many of them as we can find. But it's been getting worse."

"Because of Frost?"

"Frost's body count keeps rising. Something's happening in the vampire ranks, something big. And I'd stake my life that son of a bitch is at the center of it."

CHAPTER

30

Deacon Frost watched the translation program running on the laptop computer on the big desk in his bedroom. The pages of the ancient vampire prophecy were being laid bare, byte by byte. The analogy, he thought, was properly fitting.

He pressed his fingertips together in front of him as the program ran through its final cycles. The air-conditioning blew cool against his skin as he sat in the chair, naked from the waist up. As an added enjoyment, he allowed himself to feel some of the chill.

The slender woman sleeping in his bed stirred restlessly. It was night, and they weren't used to sleeping at night. However, sex could be used as a relaxant, or a stimulant, if performed properly.

He watched her move, shedding the sheets to reveal the nakedness he'd come to relish occasionally. She was more than one of his lovers. She was a conquest, and a trophy.

She crossed the room with a liquid roll of hips that he knew she meant to be seductive. Her breasts were full, proud. Moonlight swathed the curves, and he didn't use his vision to its fullest to strip away the darkness that seemed so much a part of her. Her ebony skin remained smooth and supple despite the passage of the last thirty years added to whatever she had been.

He continued devoting most of his attention to the computer screen, knowing she enjoyed being the pursuer.

She stopped behind him and put her hands on his shoulders, tightening her fists just enough to let him feel some of the power she wielded. She moved against him, letting his head rest against the smooth flesh of her stomach. Her breast rested against the top of his head. It was an open invitation.

Frost luxuriated in the heat coming from her, peering at the laptop with slitted eyes. Abruptly the decryption program stopped, leaving only two words on the light blue screen: TRANSLATION COMPLETE.

A moment later, the screen blinked again, then the English version of the Vampire Prophecy started printing out. Frost smiled in satisfaction, giving himself over to the woman as she started to caress his face.

•   •   •

A slice of moonlight invaded Blade's room in the ironworks, and he would have banished it if he had felt like getting up to close the window completely. Instead, he huddled in the corner on the floor, willing his body and the Thirst to give in to the serum one more time.

Footsteps too light to be Whistler's approached the room. Then Karen was at the door, pushing it open. "Blade?"

He didn't answer, not wanting to deal with her or her questions. Blade knew he was mostly healed now, and the shakes weren't as debilitating. He hated being wounded this badly, because he had to remain idle for the healing process to kick in and be at its most effective. He avoided looking at her.

"It's dark in here," she said.

He felt her eyes looking at him, knowing there was no way to avoid her completely. "You get used to the darkness," he said softly.

Karen stepped into the room. She walked over to the small table and touched the driver's license there.

Blade almost felt invaded. The license was his personal property, all that he had left of his mother outside of memories.

"Whistler told me what happened," she said. "And about your mother."

That wasn't part of the deal, Blade thought. The old man overstepped his bounds.

Whistler had been supposed to tell the

woman enough that she took the hint and got the hell out of Blade's life. "Whistler talks too much," he said.

Karen turned to Blade, her eyes regarding him. "I know what you are now."

Blade's voice came out harsh, angry. He'd been using the anger as a focal point again, and he wasn't going to give it up easily. "You don't know me. You don't know anything about me. I'm not even human."

"You look human to me," Karen insisted.

"Humans don't drink blood. I'm different. I always have been. I remember from day one. People staring at me, sensing I wasn't like them." Blade forced himself to breathe, feeling the anger squirming around inside of him as he tried to pin it down. "You don't get over something like that."

Karen's voice got harder. "Maybe you should try."

Her statement stung Blade. He concentrated on the anger again, using it to ferret out and erase any other confusion that might be raging inside him. "Maybe I don't want to." He glared at her.

Karen stood there, waiting quietly.

Her patience got on Blade's nerves. He laid it out for her, etching each word with the hatred and anger that filled him. "I've spent my life looking for the son of a bitch who killed my mother, who made me what I am. Every time I cut down one of those monsters I get a little piece of that life back. So don't talk to me about forgetting."

She tried the silent treatment a little longer this time, then finally gave up and left the room.

Blade continued sitting in the darkness. Until she'd entered and tried to talk to him, he'd never realized how much loneliness clung to that room along with the healing darkness.

CHAPTER

31

Frost paced beside the pool at the Edgewood Towers penthouse. Blade had gotten away again. It wasn't to be unexpected; the Day-Walker had proven to be a most capable opponent.

And the war was opening up on two fronts. By morning Dragonetti would know about the attack Blade and Whistler had engineered on the archives at the Black Pearl. The vampire lord would try to take advantage of what he perceived as a weakness. *That* was unacceptable.

The eternal party in the penthouse had dropped into low gear, barely an audible rumble. Most of the hangers-on had even drifted away, returning to whatever they claimed as lives when they weren't at the penthouse.

Two women who looked like recreational drug burnouts sat on either side of Quinn, re-dressing his latest stump. Mercury stood before him, in full ball-breaker mode. Neither of them sensed Frost coming.

"It wasn't my fault," Quinn said petulantly. "Deek'll understand. We got taken by surprise. We were outgunned—"

Mercury cut him off, her anger brooking no excuses. "Two of them against our entire security force? You lost seventeen familiars to the Day-Walker. I'm sure Deacon will appreciate the reduction in payroll." She wore a revealing strapless yellow dress, her hair pulled back.

"Don't try to put it all on me, bitch," Quinn snarled. "I was just doing my best, and I got stabbed in the balls for it—ouch. Stop that, you fucking skeez!" He yanked his stump away from one of the burnouts. She'd been licking at his raw flesh, her fangs extended to feed. He shoved her away.

"Ha!" Mercury laughed. "The amputee life-style really suits you."

"How'd you like a stump through that shit-eating grin of yours?"

"Face it, angel. You were sloppy; you got what you deserved."

"Yeah, well we'll see what Deek has to say about that."

"You think he gives a shit about your god-damned hand? *The only thing he cares about is Blade.*"

Ignoring the bickering between the two, Frost

stepped into view and waited for their attention to center on him.

"Deek," Quinn pleaded, "you gotta let me take this guy out. He took my fucking arm again! I owe him big-time."

Frost kept his voice low and cold, forcing Quinn to concentrate on his words to hear them. "Listen very carefully, Quinn. *No*. I want him alive."

"Why? Fer fuck's sake!" Quinn exploded in frustration. "We've been trying to nail that freak son of a bitch for years, and now, all of a sudden"— he altered his voice, trying to do an impression of Frost—"I want him alive." His voice returned to normal. "Have you lost your fucking mind?"

Frost reached out tenderly, but the slow motion still caused Quinn to recoil slightly. The big man had overstepped his bounds, and he knew it. Frost brushed the hair out of the bearded face, gentle as a lover. "Calm down, Mikey. Be patient. All will be explained soon enough."

Mercury looked at Frost, shaking her head slightly at Quinn. "It's nearly dawn," she said.

"Time to do what we have to do," Frost replied agreeably. Fighting a war on two fronts wasn't something he was willing to put up with. Since he couldn't get Blade, and he needed that opponent alive, he was left with only one other option. And he was choosing to exercise it.

•   •   •

Mercury sat in the Porsche next to Frost, applying cream from the small jar in her hands to his face. He felt her fingers against his skin, slow and liquid, making the contact more than merely functional. His confidence rose with his libido, and when she finished he leaned down to kiss her. As he crushed his mouth against hers, he felt her canines elongate and graze his hungry tongue. Then he broke the kiss, looking east out across the incoming tides. It was time to get down to business.

He stepped out of the sports car, dressed in a leather motorcycle suit according to the plan he'd set in motion during the night. Quinn and Mercury wore similar suits. Dawn was only minutes away.

Quinn dragged Dragonetti after him, leaving a sandy slug trail across the deserted beach. The vampire lord's hands were bound behind his back, and he wore a black hood over his head. His evening suit looked bedraggled, something Frost had never seen before.

Silently, ignoring Dragonetti's protestations, Frost led the way down the beach to the water's edge. Despite the special sunblock cream he wore, his skin prickled against the coming of the sun. Even though it wasn't an old fear for Frost, it was a strong one. The fear of extinction ran bone-deep.

Capturing Dragonetti hadn't been hard. Frost had watched the man for years, and knew most of the vampire lord's schedule. Even the men

Dragonetti had around him had posed no real threat.

Once they'd stopped again, Dragonetti's questions had started back up. "What is this? Where am I?"

Stepping forward, Frost stripped the hood from Dragonetti's face.

The vampire lord blinked against the brightening sky across the ocean. A look of horror etched his features.

Frost had to respect the old vampire for his ability to face what was coming. He'd never thought the man a coward, only fearful.

"Morning. When was the last time you stopped to appreciate a good sunrise, Gaetano? You ever surf? You know, *catch a wave*?" Frost taunted. Then his tone turned to acid sarcasm. "Oh, that's right, you were *born a vampire*. You've never had the pleasure, have you? Well I'm glad the two of us could share this moment together. Really, you don't know how much it means to me. See, deep down in my heart, I'm actually a fairly sentimental kind of guy." He checked his watch. The meteorologists had gotten so precise these days they could time a sunrise to the second.

A sliver of gold appeared out above the hills, knifing into the heart of the gathered clouds.

Frost saw the fear touch Dragonetti, but the vampire lord didn't beg. Frost ripped the man's coat from his shoulders, unveiling more of him. As the weak sunlight touched Dragonetti, it made his skin blacken and smoke in spots, acting as though live coals were buried deep in the wrinkled flesh.

"Do what you want, Frost," Dragonetti said in a calm voice. "It won't make any difference."

"That's just it, Gaetano. I don't want to do this. But you give me no choice. You just don't fucking get it."

"You'll *never* be a pureblood. You'll never rule us!"

The stated accusation cut Frost deeply, more than he would have thought possible. Still, he made himself ignore it. He took a pair of pliers from his back pocket, showing them to Dragonetti. "Hold him," Frost told Quinn.

The big vampire seized Dragonetti from behind, pinning his arms. Frost stepped forward and forced the vampire lord's mouth open. As Dragonetti shrieked in pain and anger, Frost moved quickly, clamping the pliers on each fang, then wresting them from their fleshy beds. Blood dribbled from Dragonetti's mouth.

Finished, Frost forced the vampire lord to his knees in the incoming tide. Dragonetti's face charred in earnest now, chunks of it peeling away, leaving burning bone beneath.

"Time's up, pureblood," Frost said.

"Guess you just got a little too long in the tooth," Quinn said.

Mercury shook her head at Frost as he put on his motorcycle helmet and left the visor up.

"Sorry," Quinn said. "Couldn't resist."

The first rays of daylight fell upon the old vampire, eliciting howls of pain, rage, and fear. He skin sizzled and smoked, finally catching fire in a half dozen different spots.

Frost flipped down his visor, totally secure inside the motorcycle helmet. The vampire lord seized Frost's hand, trying to pull himself up. Frost watched as Dragonetti exploded in a flash of blinding white light like nothing he'd ever seen before, a definite reminder of how old the vampire lord had been. Curiously, Frost felt a small pang of remorse, but the feeling quickly ebbed when Dragonetti finished burning.

The ash drifted out on the tide.

The other eleven vampire lords were already in the conference room when Frost arrived. They all watched him as he walked around to the vacant chair at the head of the table. He smiled confidently, then sat in Dragonetti's chair.

They all knew what it meant, even Pallintine, who appeared the most disappointed of all. "What have you done with Dragonetti?" the second-in-command demanded.

Reaching into his pocket, Frost took out Dragonetti's bloody fangs. He tossed them casually onto the tabletop, watching as they skidded across the polished veneer of the wood.

"Dragonetti is dead," he stated.

The fangs came to a stop in front of Pallintine,

who for the first time that Frost could recall, showed signs of fear.

Silently, Frost gazed into the eyes of each of the vampire lords gathered at the table.

No one said anything.

Frost nodded, making sure they all understood. "You're all working for me now."

CHAPTER

32

Struggling with a control panel for the centrifuge Whistler was helping her take out of the back of a van, Karen Jansen saw Blade emerge from his room. He watched them as she and Whistler lowered the centrifuge to the floor.

Tight and compact, Blade looked both unforgiving and unforgiven. His attire was still black, but geared more for casual strolling through the streets. He glanced at the centrifuge and other medical equipment on the floor of the workshop. Then he flicked his black-lensed gaze back up to Karen as he strapped on his bandolier of silver stakes and secured the sword scabbard down his back.

He took a piece of paper from his jacket and handed it to Whistler. Seeing the curious glyphs on it, Karen recognized the paper from the ancient book last night. She hadn't even thought to ask if Blade had shown it to Whistler. In all the confusion, she supposed it had been forgotten. But then Blade hadn't exactly been sociable since their return, either.

"Written in blood," Whistler commented. "What is this?"

Blade shook his head. "I took it from the archives. It's from the *Book of Erebus*. I think it's what Frost has been working on. Can you read it?"

Whistler stared more closely at the page, pulling it back and forth, and turning it from side to side. "It's something about the Blood God, the Chosen One setting him free." He finally gave up and shook his head. "I don't know. I can't make the rest of it out."

Blade handed over the zip drive that Karen remembered him taking from the fat Asian vampire's computer. "Maybe this'll help," Blade said.

Laying an affectionate hand on a newly installed computer, Whistler said, "We'll figure something out." Then he looked deliberately at Blade.

Blade looked at all the equipment sitting around the room. "What's all this?"

"We made a trip to the hospital last night," Karen said, "and borrowed some equipment."

Blade shook his head. "For your miracle cure?" he asked sarcastically.

Karen's anger sparked and turned white-hot in an instant. But before she could respond, Whistler stepped between them, setting toolboxes filled with parts on the centrifuge.

"I think she's onto something, Blade," the old man said. He turned to Karen. "Show him."

She stared at Blade, daring him to say no.

Blade waited a beat, then shrugged.

Karen crossed to the operating theater and opened the refrigerator. She pushed aside steaks and vegetables she and Whistler had also bought while they were out all night. Today was going to be an all-work day, with no outside interruptions. She took a syringe filled with blue fluid from a foam-rubber-lined protective plastic case.

"This is EDTA—ethylenediaminetetracetate," she said. "It's an anticoagulant. We use it to treat blood clots. Vampire blood is thinner than humans', though. Watch what happens when I introduce some into a sample." She put a slide under the microscope. "This is vampire blood, from a sample Whistler had on hand. Take a look."

Reluctantly, Blade moved forward and peered through the microscope.

"Now watch." Karen injected the contents of the syringe onto the slide.

Immediately, the blood on the slide atomized, exploding outward in a fine mist that also managed to burst apart the glass lens of the microscope.

Blade pulled back. "Some cure."

Whistler chuckled and limped away to a customized street bike he'd been working on lately.

The motorcycle sat in one corner of the big room, nearly finished and looking like a gleaming, flexed muscle.

Karen wanted nothing more than to tear the cold smirk from Blade's face. "I'm still working on it," she said.

Blade turned to go.

Karen stopped him. "Wait. I need a sample of *your* blood."

"Later," he told her. "I'm going downtown. I need more serum."

Whistler wheeled around, still close to the motorcycle. His voice was stern when he spoke. "The serum can wait. This is more important."

Grudgingly, clearly indicating that he thought she was wasting his time, Blade faced her and rolled up his sleeve.

Karen gazed at him, marveling at his body's constitution. There weren't even any scars left over from the previous night. She took a fresh hypodermic from one of the boxes she'd brought from the hospital, located a vein, and pushed the needle home.

Blade didn't move at all as the vacutainer began to fill.

Behind him, Karen saw Whistler bring a handkerchief to his lips and begin coughing. The spasm wracked his body, almost doubling him over. She'd noted the coughing fits during their talks last night, but this was worse.

"I noticed he seemed ill last night," she said to Blade. "Is he sick?"

"Cancer," Blade answered.

A cold chill of dread filled Karen as she heard the word. She slipped a new tube onto the Vacutainer and began to fill it as well. "You care about him, don't you?"

"We've got a good arrangement, that's all. Whistler makes the weapons, I use them, the vampires die. End of story."

Karen finished the third sample and took the needle from his arm. She directed her hard gaze on the black-lensed stare before her. "My mother used to say that a cold heart is a dead heart."

Blade rolled his sleeve down. "Your mother sounds like a Hallmark greeting card." He slipped his MACH pistol into a shoulder-holster rig, then shrugged into his leather jacket. "I'd wish you luck, Doc, but I never put much stock in optimism."

She watched him head toward the Dodge Charger. Then she turned and went to help Whistler with the medical equipment again. The wound on her neck burned with a new life, causing a spasm to rip through her stomach. She walked toward the bathroom, afraid that she wouldn't make it before she purged. And afraid of what it all meant. They were *all* living on borrowed time.

CHAPTER

33

Blade noticed Karen's distress at once, and the sympathy he felt for the woman deflected him from his course. He wanted nothing more than to get the hell out of the ironworks and back on the road for a while. Driving relaxed him, and he hadn't had the chance to air out the Charger in a long time.

Instead of getting into the car, he glanced at Whistler, wondering if the old man had noticed the change as well.

Whistler nodded back, then dropped his head.

Blade felt a chill of dread run through him, something he hadn't experienced with such intensity in years. He looked back at Whistler.

"Yeah," the old man said, polishing one of the motorcycle's mirrors. "Know how you feel. She's a good kid. Been working her ass off."

"Dammit," Blade said. He knotted his hands into fists.

"Somebody's going to have to tell her," Whistler said.

"Better not to," Blade replied.

Whistler lit up a cigarette. "Maybe. But she's smart, my friend. She'll figure it out for herself, and it's going to be worse if she knows but doesn't know if she knows for sure."

Blade said nothing.

"She's a strong girl," Whistler said. "Everything she's seen the last couple days, she'll do okay with it."

"And if she decides to run?" Blade asked. "If she decides she's got more to fear from us than from what's inside her?"

"We can't let her do that," Whistler said.

"No."

Whistler took a deep pull on the cigarette, which led to a coughing fit. It took a long moment to subside. "You want me to tell her?"

"No."

The old man nodded, then dropped the cigarette on the concrete floor and crushed it out with his boot. "If you don't, I'm going to. I respect her too much to let it go down any other way." He turned his back and went to work on the motorcycle in front of him.

Blade watched Whistler work. Ever since Blade had known him, the man had amazed him. Whistler had gone through trauma that would have reduced most other men to shells of themselves. Whistler had only gotten stronger, harder, more knowledgeable. He was the most complete man the Hunter had ever met.

"She's been some kind of lady," Whistler said. "Hasn't she?"

Blade remained silent, his thoughts churning. He had to keep himself centered to keep from thinking about Karen—about the woman—too much.

"I knew you thought so, too," Whistler said. "Would have been nice to get to know her a little longer. She showed a natural talent for this line of work." He cleared his throat. "Waiting ain't going to make it any easier."

Chastised, Blade turned and walked to the bathroom, reaching up behind him to adjust the sword in its sheath. Cursing himself for a fool, knowing he was only asking for more trouble, he followed Karen into the bathroom off the workroom. He went through the door after the sound of retching had passed.

She looked pale and wan, her hair was a mess, and the whites of her eyes held streaks of red as she blotted her mouth with a tissue. Peeling the dressing from her wound revealed an infected, gangrenous mass centered around the bite marks. She ran water over her hand, then rubbed it onto her face, catching his reflection in the mirror in front of her.

Blade felt sorry for her then, felt bad about the

way she was determined to beat her head up against a stone wall. There was no cure. If there had been, Whistler would have found it. No one knew vampires better than Whistler.

"You don't look good." He meant that to come out differently, softer. But he wasn't used to working with those words. He waited for her attack.

She didn't, though, looking at him as if she read his intent instead of hearing his words. "I'm just tired, that's all. We've been up all night." She massaged her throat as she spoke, and the effort looked like it brought her pain.

"It's started," Blade said. He moved quickly, seizing her jaw in his fingers. "You've got another day or two at most."

Wordlessly, Karen pushed past him, headed back for the door.

He grabbed her wrist, gently restraining her, wishing there was something he could say to make everything better. All he said was, "For what it's worth, I'm sorry."

"You make it sound like I'm already dead."

Blade didn't say another word, but in his mind, maybe she was. He glided from the room, never looking back.

CHAPTER

34

Blade made his way through the open-air market in Chinatown, listening to the voices of sellers and buyers as they haggled and tried to find a common meeting ground. The wares included exotic vegetables, clothing, cheap curios, and electronics. Nearby butcher shops held rows of roast ducks in the windows.

No one bothered him, including the street gangs whose paths he crossed. No one tried to talk to him.

He cut into the dark alley to the right, then ducked into the doorway of an herbalist well off the beaten path. The bell over the door jingled as he walked through. The room was dark, like a small cave, with the smell of dust laced with spices and incense permeating everything. Bottles lined the shelves, and joss sticks burned in their holders.

At the back of the shop, an elderly Chinese man in a cardigan filled a prescription behind a scarred and weathered desk.

"How's it going, Kam?" Blade asked as he stopped at the counter.

Kam glanced up at the calendar on the wall over the television. "You're a week early."

"I was in the neighborhood." Blade felt uncomfortable admitting the serum wasn't working as well as it had in the past.

"That bad, huh?" Kam took the envelope Blade offered and looked inside. His thumb grazed the sheaf of money inside, then he nodded and took a bottle down from one of the top shelves.

The Hunter opened the bottle and looked at the white powder inside. It looked so ordinary, yet it kept the edge off, let him walk that much closer to human. He recapped the bottle and dropped it into a pocket. "Whistler says I'm building up a resistance to it," Blade said.

"I was afraid that might happen." Kam shook his head sorrowfully.

"Maybe it's time to start exploring other alternatives."

Kam stared at him, his eyes narrowing. "There's only *one* alternative to the serum."

"Yeah. I know." Blade definitely knew what the alternative was, and it was unacceptable. The unsaid words between them hung uncomfortably. The old man had been as much a part of his war against Deacon Frost and the other vampires as Whistler. And Kam had his own reasons for fighting the bloodsuckers. "Thanks, Kam."

"You take it easy," Kam replied.

Blade cleared his mind and headed for the door. He wasn't a student of optimism, just as he had told Karen Jansen. But nor was he going to give up on himself till it was time.

Getting the Charger in and out of the market was hard, and Blade had learned during his visits to Kam's shop to leave it at the nearby park. Noonday sunlight filled the open area, chasing away the shadows as he crossed between the trees and playground equipment.

"*Blade.*"

He stopped, balancing himself automatically, senses at full alert. He spun, scanning his surroundings, not sure if he'd really heard the name or it was just the fragrant wind blowing over the overflowing Dumpsters.

"Over here."

The Hunter was certain he'd heard it this time. And it came from in front of the alley. He walked back, stopping in the middle of the market area. His hand drifted under his jacket, closing on the butt of the MACH.

"Here," the voice said.

Blade let his gaze settle on a male sitting on a bench in the deep shade under the green-and-white-striped awning of a takeout restaurant. A Chinese newspaper obscured the face. A little Chinese girl in a purple shorts set sat stiffly beside the speaker. She looked all of six or seven years old, with raven's-wing black hair square-cut to touch her shoulders. Her face still held baby roundness, but pure terror was written across her features.

The Hunter's stomach turned cold. It wasn't a surprise to find vampires using children in their feeding. The blood was stronger, richer. But it was the first time one had ever been used as a shield against him.

"How's it going, chief?" The speaker lowered the newspaper, revealing the familiar face behind dark wraparound sunglasses.

Blade's stare hardened as he recognized Deacon Frost. Without wondering how Frost had managed to put in an appearance in full daylight, the Hunter started to pull the MACH.

"Easy," Frost advised. In an eye blink, Frost's hand was resting casually at the back of the girl's neck. The hand morphed, stretching claws forth that caressed the flesh beneath her chin, an obscene imitation of the attentions paid by a favorite uncle. "Wouldn't want our little friend here to wind up on the back of a milk carton, would we?"

CHAPTER

35

"**B**eautiful day, isn't it?" Frost went on. He appeared totally nonchalant, his razor-sharp talons sliding along the vulnerable flesh of the little girl's throat.

Blade pushed the pistol back into the shoulder holster. No one on the street paid them the slightest attention. He breathed out, working to keep himself calm, trying to focus on his anger, not the little girl shivering in fright beside Frost. "How can you be out here?"

"I dabble in pharmaceuticals, medical research. We've developed a type of sunblock using octyl salicylate, a few other things." The vampire touched a finger to his cheek, then rubbed the translucent lotion between his fingers. "It's not very effective in direct sunlight, but it's a start. The goal, of course, is to be like you, *the Day-Walker*."

Frost smiled. "It's nice to finally meet you. I've had my eye on you for years. I know all about you—your serum, Whistler, *everything*."

Blade worked to keep the surprise from his face. It wasn't stunning that Frost had heard of him. He'd been killing vampires for years. But the vampire shouldn't have known of his serum.

"You've got the best of both worlds, don't you?" Frost went on. "All of our strengths and none of our weaknesses."

Blade stood in the flow of people walking by him in the park, getting no one's attention. "Maybe I don't see it that way."

"Oh, so it's back to pretending we're human again, is it?" Frost gave him a bored look. "Spare me the Uncle Tom routine. You can't keep denying what you are." The creature leaned forward conspiratorially. "You know what your problem is? You hate yourself. Now me, on the other hand, I love what I am."

Blade remained silent.

"You think the humans will ever accept a half-breed like you? They can't. They're *afraid* of you." Frost regarded him full on. "And they should be. Look at you. You're an animal—you're a fucking maniac."

Blade scanned the surrounding park attendees, knowing Frost wouldn't have walked into this situation without backup. It was just a matter of pinpointing who they were and working up a plan to nullify them. He tried to make himself believe that it would be as easy as that.

"Now look at them," Frost said, indicating the people milling around. "They're cattle. Fucking pieces of meat. What difference does it make how their world ends? Plague. War. Famine. Morality doesn't even enter into it. We're just a function of natural selection. The new race."

A bead of sweat ran down Frost's neck, washing away a layer of the sun-blocking cream. Smoke curled up from his flesh, and the small portion of skin blackened immediately.

Blade showed the vampire a cold smile. "Looks like your mascara's running."

Seeing the smoke, and evidently feeling the pain, the vampire reached a hand to his neck, covering the spot, then gazed up hatefully at the sun. Then he switched some of those feelings to Blade. "I'm offering you a truce," Frost said. "I want you with us."

Blade shook his head. "Do you think I'm stupid?" He reconstructed the words in the vampire language Pearl had said. "The Blood God comes."

Surprise filled Frost's features. "You know about the Blood God?" the creature asked in the vampire language.

Hearing the interrogative in the man's speech and recognizing some of the words, Blade guessed at the rest. "I know enough. You're up to something, Frost. I don't know what you need from me, I don't know what your game is—but when I find out, I'll take you apart, just like all the others. You're nothing to me. Just another dead vampire."

Coldness lit Frost's eyes. "You're an idiot, you know that? I came here offering you an easy way out, and you spit it right back in my face."

Making his decision, thinking of Karen succumbing to the bite that had infected her, thinking of all the lives that Frost would destroy if he could, Blade swept his coat back to reveal the MACH. He laid it on the line for Frost, letting the vampire know how far he was prepared to push the confrontation.

Frost moved the little girl, using her to shield himself. "*Careful*," he admonished.

"What do I care?" Blade asked in the coldest voice he could manage, trying to make Frost believe he meant it. "They're cattle. You said so yourself."

Disgust showed plainly on Frost's face. "If you want to take the hard road, be my guest. But I promise you, when this is all over, you're going to wish they'd never cut you from your mother's womb."

Blade drew the MACH from the shoulder rig with blinding speed, firing from the point. The round blurred by the little girl's head, narrowly missing her and streaking for Frost's face.

Frost jerked his head away, only his vampiric speed saving his unlife. Even then, the bullet sliced across his cheek, splitting the lotion-covered flesh open. The vampire continued dodging. His head turned slightly as a city bus rumbled by. Without any betraying motion, he hurled the little girl forward, out in front of the oncoming bus.

Blade fired three more rounds, but none of them touched Frost. Moving without hesitation, Blade went for the uncertain save rather than the certain kill. Even then, even with his incredible speed and abilities, he didn't know if there was enough time. He dived forward, scooping the little girl into his arms, continuing the roll to take them from in front of the bus. Hot air and exhaust stink enveloped him as he lifted the little girl and dived clear of the multi-ton vehicle.

He felt her heart beating against his chest, her arms tight around his neck. And he sat there on his knees for a moment, just holding her, aware of how close they had both come as the bus continued on its way.

Frost was already gone. He knew that before he even looked.

"Are you okay?" Blade asked the little girl, from his meager supply of Chinese. He repeated it again, smoothing her hair.

She only stared back at him, afraid of him; it was apparent in her eyes. She recognized no safety in Blade's arms, only more horror. She backed away from him when he let her go, then she bolted and ran into the crowd. The people fell in protectively behind her, defending her even from the Hunter.

With easy grace, Blade stood and started walking. He had the fire inside his belly, hotter than it had ever been before. It was the old anger, born of the fact that every normal person would know he was not one of them, and that he never could be.

Instead of giving in to it, he concentrated all his thoughts on Frost. If he was going down, a victim of the Thirst that waited to rage inside him, he was going to bring Frost down first. That was a promise he made to himself.

CHAPTER

36

Daylight streamed against the windows of the ironworks, little of it getting through the layer of paint covering them, hardly enough to fragment the heavy darkness determined to haunt the place.

Karen stared through the microscope at the blood smear on the slide. Whistler sat beside her at the worktable, as bone-tired as she was, but for hours his attention had been riveted on the compact disk Blade had given him. Her neck burned, the irritated area seeming to grow by the minute, and it gave her chills to think of what was taking place in her body. She felt the fever burning under her skin.

"Run me through that again," Whistler asked.

She didn't get mad at him for his inattention. Both of them were working on areas that might help them all. Neither avenue could be ignored at the moment.

"All right," she said, having to work to make herself think clearly. "It's simple and elegant. Why do vampires need to drink blood?"

"Their own blood can't sustain hemoglobin," Whistler replied.

She knew she must have asked him that question at least a dozen times before, but he didn't show any impatience with her asking it again. And the answer helped her keep her focus when her mind wanted to concentrate on her own problems and where Blade might be at the moment. "Right, so vampirism is a genetic defect, just like hemolytic anemia."

Whistler nodded, his eyes still scanning the decrypted pages of the vampire Bible. Since the beginning, Karen had been very impressed by the old man's knowledge. For someone who hadn't been grounded in chemistry or biology other than high-school classes, he was amazingly well taught. But then, the man had possessed an incredible motivation.

"That means we have to treat it with gene therapy," she said. "Basically you'd have to rewrite the victim's DNA with a retrovirus. It's injected into the bone-marrow cells. It causes the host's DNA to mutate. They've been using it to treat sickle-cell anemia." She rolled up her sleeve and reached for a prepared syringe.

Whistler turned from the computer monitor at

once, hesitation flickering across his craggy face. "You sure that's safe?" He nodded at the microscope on the table, the one that had been destroyed earlier by the chemical reaction.

"No," she admitted, "but since there don't appear to be any other guinea pigs around—" She left the rest unsaid, both of them knowing that the disease in her own system was advancing. She had no choice: The serum *had* to work.

Whistler got up and walked over to her, and for a moment she was afraid that he would try to stop her. She saw the effort it took for him to stop himself. "You actually think this could work?"

Karen injected herself, feeling the dose knot up under her skin. Then it began racing through her system, running hot and cold. "On *me*, yes. On Blade, I'm not so sure." The first effects of the inoculation passed, leaving her only a little light-headed. "I think I can cure anyone who's been bitten. Blade's more difficult. He went through the change in utero—the virus is part of his DNA. I probably can cure him, but it's going to take some time."

"Damn." Whistler's curse sounded tired and old. He tried to cover his feelings by lighting a cigarette.

"I can keep trying," Karen said.

Whistler shook his head, turning his attention back to the computer he was working on. "We're out of time." He pointed at the monitor. "You saw what was on that disk Blade brought back. We *know* what Frost is after now."

Suddenly, an alarm sent a strident squeal speeding through the ironworks. The sound of breaking glass followed on its heels.

"What's wrong?" Karen asked.

Whistler scrambled, getting the most out of his injured leg. "*Shit*, it's the motion sensors." He reached for a stake-shotgun and lowered his voice to a whisper. "Get out of here!"

But before she could move, a black-clad figure wearing a motorcycle helmet rushed at them with supernatural speed. It leaped for them.

Moving with a quickness that most people wouldn't have given him credit for, Whistler pulled the shotgun up into the crook of his arm and racked the slide. He fired, and Karen saw the black-clad figure double over in midair. In the next heartbeat, the black-clad figure turned into a tower of ash and scattered. By then Whistler was already firing at the next opponent, putting a silver stake through its head.

Even if Karen had been willing to leave Whistler, she couldn't have. Everywhere she looked were more of the black-clad figures. They even smashed in through the windows, streaking for them.

She pulled the Glock Blade had given her from the lab-coat pocket and fired. It was almost impossible to miss someone in the army of darkness that swept toward them.

One of the attackers somersaulted across the floor, staying just ahead of Whistler's marksmanship. Then he dropped his pistol into place and fired.

The bullet cored through Whistler's good knee, knocking the old man from his feet in a tangle of flailing limbs. The shotgun skittered from his grasp.

Karen turned to fire at the creature who'd shot Whistler, but a fist suddenly exploded against her jaw. She flew from her feet and landed on the floor hard enough to knock the wind from her lungs. She tried to curl her hand around the Glock again, but the black-clad attacker kicked the pistol from her grip. Before Karen could get up, her attacker put a motorcycle boot against her stomach, holding her down.

The black-clad figure who'd shot Whistler took off his helmet. Karen recognized Quinn immediately. Deacon Frost was behind Quinn, stepping out of the shadows to tower over Whistler.

The old man was bent in agony, trying to staunch the bleeding from his ruined knee. But he didn't turn away from Frost's malevolent gaze, meeting it with a force of will.

"Nice place," Frost said, looking around. "Took us a while to find it."

"If you're gonna bite me, get it over with, you snot-nosed sack of shit," Whistler growled.

Frost bent over and slapped the old man in the face, snapping Whistler's head back against the concrete floor. "Bite you?" Frost asked. "That'd be like chewing on a fucking piece of beef jerky."

Frost planted a bootheel in Whistler's stomach.

Karen heard the snaps of several ribs breaking. Whistler doubled over and gasped in pain.

Then Frost gave himself over to the attack, kicking the old man again and again. Karen tried to turn her head away from the sickening violence, but the creature holding her down made her watch. It seemed to go on forever.

Driving to the elevator that would take him to the workshop, Blade spotted the Porsche and a number of other cars peeling away from the ironworks through the broken windows. A glance showed him that the outer security systems had been forcibly breached, the gates reduced to a twisted mass. He pulled into the elevator and triggered the remote control. It seemed like forever before the door opened again.

Senses electric with adrenaline, survival, and fear, Blade stayed inside the Dodge Charger when he saw the first of the damage in the workshop. He pulled the shotgun from the sliding rack under the backseat, then laid it against the dashboard. He switched on the car's headlights, chasing away the few shadows remaining in the room.

He waited for a time, growing more impatient

when nothing happened. His imagination, fueled by every cruel vampire attack he'd ever seen, ran rampant. Unable to wait any longer, unable to sense any of the creatures remaining in the workshop, he opened the door and got out. He kept the MACH at the ready, holding it in both hands as he walked through the large room.

"Whistler? Karen?"

There was no response to his calls.

Nothing had been left untouched. It looked like a major force of nature had whipped through the workshop, leaving a stream of wreckage in its wake.

But there were a few bodies, too, all dressed in black motorcycle suits. He checked a couple of them, finding Deacon Frost's vampire glyph marking the backs of their necks.

Still, Blade had hopes that the old man had gotten Karen to safety before the vampire army overran the ironworks. There were hiding places they'd built into the building, taking advantage of the architecture that already existed.

"Whistler?" He heard the desperation in his own voice then, and he hated it.

A figure took shape in the medical restraint chair against the far wall. He raised the MACH, taking aim. When he got closer, he saw that it was Whistler, though Blade was barely able to recognize the man under the bloody white sheet.

"Whistler," Blade said in a harsh voice. Dropping the MACH on the ground at Whistler's feet, Blade pulled the sheet from his friend. The fang marks on his neck stood out prominently, already in an advanced gangrenous state. His broken good leg was folded under him at an awkward angle.

There was also a bloodied videotape tucked into Whistler's shirt pocket. PLAY ME was written on the cassette case. Blade pulled the tape out and tossed it aside, needing to take care of the old man first.

Anger made Blade's voice work when he thought he couldn't speak. *The bastards had taken away his last leg.* "Whistler—I'm gonna take these motherfuckers apart."

With great effort, Whistler opened his eyes and struggled to speak. "Frost took her," he said. "Listen to me. The disk, we decoded it—" A coughing spasm took away the rest of his words, causing him to wince in pain. He continued. "Frost is trying to trigger a fucking vampire apocalypse. Calls it the Blood Tide. There's some kind of vampire god he's trying to resurrect."

"LaMagra," Blade said. "How?"

Whistler breathed through clenched teeth, fighting down another surge of the pain that wracked him. He opened his eyes again and focused on Blade. "You're the key to making it happen," the old man warned. "He needs *your blood.*" He gasped with the effort of speaking, blood flecking out with his breath. "Blood of the Day-Walker. You're part of the prophecy. You're the Chosen One."

Blade's mind reeled as the pieces fell into place. He represented the next evolution of the vampire, a nightbreed who didn't have to fear the sun. That was why Frost had been adamant about not killing him when the opportunity had presented itself. The Hunter had trained himself to be the downfall of the vampires he stalked; yet, he was their salvation instead. The irony was too much.

Whistler clutched his arm, struggling harder to speak now. "Listen to me, Blade. *You can't go after him.*"

"Bullshit," Blade said. There was no way he couldn't. Not after what they'd done to Whistler, and not as long as Frost had Karen Jansen captive.

"Forget the girl," Whistler ordered. "Walk away from it."

"I can't do that."

"*You have to.* If Frost gets his hands on you— it's all over. He'll be able to resurrect this thing— he wants to become the Blood God. A tide of blood. There'll be armies of the motherfuckers."

Blade looked away from his friend, not wanting Whistler to waste his strength on the argument. And he knew the old man would see the angry frustration in his eyes despite the sunglasses, and he'd see the rebellion there as well. Blade wasn't about to let it go.

Shaking, Whistler's hand lost strength enough to hold on. His hand dropped away from Blade's arm. "Ah, shit," the old man said. He took a deep breath. "You're gonna have to—finish me off. Don't want me coming back."

The Hunter felt tears burning at the back of his eyes, felt his throat close up as if a vise were tightening on it. He remembered clearly how alone he'd been before Whistler found him, and how afraid. It was all coming back to him now in a nova-hot rush. Blade spoke past the rock in his throat, denied everything that he knew to be true. "*No.* We can treat the wounds."

Whistler looked at him, tears in his eyes, too. "Too far gone, and you know that." He took in another breath, fighting for it. "Give me your gun."

CHAPTER

38

Blade struggled to make his voice work. "Whistler, I *can't.*"

The old man gripped Blade's arm, but the hold contained only a shadow of the strength the Hunter remembered. His words carried conviction, and the knowledge of what he was asking— for both of them. "*Give me the goddamned gun. I trained you for this, dammit. Don't you dare be weak. I need you strong.*"

Blade held his friend a little longer, feeling the life ebb from Whistler. And once that slim mortal coil was cut, it would leave only hellspawn in its place. There was nothing else to be done. He picked up the heavy MACH from the floor and handed it to Whistler, feeling himself growing dead inside. The pistol had never felt harder or heavier, and there were no illusions about its being something only vampires needed to fear.

"Now walk away, you stupid son of a bitch," Whistler ordered. *"Walk-the-fuck-away."*

Tears ran down Blade's face, skidding out from behind the wraparound sunglasses. But he made himself turn around and walk away.

The sound of the shot filled the ironworks, echoing for a long time.

Blade shoved the VCR tape into one of the units in the workroom, then pressed PLAY. He stood as the tape spun out.

Deacon Frost, looking calm and debonair as ever, filled the screen, a mocking smile touching his lips. "Hello, Blade," Frost said. "By the time you watch this, Mr. Whistler will no doubt be dead." The person working the camera had zoomed in closer, filling the screen with Frost's face. "If it makes any difference to you, he put up quite a fight." The camera tightened up till only Frost's eyes were visible, flashing magnetic black. "You can find us at the Edgewood Towers. We'll be waiting. By the way, we've got your girlfriend."

The screen grayed out with fuzz, continuing to spin. Blade didn't bother to shut it off.

Blade went to the hidden lockers and brought out the heavy-duty armor. It was in pieces, but made a cohesive whole. By the time he finished suiting up, he looked like a riot cop. Black-leathered Kevlar covered him from head to toe, turning him into a high-gloss shadow warrior. But the armor was put on in specific layers, leaving his movements open to him.

He worked the leather and Kevlar joints, using the sword as he went through his katas. His body programmed in the extra weight, the small limitations that were imposed by the armor. Perspiration filmed him. He used the exertion to hone his rage and anger, focusing on those emotions and making them one, so that he could better wield them against Frost and his vampire army.

The void was the perfect state in martial arts. Death did not exist, fear did not exist, and hate existed only as a fuel. He was centered, the best that he could be, and fully committed to his chosen quest.

With a final flurry of swings, he sheathed the sword in the scabbard across his back. He crossed the room to the medical supplies Karen had brought to the workshop, not letting himself think about the things Frost and the other vampires might be doing to her even now. A quick search through the boxes turned up the canister of EDTA.

He took it to a workbench, then filled the vials that went with his serum injectors with the blue fluid. When he had as many as he could fit into a belt-pack, sliding them into the leather loops that normally held silver stakes, he belted it on.

All his gear in place, he walked over to the corner where Whistler had the motorcycle. He stripped back the dustcover, revealing the gleaming hunk of street bike painted in gunmetal gray. The bike left him more vulnerable than the Charger, but the bike also gave him more maneuvering room and quick acceleration.

He threw a leg over the motorcycle, squeezed in the clutch, and thumbed the electronic ignition. He rolled the throttle as the engine caught, filling the ironworks with the full-throated roar of the mechanical beast.

Letting the clutch out fast, he leaped from the corner and sped toward the ironworks door. He was hell on wheels, death come a-walking.

CHAPTER

39

Karen looked across the expensively furnished room where she had been held for the last few hours and saw the blond vampire standing in the doorway. She hadn't even heard the woman open the door. At first, Karen ignored the vampire, but the cold glass and slate of the penthouse left her little to focus on. Frost's taste were artistic minimalism. She tried in vain to find a comfortable position on the couch.

Quinn and Frost walked into the room, followed by a number of men who stood guard.

"Why am I still alive?" Karen demanded of Frost.

The vampire chief grinned at her lazily, taking a seat across from her. "I want to talk to you," Frost said. "Get to know the real you."

"Bullshit. You're hoping Blade'll try and save me."

Frost shrugged. "Of course. He did it before. He'll do it again. Now why is that?" The vampire leaned across the intervening space, making what would normally be a gesture of polite interest into a threat. "You doing him? Is he good? Does he make you happy? You should be happy. You're a beautiful woman. Sexy, nice skin."

"I'd do her," Mercury said, licking full lips.

Karen ignored the revulsion that filled her at the female vampire's display and stubbornly held on to her courage.

"Me too," Quinn said, with a ˉgnashing of teeth.

"You'd do my dog," Frost said to the big vampire. The creature turned his attention back to Karen, speaking softly. "You *should* be happy, Karen. I'd hate to see such glorious bone structure go to waste."

Karen put her fear aside, reaching for sarcasm instead. "Is this the part where you offer to turn me?"

"It's either that or a body bag, sweetheart."

"Go ahead," she told him. "Bite me. I'll just cure myself. I did it once, I can do it again."

The vampire leaned back in the sofa, shaking its head almost imperceptibly. "There's no cure."

"Quinn bit me," she said triumphantly. It felt good to prove him wrong, to undermine his confidence. "And now I'm cured." She twisted her neck, exposing the healing flesh where the bite mark had been.

"I did bite her," Quinn said, leaning in. "She should be well into the Change by now."

"But I'm not," Karen told them all. "There's a cure if you've been bitten, if you were *once human*." She pointed to the scar on Frost's eyebrow. "How'd you get that scar, Deacon? A born vampire would have the power to regenerate from birth. You must've got scarred *before* you were turned, isn't that right? Vampires like you aren't a species, you're just *infected*, a virus, a sexually transmitted disease."

"I'll tell you what we are, sister, we're the top of the fucking food chain," Frost snarled with venom. "The Blood God LaMagra's coming, and after tonight, you people are fucking history! The Blood Tide is coming, and you better get ready for your worst nightmares." The creature reached out faster than she could react to him and put a forefinger against her temple.

At his touch, his hand resting on her temple, electrical explosions occurred in Karen's brain, taking her away from the room. A whole new world was built around her, and all five of her senses were plugged into it. She knew it couldn't be happening; she still had to be back in the room where they held her captive.

But for the moment the only real thing to her was the underground chamber she stood in. It looked like some kind of coliseum. Across from her was a deep, dark throat of a tunnel that belched forth gurgling noises.

Everything in Karen screamed at her to run, but she was mesmerized by the sound of the gurgling growing quickly and steadily louder. Dark liquid exploded out of the tunnel in a scarlet-tinted rush, revealing itself to be a roiling wall of blood racing for her.

"LaMagra's a hurricane," Frost told her, sounding far away. "An act of God. Anyone caught in *his* path will be *turned*."

Just before it touched her, the blood cycled up, captured in the grip of cyclonic winds. The blood fed up through the eye of the cyclone, filtering out into a red mist that filled the chamber.

Karen drew back from it, only she drew back much more quickly and distantly than she'd imagined. She stood in the center of a city, dozens of people scurrying in fear around her. The Blood Tide washed over the rest of the city, spreading outward at an increasing rate. She couldn't believe the amount of blood involved.

When the Tide subsided, all that was left was a crimson wasteland.

"Everyone you've ever known, everyone you've ever loved," Frost said. "I'm talking about Planet of the Fucking Vampires!"

Out of that crimson wasteland, people began to rise and take their first shambling steps through fire-covered lands. Then Karen realized they weren't people anymore. They were *vampires*, an endless army of them.

"It won't matter who's pureblood and who's

not!" Frost roared. "How are you gonna cure the *whole fucking world?"*

Horrified, Karen tried to move again, this time succeeding in breaking the contact Frost had with her. She gazed up at the vampire, realizing the full extent of the enemy Blade and Whistler had stood against. Her head hurt from the electrical impulses that had jumped through her brain, and from the adrenaline overflow that had slopped ·through her body.

"And Blade's blood is the key," Frost went on. "That's the beauty of destiny. We've been trying to kill this idiot for years, and he turns out to be our salvation. I love this guy."

"If you turn everybody into vampires, whose blood are they going to drink?" For a moment, she thought she had the creature. Even megalomaniacs couldn't plan for everything.

But his smile sent cold chills through her. Frost stood, and told Quinn, "Bring her."

Frost led the way through the penthouse, moving surely in spite of the near-nonexistent light. Karen noted that heavy shutters covered all the windows.

They came to a stop in an immense kitchen furnished in unblemished white tile that somehow seemed obscene, in front of a large, stainless-steel walk-in freezer. Frost pulled the door open, revealing the horror that lay inside.

Human beings hung in the freezer, suspended

by harnesses, looking like broken angels in a demonic child's mobile. Hooked up to IV feeds that dripped into their veins and to medical monitors, their physical needs were being met. Their forearms held implanted shunts that served as taps.

"Neat, huh?" Frost asked, laughing at her disbelief. "I can keep them alive for years, producing anywhere from ten to fifteen pints of blood a day. Of course, this is just a pilot program. Once the Tide comes, we'll have to institutionalize production."

Revulsion filled Karen, and she turned her head. She knew what the process most reminded her of: concentration camps. "You're disgusting," she said.

Frost smiled coldly. "Why? Because we live at another species' expense? Your people rear cattle. How is this any different? It's called evolution, nature, *survival of the fittest.*"

While Karen tried to think of a response, the door flew open and a Kevlared guard rushed into the room. "We've got an intruder," the man announced.

Frost smiled. "Let me guess."

Karen's heart increased its thudding speed inside her chest. Blade was still alive. Frost and his people hadn't killed him.

But the odds against him were phenomenal. One man, against an army of vampires.

CHAPTER

40

Deacon Frost watched the security monitors on the console in front of him. The whole penthouse was wired for audio and video transmission. Despite the manpower and the technology, he was irritated that he didn't feel as confident as he should have.

On-screen, ten men zipped through the labyrinth of corridors honeycombing the huge penthouse. The four unit leaders were equipped with SWAT-styled battle gear.

They patrolled the main room, the one Frost had specially commissioned to be filled with waterfalls. Heavy bribes to the building's owners and the city and state building-permit agencies had gone into the creation of that room. But he'd made it into one that no one ever forgot once they saw it.

Frost was conscious of Karen standing behind him, Mercury holding on to the woman. Her story about curing herself had been somewhat disconcerting. He'd never read anything about that in any of the vampiric lore. But it didn't matter. Now he had the truth about LaMagra and the Temple of the Night. Dragonetti and the other purebloods had never found either.

An elevator's arrival bell dinged, echoing in the room even over the sound of running water. The squad changed directions, zeroing in on the corridor containing the elevator.

Using the fingertip toggle, Frost selected the camera view over the elevator. The scene came on just in time for him to see the elevator doors closing on the empty cage. The security unit appeared nervous, not knowing what to do.

Frost grabbed a hands-free headset that connected him to the frequency being used by the teams inside the penthouse. "Get to it," he ordered.

"Yes sir," one of the commanders replied.

The ten men split up, one of the groups going back to the waterfall room.

Frost left the security command room. Blade was here, inside the penthouse. The vampire could feel it. "What's taking so long?" he demanded. "Is he down yet?"

"He's not exactly a pushover, Deek," Quinn volunteered behind him.

"Shut up," Frost said. He keyed the headset

again. "Take him out, people. I'm warning you. He's just one guy on foot—"

Blade watched five of the security guards reenter the waterfall room of Frost's penthouse. Behind the frosted glass, he sat motionless on the motorcycle.

The elevator he'd used to get to the penthouse had some natural weaknesses he'd exploited. First of all it was a freight elevator that led to the underground parking garage. It was also privately maintained and operated by Frost, which meant there'd been no innocents involved when Blade had killed the familiars guarding it. Neither of them had gotten a chance to relay a message.

However, he hadn't known the security access code that shut off the alarm system announcing his arrival at the penthouse floor. He'd arrived, and the alarm had gone off, but he'd still been fast enough to get away from the patrol.

Now it was time to turn the tables.

Memorizing the positions of the men spread out before him, Blade drew the clutch in, then pressed the electronic ignition. The motorcycle fired to life at once, and he popped the clutch as he twisted the accelerator.

The big bike reared like a stallion and charged through the frosted glass into the waterfall room, surprising the hell out of the security personnel who thought they'd been hunting him. The bike came down hard and heavy in the middle of them, landing on one of the humans and killing him instantly.

Skidding away from the bike and the dead man, Blade pushed himself up, filling his hands with the MACH and the shotgun. He triggered rounds automatically, a killing machine working his way through a thorough agenda. The security team were a mix of vampires and familiars, and the way they fell or blew apart told him which were which.

Not a single shot hit him in return.

Everything grew still except for the hiss of the water—and the lone man who'd fallen into the pool around the big waterfall.

Blade walked over to him, reloading both weapons. He sheathed the MACH and kept the shotgun in both hands. Peering down into the water, he saw a human male attempting to get back up, his features blurred by the rippling water. There was no pity in the Hunter. Every man there was there by choice. Frost had no innocents around him.

Blade swiveled the shotgun muzzle against the familiar's forehead.

The man's eyes grew wide, frightened. "Please, no," he begged, still underwater. His words bubbled out in the liquid. "I'm human. I just work for them."

With no trace of mercy in his heart, Blade squeezed the trigger and turned the pool of water the color of blood.

•   •   •

The sound of small-arms fire reverberated in the penthouse corridors, reaching Frost as he sped through the dining room, with Quinn and Mercury behind him. Two of the guards dragged Karen Jansen along, and she was fighting every step of the way.

Frost tapped the headset. "Do I hear gunfire? Did I tell anyone to start shooting? Jesus Christ, you assholes. I NEED HIM ALIVE!" Clicking out of the frequency, he turned to one of his personal bodyguards. "Send the A-Team. And lock down the shutters."

Blade wasn't going to escape, dammit, he thought. This was a trap, his trap, and it was foolproof. The Day-Walker had nearly taken his last step.

CHAPTER

41

Blade listened to the series of massive slams echoing around him. He raced through the corridors, spotting shutters on windows shutting all around him. Frost had chosen to lock down the penthouse. The Hunter thought that was fine; it meant Frost couldn't get away from *him* either.

The penthouse level was a maze of rooms and walls. He had expected no less. Deacon Frost wouldn't have thrown down the challenge and invited him into his territory without being certain of maintaining the upper hand.

Two vampires carrying assault rifles raced at him from the other end of the room, baying their challenge. A door behind them was just closing, much smaller and less ornate than the penthouse's main door in front of the elevator.

Blade racked the shotgun's slide and targeted

the running vampires. He blasted them both with stakes, and they fell like flaming scarecrows.

Racking the slide again, the Hunter heard the whisper of movement overhead. He looked up, bringing the shotgun up with him, but couldn't get the barrel around in time to shoot the vampire dropping down on him from the ceiling.

He met the vampire's fall with the shotgun's barrel, slamming it into the creature's face like Griffey, Jr., going for the upper deck. Teeth shattered, and the vampire's head jerked violently to the side.

Incredibly, the creature took the damage and rolled to a standing position on the carpet as soon as he touched down. The vampire leaped at Blade again, his features masked by rage and pain, mouth distended wide open to reveal only one fang left.

Holding the shotgun with a fist, Blade filled that gaping mouth with a silver stake that exploded the creature's head.

The penthouse door opened in front of Blade. He whipped the shotgun up and fired instantly. The door partially protected the vampire taking cover behind it, but didn't manage to conceal him completely. The stake tore the vampire's face away in a flaming rush of destruction.

Running to the door, Blade jammed his foot against the doorsill before the lock could catch. Another vampire stood on the other side of the door and fired a handful of rounds at the Hunter. Blade felt two of them slam into his body armor, knocking him back several inches. He kept his foot in place and thrust the shotgun's barrel into the room.

The first charge took the vampire in the chest, ripping a burning hole where his stillborn heart lay. As he crumpled, Blade fired again, taking out another vampire behind him.

He kicked the door open and stepped inside. The room before him was filled with expensive and elegant furniture. Deacon Frost had been living well. Shadows moved and twisted inside the darkness.

Blade tracked them without mercy, becoming everything Abraham Whistler had ever taught him. The shotgun banged steadily into his shoulder, three more rounds. One of them took out a vampire who had leaped behind the large couch. Another round blew up an ornate Japanese vase, showering orchids all over the room. The third slammed through the double glass doors leading out to a balcony area. Then the shotgun's breech locked back empty.

Not having any time to reload, Blade slung the weapon and drew the MACH. He crossed the room at a run, trying to figure out where Deacon Frost would be. The Hunter didn't plan on making it out of the penthouse alive, but he didn't plan on Frost doing so either.

From his estimate, the penthouse had three floors. Plenty of rooms for Frost to hide out in. He went through the double-wide doorway at the back of the first room, noticing the security cameras with overlapping visual fields.

A pair of vampires confronted him in the next hallway, lifting their weapons and unleashing a barrage of fire.

Blade dived back behind the wall, feeling it shudder as it absorbed the impact of the bullets. When the autofire died down, he whirled around the corner and leveled the MACH before him. He squeezed the trigger twice, putting bullets through the hearts of both creatures. They staggered back and went down as the silver-tipped rounds continued their lethal attacks on their systems.

Hurrying down the hall to the left, he found only an empty den. Turning back, he faced another vampire with a shotgun.

Blade threw himself at the ground as the burst of buckshot cut through the air over his head. The pellets blew fist-sized holes in the wall behind him. The Hunter brought the MACH up and put a bullet between the vampire's eyes.

The impact rocked the vampire back, but the creature turned to swirling ash before he hit the ground.

Gathering himself, Blade ran down the hall, loosing the final rounds to nail a vampire trying to escape. He holstered the pistol as the door in front of him swung open.

He faced the entrance, seeing the two black-suited vampires waiting for him inside. Both of them moved sinuously, their arms waving in martial-arts katas.

Staying wary and circling his opponents, Blade stripped off his jacket, revealing the EDTA injectors strapped to his biceps. Before the tossed jacket hit the ground, the first vampire attacked.

Blade parried the blows with rapid-fire syncopation, the sound of flesh striking flesh louder even than his breathing. He crossed, barely avoiding a spinning backfist that would have taken his head off if it had landed. Slipping one of the injectors from the biceps strap, he fisted it and stabbed it into the vampire's eye before he could get way. Blade depressed the plunger, flooding the vampire's system with EDTA.

Instantly, the vampire atomized from the shoulders up, becoming a bloody volcano that erupted the unlife right out of him.

The second vampire attacked at once, stepping through the blood flying from the remnants of his companion. Only the creature found Blade waiting for him when he arrived. The Hunter ducked under a sweeping leg kick and moved to the attack, but the vampire was already moving away from him. With no soft tissue available as a target, Blade swung the injector into the vampire's chest, hoping the needle wouldn't snap off. Instead, it penetrated the flesh, sliding between ribs and around the breastbone.

When Blade pressed the plunger this time, the vampire screamed in agony as his chest melted

away. Before it could stumble more than two
steps, the creature boiled into pieces, becoming a
fine-beaded spray of blood-mist that fell to the
floor.

Eyes on the doors across the room, Blade
approached them. There was no one else to stop
him, and he couldn't think of another place where
Frost would be hiding. He hoped that Karen
Jansen was still alive.

CHAPTER

42

Frost ran through the penthouse complex, listening to the reports over the headset radio. Mercury and a dozen vampires trailed behind him as he descended the stairs and raced for the rooms where Blade was sighted.

"Where is he now?" Frost demanded.

"Your sleep chamber," Mercury replied.

Frost grinned, thinking about what—and who—Blade was going to uncover there. "Perfect. He's in for the shock of his life."

Blade reloaded his MACH and continued going forward.

Beyond the doors was a vault. A huge stainless-steel rectangle covered the floor, looking decidedly like a coffin. A small faceplate window allowed viewing. Biting cold filled the room.

"Erik," a woman said in a soft voice.

Blade whirled around, bringing the MACH up in spite of the confusion that suddenly filled him. "Mother." The word was torn from his lips before he knew it. His hands trembled, holding the pistol at the woman's chest.

Lithely, impossibly, she rose from the stainless-steel coffin. And she was his mother, looking just as she had in the driver's license picture thirty years ago. He knew immediately there was only one way that could happen.

Haltingly, Blade took a step back. He didn't know if the name was his or not. The orphanage where he had first grown up had assigned one to him. When he got out on his own, he rejected it, not choosing a true name till after Whistler found him and trained him for his mission.

Vanessa moved closer, arms outstretched to embrace him.

Blade let the vampire approach, trying desperately to get a grip on the quicksilver slip of emotions flashing through his mind.

Vanessa smiled, looking into his eyes with a hypnotic quality, capturing his whole attention.

Blade backed away from the creature, lifting the MACH back on target. It wasn't her, he told himself, wasn't really his mother.

Before he could figure out if he was actually going to pull the trigger, something set off what felt like a nuclear weapon inside his head. His muscles contracted, dropping him to the floor on his knees. As he fell, he saw Frost step into view, holding a stun gun. Through it all, though, Blade fixated on the vampire standing before him who couldn't be his mother but somehow was.

"But you—died," he protested.

Vanessa smiled, and it held only demonic gleams. "I came back, Erik. That very same night. And Deacon welcomed me into his arms."

The words slapped into Blade like blows, bringing pain with them even though his paralyzed nervous system read only numbness over his body. His concentrated anger, fostered for years and given shape by his hunt, honed by what had been done to Whistler, shattered inside him. Even hope to make Frost pay for what Frost had done dwindled and died inside him.

He hadn't even known everything Frost had done.

Frost stepped next to Vanessa, wrapping a proprietary arm around her waist. He deliberately kissed the nape of her neck, then held her as she leaned into him in response, something she was obviously comfortable with.

"Why wouldn't I welcome her back?" Frost asked. "Just look at her." His hands dropped across the very feminine curves, and he grinned. "She belongs to me."

Blade struggled to get at the monster, willing his body to obey his demands.

But Frost met him with the stun gun again, continuing to administer the voltage this time till it left Blade in a prostrate heap on the floor.

"Jesus Christ," Frost exploded in mock severity. "I thought you'd be happy. You're finally reunited with your mother, and this is how you act? Give it up, Blade, it's over."

"Listen to your father, Erik," Vanessa ordered in a stern voice. "It's going to be a better world."

Blade looked at Vanessa, not understanding. Then he *knew*, and the surprise left him breathless.

"It's true," Frost said. He pointed at Vanessa. "Mom." Then he pointed at himself. "Dad. You've got *my blood* running through your veins."

"No," Blade groaned in denial. But the truth was so evident, standing there in undead flesh before his very eyes.

"Don't be so surprised. You've spent your life looking for the vampire who bit your mother." He reached down and gripped Blade's chin cruelly. "Well, here I am." Then he used the taser once more to take away whatever strength Blade had regained. "I've known for a while, of course. Once you made yourself known to us, I was able to put the pieces together. Who would've guessed you'd ever survive your mother's death? But you did, and here we are." He grinned evilly. "One big happy fucking family."

Without warning Frost put his foot on Blade's jugular and pressed down. Blade fought to move, but it was impossible. The taser had taken everything out of him. Darkness clouded his vision, then finally took him in. At least the pain disappeared with the rest of the world.

CHAPTER

43

For a long time, Karen Jansen thought Blade was dead. He still breathed, occasionally, but she considered it possible that he was brain-damaged. Blood covered the black leather he wore like armor, and she couldn't tell how much of it was his.

She shivered, feeling the headache throbbing at her temples. Quinn had held her in the back of the vault room with a hand over her mouth to keep her from crying out a warning to Blade. She had seen the stun gun used on him, had seen the electricity dancing from his teeth as he opened his mouth to scream. Then Frost had stepped on his throat, shutting off the blood flow. Mercury had waited until Blade went limp, then stepped forward and backhanded Karen into unconsciousness as well. But she'd come to; Blade hadn't.

She knew how strong the vampires were. It was possible that Frost hadn't taken time into account, and Blade's brain had been damaged by cutting off the circulation too long in his weakened condition.

His skin was gray, his breathing shallow, and he was covered with beads of sweat. His hands were secured tightly behind his back with manacles and chains.

She sat near him, her back to the cab of the armored truck the vampires had put them in, as the truck moved through the city. Her face still hurt from the blow she'd received. She could hear the sounds of traffic outside.

She wished she knew what to do. Whistler was dead, and no one else even knew about the vampires infesting the city. She saw no hope for Blade, or for herself, but didn't want to be alone at the end.

Blade's eyes snapped open, looking bloodshot and jaundiced. He looked at her for a moment, then tried to get up, finding he was too weak and that the manacles prevented him from using his hands. He gazed around the back of the truck, pure hatred written on his features.

"Are you all right?" Karen asked.

"I've been better," he admitted weakly. "How long have we been driving?"

"I don't know. I woke up just before you did."

He struggled to sit up again.

Karen moved over to him, helping him into a

sitting position. The movement didn't come without cost, though. His eyes closed, and his face knotted up into a tight fist of pain.

"Is it bad?" she asked.

Blade nodded. "I need my serum. We get out of this alive, maybe I'll take that miracle cure you think you can make."

Her voice was quiet when she spoke. "There's just one catch."

His look told her that he wasn't surprised, that his whole life had been constructed out of *catches* that had been neither fortunate nor pleasant. She knew he would have berated himself for showing his feelings so openly. He remained silent, though, making her say it.

"If it works, and I *do* cure you, you'll be fully human. You won't have their strength anymore."

He lay back, looking away from her, his eyes fixed on the roof of the armored truck. She felt him pull away from her, and she wished she had something she could tell him. But she thought she knew what was on his mind. Whistler was dead, and going back into the war against the vampires as a normal human just wasn't going to cut it.

And becoming human didn't mean he was going to be able simply to fit in as a human. What kind of résumé did an ex–vampire hunter fill out?

Before she could say anything, even if she could have thought of something, the truck lurched to a stop. She heard the engine die, followed immediately by footsteps approaching the rear of the armored truck.

A guard armed with a taser opened the doors, then stepped back to reveal a small army of vampires standing there. All of them flicked tasers warningly.

"Let's go," the leader said. "Get them out of the truck."

Karen kicked at them as they easily dragged her out of the armored truck. They removed Blade, but he managed to head-butt one of them and break the guard's nose, then kick two others. They used the tasers on him without mercy, leaving him hardly strong enough to stand on his own.

Cursing but cautious, the guards dragged Karen and Blade toward a construction site deep in the shadows of the city. Red-and-white-striped sawhorses and yellow tape marked the dangerous area around the gaping hole in the center of the site. Mounds of red clay packed with rock and stone chips that looked pale in the moonlight ringed the hole.

Excavation equipment occupied the area, huge yellow earthmoving machines that dwarfed the humans drifting in among them. The smell of freshly turned earth and diesel from the equipment still wasn't strong enough to mask the other smell.

And Karen knew that odor well from college forensic classes. The scent belonged to a just-opened grave that had been sealed for a long time.

CHAPTER

44

Their captors forced them into the hole at the excavation site. As she went past the edge, Karen saw the tunnel mouth to the right. They turned her toward it, staying close to her and following her in.

Vague illumination shone from inside the tunnel, bright enough that she could make out the thick collection of electrical cables snaking into the throat of the doorway. Lights strung across the top of the tunnel lit the way.

She studied the stone walls as she passed them, seeing various pictographs and cuneiform alphabets chiseled in the walls. All of the walls showed signs of recent sand-blasting.

They went down and down into the tunnel, dropping well below ground level. More of Frost's armed guards stood along the way, gazing at Blade with contempt as he passed. Karen gave up trying to keep count of them; she'd passed way too many sometime back. Even if they somehow managed to get loose, they weren't going anywhere.

The tunnel veered again. Rather than submit to entering the next doorway, Blade rammed his shoulder into one of the guards and tried to rip free the knife sheathed on the man's leg. Before his fingers could do more than touch the hilt, the tasers sank electrical fangs into his flesh again. Once he fell inside the doorway, they threw Karen after him.

She slammed painfully against the stone steps, rolling after Blade. They ended up on a low, wide gallery that overlooked a vast cylindrical coliseum. Passages and catacombs webbed off the gallery in all directions.

Pushing herself to her feet, Karen thought she recognized some of the architecture from her university days as pre-Christian Egypt. Staring out at it, seeing the immensity of it, she felt lost and alone. The whole chamber seemed like it had been hammered out of stone and darkest night.

She glanced at Blade. It was even more unsettling to see that he was surprised enough to show it.

Frost stood near the gallery's railing, looking with pride and triumph down into the open space beyond its edge. Quinn and Mercury stood near Frost. Quinn wore Blade's sunglasses, and the female vampire had Blade's sword belted around her hips.

Men and women stood against a wall to the left. Guards held weapons on them, making it apparent that they were prisoners as well.

But when Karen looked at them, she saw only vampires' eyes looking back at her. She'd learned to recognize that look. A shiver uncoiled down her spine as she moved over to Blade's side.

Frost turned, smiling magnanimously. The vampire chief was feeling good and didn't mind showing it. "Blade, Karen," the creature said, "glad you could join us."

"Yeah," Quinn said, "and thanks for the shades." He tipped them at Blade and smiled evilly.

Frost gestured at the guards, who immediately grabbed Blade and threw him facedown onto the gallery's stone floor. He struggled, but Karen got the feeling that he was struggling against the Thirst as much as he was against the men who held him.

"You haven't met our other guests, Karen," Frost said, waving toward the vampires under gunpoint.

All of them looked nervous and uncertain. Karen couldn't find it in herself to feel sorry for them.

"Rather than bore you with their names," Frost said, "I'll announce them collectively as the Vampire Lords of the House of Erebus. Purebloods, every one of them. You're in the company of royalty." Frost smiled coldly. "Not that I much give a damn."

Karen watched the shadows move on the other side of the gallery, almost getting the feeling that they were alive. And maybe hungry. The guards forced her forward, nearer Frost. As she looked out over the gallery railing, she knew from the lights below that the shaft had to be at least a hundred feet deep.

Turning back to look out over the gallery himself, Frost said, "Our ancestors called this place the Temple of the Night. Nice, isn't it?" Frost waved at the vampire lords. "Apparently these geniuses forgot it even existed. Can you fucking believe that?"

Blade shifted under the weight of the guards holding him down. Animal savagery filled his bloodshot eyes.

"Fortunately for us," Frost said, turning to look at Quinn and Mercury, "I'm what you might call a student of history." The vampire looked at Blade and grinned again. "So why are we here? Read the prophecy. This place was built for one reason, one glorious moment—this night, the Blood Tide."

Without warning, Blade broke free of the guards holding him down. He exploded into frantic motion, lunging at Frost. The vampire didn't move and stood waiting. Only before Blade's hands could find Frost's throat, Quinn stepped in behind Blade and slammed a pistol butt into his head.

His charge broken, Blade groaned in pain and sank to his knees.

"Thank you, Mr. Quinn," Frost said, turning to Mercury. "Let's see this sword of his."

Karen's heart hammered in her chest, thinking that Blade wouldn't be able to defend himself against Frost's attack. She started to step forward, but Mercury blocked her way, followed by two of the guards.

Mercury drew the sword and handed it to Frost.

Taking the blade, Frost sighted down the length of the sword and tested its weight with a few swings. "Oh wow. Still quite sharp I see. Nice balance to the blade."

Karen heard the familiar click of the booby-trap mechanism activating. She waited, her breath tight in her throat, knowing that Frost was about to get maimed.

"Titanium, isn't it?" Frost asked as if he was picking out a rental car. "Acid-etched? I could get used to a weapon like this." The vampire whipped it through the air a few more times, then pressed a stud on the sword hilt.

Karen still waited, but it became immediately apparent that the booby trap had been deactivated.

"You think I didn't know about that?" Frost asked sarcastically. "I know *everything* about you, Blade."

Buried under the guards on the floor, Blade gave up the struggle.

Pulling back from Blade, Frost shifted his attention to Quinn. "Hold out your arm."

Karen's stomach turned flips as she considered Frost's order. Quinn didn't look too happy about it either. The creature finally had two complete arms again.

"What?" Quinn asked, drawing his arms in protectively.

"Hold out your arm," Frost repeated.

Reluctantly, Quinn stuck his arm out. Quinn's eyes tightened and his mouth curved down as Frost laid the sword's edge against the vampire's forearm.

Frost stepped back, then raised the sword, getting ready to swing. Karen gagged, almost purging, knowing that cutting Quinn's arm off meant nothing to Frost.

But Frost didn't swing. Instead, the vampire chief pulled the blade away. "Just kidding."

A relieved look filled Quinn's face, and he didn't hesitate in pulling the arm back to safety.

Mercury and some of the vampire lords laughed as Quinn looked sheepish.

A relaxing spasm shivered through Karen's stomach. She gulped in air, forcing herself to take it slow and breathe through her nose.

Frost tossed the sword back to Mercury, who deftly caught it and sheathed it again.

Blade groaned in pain.

Karen took a step in Blade's direction, instinctively trying to go to him, but Quinn grabbed her, holding her tight. "Blade."

Frost regarded her. "He can't hear you, honey. The Thirst has got him now." Frost snapped his fingers, and one of the guards brought over the serum injectors Karen recognized from the workshop. Two of them were missing, but six remained. Frost slipped one of them free, then motioned to Quinn.

The big vampire reached down, dragging Blade's head up by his hair, so Frost could address him.

"What do we have here?" Frost taunted. "Your precious serum?"

Blade didn't respond, and Karen wasn't sure if the Hunter didn't because he chose not to, or because he was beyond hearing.

"How long has it been since you shot up? Twelve hours? More? I'll bet you're just *dying* for a drink." Frost crouched, getting eye-to-eye with Blade. "What does it feel like? Is your blood on fire? Are you burning up inside?" The creature waved the glass-tipped injector in front of Blade's face.

"Try some, you might like it," Blade stated in a weak voice.

For the first time, Karen realized that the serum in the injector wasn't Blade's serum. The color was blue, not pink. It was the EDTA. And she had no problem imagining what would happen if Frost *did* use the injector.

Frost shook his head. "Thanks, but I prefer the real thing. In any event, I don't think you'll be needing this anymore." He tossed the injector cartridge belt over the gallery railing, then followed it up with the loose injector.

Blade shivered and gritted his teeth, like he was going through withdrawal. Karen had seen similar reactions in junkies in the ER. "Go to hell," Blade said.

Frost stood up, motioning to someone standing behind Karen. "Get him out of here."

A female vampire stepped forward, dressed in a sexy sheer number and moving with the grace of a trained dancer. Karen stared at the woman, knowing she'd seen her before in Frost's house. Her name was Vanessa, and now that she got a really good look at the vampire, Karen realized that she looked exactly like the woman in the blood-spattered driver's license in Blade's room. Even had the same name. She wished she knew what the woman in the picture meant to Blade but Whistler hadn't mentioned the connection.

Vanessa motioned to the guards gathered around Blade, and they lifted him from the ground. Then they dragged him off, following the woman.

Karen watched him going, feeling the need to say something, but having no clue at all what to tell him. She didn't even know if she'd see him again.

CHAPTER

45

As Blade was being dragged away, Deacon Frost turned to face the vampire lords. They gazed at him hotly, hate in their eyes. He grinned in spite of it. Being in the Temple of the Night, knowing what he now knew, their hate couldn't touch him. He was far more cunning than they were, far more dangerous. And he wasn't afraid to spill blood. There'd be plenty of that before he was finished tonight.

"And get these bozos downstairs," Frost ordered Mercury.

Mercury moved to comply, motioning to the guards covering the vampire lords. With the guns trained on them, knowing the ammo was silver- and garlic-tipped and would kill even them, they started moving.

Only Pallintine and Reichardt refused to move.

"How dare you bring us here under duress, Frost," Pallintine accused.

Frost approached the vampire, never feeling more confident in his life or unlife. "I wanted to share this moment with you. I mean, come on, tonight is a big night, isn't it? What we've all been waiting for, right?"

Reichardt thrust his chin defiantly out toward Frost. "Pah!" the German said. "Watch your back, boy. You won't get out of here alive."

Frost grinned at the creature in true amusement. "Is that so?" He waved to the guards, who forced Reichardt to get moving. "Bye." Once they were gone, he turned his attention to Karen Jansen. Sadly, he no longer had time or the inclination to watch the woman's suffering. Of course, that didn't mean it wasn't going to stretch out all the same. "Don't worry, sweetheart. I haven't forgotten about you."

"Yeah," Quinn agreed, "we've got something real special planned."

To her credit, the woman didn't break down. Maybe, Frost considered, she had no inkling of how much worse things could be. But she was about to find out. He smiled at the thought, watching as Quinn dragged her away, then fell into step with them.

"So there was this guy I bit one time," Quinn was saying as it led Karen through a narrow passageway, "ripped his throat out, bled him dry. Figured he would turn, right?"

Karen knew they were only trying to scare her, to make the whole experience they'd planned for her somehow worse than it was going to be. She didn't see how that could happen: She was already as scared as she thought she ever could be. She didn't look at them, watching the shadows that dodged around her as she passed under the jury-rigged lights suspended from cables along the ceiling.

"Only the guy didn't turn," Frost went on, joining in the story. "He was stuck in some kind of—zombie state." He sounded uncertain, which made the whole story somehow even more horrifying. "For whatever reason, some of them reject the change. It's pathetic, really."

Abruptly, the passageway they'd been following widened into a small chamber. Four gaping holes were open in the chamber's floor.

Karen's instincts warned her away from those holes. She dragged her heels, giving in to that primitive warning system.

"The poor fucks are completely stupid," Quinn said. "They'll feed on anything, given the chance: animals, corpses, even other vampires."

"That's a plus," Karen made herself say. No way was she going to give either one of the bastards holding her the satisfaction of seeing her cry—or beg.

It was wasted effort as far as Frost was concerned. "Bearing all this in mind," the vampire said, "I'd like you to meet an old friend of yours."

Quinn shoved Karen forward, toward the gaping holes in the chamber floor.

Stumbling, she stared down into the mass of shadows that filled the nearest hole, knowing it was deep. The lichen-encrusted stone walls had been worn smooth over time. Too smooth. Her feet wouldn't stay under her, and she plunged into the hole.

She fell for a short time, lost completely and disoriented in the shadows. A moment later, the breath was knocked out of her body as she landed hard, ending the scream she had started. Loose debris rattled around her, felt like it was filled with angles and edges. She groaned and sat up gingerly, recognizing the shapes as dry and brittle bones.

Frost's voice sounded loud above her even though she couldn't see the creature. "Shame. She was hot."

Karen forced herself to her feet. There had to be some way to escape. She couldn't just give up. She put her hands out, moving like a sightless person through the gloom, hoping her eyes would make the adjustment so she could take better stock of the pit.

She also had the distinct impression that she wasn't alone in the pit. Frost *had* mentioned meeting an old friend, hadn't he?

CHAPTER

46

Blade fought against his captors, but no strength remained in his body. He was all tapped out, weaker than he'd ever been in his life.

They dragged him deeper into the Temple of the Night, up a flight of stairs that led to a circular antechamber directly above the galleried sanctuary where Frost had been waiting. He tried to fight again as they reached the next doorway, trying to use the narrow opening to his advantage. He also thought about what Quinn and Frost were probably going to do to Karen, what they'd already done to Whistler. Even with that, his anger wasn't enough to kindle the kind of strength he needed to break free.

They pulled him inside the room with only a little trouble.

He noted the circular structure of the stone

room at once, his eyes drawn to the huge marble blocks in the center. One block sat on the floor, positioned to fit perfectly with the scheme of the groove cut into the floor. The other block sat farther up the incline, looking like it would slide right on top of the first one and join together seamlessly.

Blade got a bad feeling when, upon closer inspection, he spotted the man-shape cut into the bottom marble block. Looking back at the other block, he saw the man-shape repeated on it, as if they clapped together to make a mold.

The guards pulled him farther into the room, acting as if the struggle he managed to put up was nothing. He saw the razor-edged blades in the block's man-shape, built into the stone at the wrists.

While the guards held him, Vanessa stripped him of his body armor. Then the creature took a knife and cut his tank top away. He stared into the vampire's eyes, so like his own, but couldn't find any answers there. There wasn't any emotion either.

In spite of the slight struggle he was able to put up, the guards strapped him into the marble block on the bottom. Eerily enough, the man-shape seemed to be an exact fit.

Vanessa peered down at him, running fingers over his body and noting how well he fitted into the block. "A perfect fit," the creature said. "They knew you were the one, Erik. The Day-Walker. They foresaw your coming, all those millennia ago." Vanessa waved at the guards, sending them away.

For a moment, a tiny crust of hope entered Blade's heart. But Vanessa's words took it away at once.

"You poor child," she said, taunting, an evil gleam in her eyes. "You're so sick. So thirsty." She ran her fingers across his brow.

The caress chilled Blade's heart. "Don't touch me," he said.

"Erik, these are my people now. *I'm one of them.*"

"You can't be." Blade's voice was soft. He knew he wasn't trying to convince this creature; it was himself he was trying to convince.

The vampire leaned over him more closely, her lips almost touching his. He felt the coldness coming off the creature, felt the barrenness, but Vanessa spoke with passion. "You don't understand," the vampire said. "Your mother died a long time ago. I've hunted, I've *killed*, and I've *enjoyed* it. Haven't you? Sooner or later, the Thirst always wins."

"I don't believe that," Blade gritted, but even as he said it, he felt the fire in his belly that was threatening to consume his backbone. He felt like he was burning up.

Slowly, the emotion drained from the vampire's face as Vanessa stepped away. "You will," she replied coldly. Then she was gone, moving into the shadows and disappearing from sight.

Blade screamed in frustration, trying to break the fever that was burning him up. He tried to pull out of the marble block, but he was too weak. He sagged back in total exhaustion as the guards took their places at both doors leading out of the chamber.

In everything he'd learned about the vampires while fighting them, he'd never heard anything about the Temple of the Night. It was hard to imagine that anything as large as the temple had gone unnoticed under the city, but then, vampires weren't common knowledge, either. Judging from the architecture, he knew a vampire family must have brought the whole temple overseas at some point, then hidden the thing in the ground. Hidden it so well, in fact, that it had taken Deacon Frost years to find it.

The Hunter thought about the groove cut into the stone floor, and the blades already nestled tight against his wrists. It didn't take him long to reach a conclusion what they were for, and he didn't like what he came up with.

CHAPTER

47

Karen had to move cautiously in the pit, still hurting from the jarring fall she'd taken. Bones slid out beneath her, causing treacherous footing. Even when her eyes adjusted, vision remained a problem. She hacked and wheezed, holding a hand over her mouth so she wouldn't suck too much of the raised dust into her lungs.

The room had a low ceiling that prevented her from standing too straight. Despite the debris scattered around the chamber, she made out hemispheres cut into the floor. They circled a larger central hemisphere, leading her to believe that the chamber was once a map room of sorts.

All she could really see clearly, because the whiteness of bone somehow seemed to glow like neon in the blackness of the pit, were skulls, rib cages, femurs, tibiae, and other bones she could identify because of her profession. All of them were picked clean of flesh, and some of them showed what looked like human teeth marks on them.

A few of the skulls had large caninelike fangs. She guessed that those were the remnants of the dead who hadn't quite made the crossing over to become vampires.

She continued feeling the wall, hoping to find some imperfection that might give her purchase and possibly lead her to another hold higher up that would allow her to reach one of the four shafts leading from the chamber. It didn't seem likely at this point, and she was beginning to think she had already been completely around the pit at least once and hadn't realized it. But she had to try.

A whisper drifted through the pit.

Karen stopped what she was doing, hoping that she was wrong and it was only a stray gust of wind.

The whisper repeated, carrying with it the sound of shifting bones this time. And the whisper sounded closer.

"Trying to understand what's happening to me," the whisperer mumbled. *"No pulse. Then there's the question of lividity."*

Turning, Karen looked into the darkest pocket of shadows in the bottom of the pit. Fear struck her mute, paralyzing her.

A pallid face emerged from the darkness, desiccated flesh hanging on the skull. Lidless eyes looked like dark cigarette burns, black marbles slick with Vaseline, in the cadaverous features. The twisted mouth resembled a raw wound.

Recognizing who the man was, recognizing what he was, Karen backed away. The wall came up quickly behind her. "Curtis?"

"*Karennnnn,*" the undead thing gasped. "*I never thought I'd see you againnnnn.*" The thing that used to be Curtis Webb, forensic pathologist and former lover, snarled. He swung a fist at her, the flesh already peeling off of it to reveal the skeletal system beneath.

The fist collided with the side of her head, dazing her and knocking her to the ground.

The corpse crawled on top of her, pinning her arms at her sides. It gurgled through its gutted trachea, gazing at her with those black, black eyes. "*Tell me, Karennnn,*" it wheezed, "*ever have second thoughts—about usssss?*"

Karen gave in to her fear, feeling the adrenaline surging through her system, intending to use it to her advantage. The dead thing lunged closer, lolling its distended tongue over her mouth, trying to bite her.

Fumbling behind her, choking as the thing tightened its grip on her throat, she grabbed hold of a human femur. She swung it upward, smashing the corpse's jaw. The thing reared back, falling to one side.

Karen crawled out from under its weight and swung the femur repeatedly. The sounds when she struck were different, bone hitting flesh, bone hitting bone, bone hitting something that she didn't even want to think about.

It howled in terror and pain, giving ground before her. A final swing and the femur shattered in Karen's hands. She backed away, watching in horror as the thing fell into the debris of dust and shattered bones.

Its head was tilted at an awkward angle, its neck broken. But it didn't move again. The broken neck had obviously paralyzed it.

Crying freely now, Karen retreated. She waited, making herself breathe, to see if any other horrors would come crawling out of the bone pile. When she had herself under control again, she returned to the wall and the search with her fingers. This time, though, she found a hole between two of the bricks, where the ancient mortar had cracked and fallen out.

She dug at the imperfection with her fingers, pulling pieces of it out. Getting an idea, she glanced down at the bone pile and found the other half of the cracked femur. She jammed the sharp end into the crack between the bricks, then used a skull to pound it in deeper.

When she had it in far enough, she put her weight on it to test it. Hope returned to her in the instant that her feet cleared the ground and she hung there.

She returned to the chamber long enough to take the other piece of the splintered femur from the floor. Back at the wall, she rammed that bone home as well. Pulling herself up, she freed the first bone and whipped it around, gaining another foot when she drove it into the wall above the second one.

Slowly, she started up the wall, her muscles blazing fire as she fought gravity. But the top of the pit grew steadily closer.

"KARENNNNNNNN!"

She ignored the cry because there was nothing she could do for the Curtis Webb she'd known and briefly loved, and concentrated on her own survival. She kept pulling herself up the wall.

Blade lay trapped in the marble block, unable to move. The Thirst was alive in him, claiming his body, staking out each new gained piece of territory from him as the blood wept from the slashes on his wrists.

His vision dimmed to a narrow tunnel directly in front of him. Quinn stepped in to fill it, accompanied by Frost.

"Been a long road, hasn't it?" Frost asked, stopping beside the marble block. "When I think of what you've become, what you *should've* become—" He cocked his head and stared deep into Blade's face. "Guess I don't blame you, though. I want you to know that. Even after all you've done. It's your human side that's made you weak. You should've listened to your blood."

Blade raised his head with difficulty, glorying

in the small success. "Say what you want, mother-fucker," he growled. "You'll be dead by dawn."

Quinn pulled a mock face. "Ouch."

Smiling, Frost stepped closer. "After tonight, there won't be another dawn. LaMagra isn't a physical being. He's a spirit that needs a host."

Cold fear raced through Blade as he realized the implication of Frost's words. "You," the Hunter said.

"Of course," Frost agreed. "Who else? It's destiny, baby. This was *meant* to be, every moment of it." He surveyed Blade's position inside the marble block. "And you turned your back on it. You're a traitor to your own race, Blade. You're too human."

Despite the fever and nausea filling him, Blade made himself speak. "You're the second person to tell me that. I didn't buy it then either, but you know what? The human side is telling me to do this." He spit in Frost's face.

The smile disappearing at once, the vampire chief stepped back and wiped the spittle from his cheek with a handkerchief. "Nice." Frost looked at Quinn. "Close the stone."

From the corner of his eye, barely above the lip of the marble block, Blade watched Quinn step on a raised golden stud protruding from the floor. In response, the other marble stone slid smoothly into place over Blade, locking him inside the marble coffin. Only the narrow slit in front of his eyes allowed him to see out.

Then the razors at his wrists bit into his flesh. Blood blazed warm across his skin, trickling down his fingers to ooze into the narrow channels cut expressly for the purpose. And it kept on flowing.

The resonant sound of the marble stones fitting together reached Mercury's sensitive ears. They'd experimented with the blocks when Frost had first found the Temple of the Night, even tried putting humans and vampires in the man-shape grooved in the rock and bleeding them dry. Occasionally, Quinn had cut off the extra pieces to make one of them fit.

But nothing had happened at those times. So they'd cleaned the blood channels again and again, waiting till they deciphered the prophecy.

Now, however, the closing of the stones had an entirely different sound. And the sound was *right*. She smiled at the thought, knowing it was true.

The vampire lords ahead of her milled anxiously, and almost got shot by the men guarding them. She got them moving again, knowing there wasn't much time left now.

The last ringing echoes of the blocks fitting together died away as Vanessa walked alone on the high gallery. She enjoyed the view, glad Frost had brought her to the temple. She didn't like remembering everything she'd had to give up to become what she was, but the temple was a definite reminder of what she'd gained.

It was too bad that Erik hadn't seen it that way. But then again, once they'd finished bleeding him, maybe he'd be more open to suggestion.

She used that thought to balance the sadness she felt.

Deacon Frost stared into Blade's eyes, having a bit of difficulty spotting them through the narrow slit left to see through. Frost grinned, watching Blade's blood fill the initial gold grooves under the marble coffin, then start spiraling out to fill the arcane designs.

"Let's have it, Blade," Frost said. "Every last drop."

The warm red liquid oozed faster now, gaining speed as it sped through the spirals. Then it disappeared through the floor, spinning into the first of the rooms it had to go through in order to activate the process.

A moment later and the blood reached the Primary Glyph. Frost knew from experience that it would fill the narrow tube, tracing the glyph, then move on.

Frost knew exactly when the glyph had filled, because a rumble began in the distance. It sounded like heavy bass, a distant thunder. Only it might not have been a real sound at all, but a resonance that had been plucked and echoed within himself. It felt like nothing he'd ever experienced before.

By now, he knew, the planets of the solar system would be lining up as well. Just as the prophecy had foretold.

Frost couldn't help himself, laughing out loud. This was success, the most fantastic success he'd ever been part of. "Amazing. It's really working," he murmured to himself. Then he turned to Quinn and the guards. "Places, everybody. We're on."

He led them out of the chamber and to the elevator hanging near the gallery. As he went, he noticed that the vibration of the thunder continued, knocking dust from images carved into the walls. It fell in growing heaps and clouds.

CHAPTER

49

Her strength flagging, Karen reached for the top of the pit. Her fingers just made it over the edge. The bone shard she held in her other hand slid away, leaving her dangling by one hand. Praying quietly, listening to the thunder of voices somewhere overhead, she flailed with the other arm and managed to grab the top of the pit with it as well.

At the same time, she spotted Frost and Quinn going by, obviously in a hurry to get somewhere else. Arm muscles screaming in silent protest, she lowered herself back down the shaft till they passed.

Then she pulled herself up, arms trembling, and managed to stretch out on the floor beside the pit. She wanted to do nothing but rest.

•   •   •

Mercury ordered the guards to put the vampire lords into position. They were in the lower part of the temple. A central dais surrounded by catacombs and a dozen secret passages occupied most of the area. The catacombs held ages-old burial vaults, the residents still inside them.

At her instruction, the guards herded the vampire lords up the wide ramp to the central dais itself. "One under each glyph, under the tombs," she commanded, pointing out the glyphs marked in the ancient stone dais. "Make it perfect."

Most of the vampire lords were in awe despite the hostility they were shown. They glanced upward, scanning the hundred-foot distance that reached back up to the sanctuary at the top. Catacombs stretched the whole distance on the walls.

Reichardt was the first to resist. He shoved back against the guards, scaring the humans among them. "You stupid girl," he said to Mercury, eyeing her over the weapons the guards held on him threateningly. "What do you think is really going to happen? LaMagra? The Blood Tide? They're nothing more than myths, vampire fairy tales."

"Then why are you sweating, pureblood? You afraid we're going to steal your soul? Your *pureblood* spirit? You should be. Read the prophecy. It's time you fucks contributed something to the cause."

"Even if Frost is right," Pallintine added, "do

you really think he cares about you? You're going to die along with the rest of us."

Angrily, knowing she had to make a statement that would push the rest of the vampire lords into seeing things her way, and not minding at all that the main subject involved in the lesson-giving was Pallintine, Mercury drew the sword at her waist. She turned and threw the sword, putting a lot of effort into the whip-crack movement.

The sword impaled Pallintine in the chest before he had a chance to move. The impact was enough to rip him from his feet and knock him back against a wall twenty feet behind him. The sword embedded in the stone wall, leaving Pallintine to hang there for a moment. Then the vampire burst into flame, and his ashes drifted away.

Mercury turned to the other surviving vampire lords. "No harm, no foul," she declared. "We only need twelve of you anyway."

The rest of them moved into position on the glyphs, offering no arguments and no delays.

Karen clutched the broken femur tightly as she crept through the passageways honeycombing the underground temple. Everyone appeared to have deserted the upper levels. Thankfully, though, the doorway she'd seen them take Blade through only led in one direction. There was no way to get lost. The downside was that the door took her away from the entrance that led back to the construction site.

She knew, however, that she wasn't going to be able to escape Frost and the other vampires without Blade. She couldn't bring herself to leave him anyway.

She followed the passageway to the big room at the end, taking note of the winding groove cut into the floor and the blood filling it. When she spotted the huge stone block in the center of the room, she knew that was where Blade had to be.

Steeling herself, remembering what had been done to Curtis Webb and knowing that the block couldn't mean anything good for Blade, she crept forward. She barely heard the whisper of breath coming from the stone.

When she peered through the narrow slit on top of the block, the darkness inside almost kept her from seeing Blade's face. At best, he looked unconscious, but with all the blood running through the groove in the floor, she knew he could also be dead.

Frantic, she glanced around the room, noting the inclined position of the floor. Then she noticed the handle on the side of the stone that held Blade captive. Grabbing the handle, she managed to turn the stone, but it moved so slowly.

Stone ground against stone as the block revolved around its midpoint, then the top portion of the makeshift coffin slid open. Blade lay inside, his skin already turning ashen from blood loss and shock.

"Blade," Karen called softly.

She couldn't believe it when his eyes flickered open, but they did, filling her with hope. Fear was in there, too, because she didn't know how to fix the damage that had been done to him. Maybe she'd only arrived in time to watch him die.

Using the jagged femur, she cut the leather restraints away. When they were gone, he didn't have the strength to hold himself up. He crumpled to the floor and didn't move.

Karen went to him, her mind flying as she tried to think of a way out. She couldn't carry Blade, and she couldn't leave him behind. She wanted to scream in frustration, but she was too scared.

Frost ran to the gallery, taking his jacket off and tossing it to the side in his haste. Below, he could see the whole top section of the temple spread out. And there, at the heart of it, was the gold ring circling the great inverted moon dome that comprised the ceiling.

Even as he watched, excitement throbbing through his veins, the golden channels of the Primary Glyph filled with Blade's blood. With the blood of the Day-Walker, he reminded himself. The red liquid fanned out in all directions, running more quickly than it had.

Quinn and the four guards spread out along the railing as well, watching in awe.

Frost turned to the closest guard. "Bring the elevator up. Hurry."

The guard lifted a walkie-talkie and spoke into it.

Unable to move fast enough now, feeling the resonance thrumming inside him, Frost left the railing and sprinted for the narrow upper gallery.

Vanessa waited for him on the other side, but he didn't care. Frost was about to become something even more than he'd dreamed. When he'd first been turned, first risen from the grave, he'd thought nothing could compare to the promise of eternal life.

But that feeling paled beside the one that filled him now. He was on the verge of godhood.

CHAPTER

50

The squeaking makeshift excavation elevator drew Mercury's attention at once. She'd been watching the blood fill the moon dome, wondering where Frost was.

The open-sided elevator shuddered as it rose along the vibrating steel cables.

The vampire lords shifted restlessly, some of them obviously more fearful than they had been. But none of them wanted to chance the guards' weapons.

She smiled as the elevator neared the top of its run. It wouldn't be long now.

By the time Frost reached the upper gallery, the capillaries framing the moon dome had nearly been filled. Only a few empty channels yet remained, but the blood seemed to be moving faster, drawn along its course by more than mere gravity.

He reached the elevator staging point and found Vanessa waiting for him.

She looked radiant, her smile filling her face. Normally the expression would have symbolized the conquest he'd made over Blade and been a source of dark pride. But he found he didn't care at all.

"It's happening," Vanessa said. "You're really making it happen." She held her hands out to him.

Frost ignored her, stepping quickly out of her reach as he watched the steel cables jerking with the strain of bringing the elevator up. "Take care of your son," he told her coldly.

For a moment, Vanessa's arms hung out before her, empty. Then she nodded and left without another word, heading back to the bleeding chamber, where Blade should have been a dry husk by now.

Frost watched the moon dome as it finished filling. The blood started to overflow at predetermined points, spilling single beads onto the top ring of tombs below.

"Where's that fucking elevator?" Quinn demanded, peering over the top railing.

Frost made himself wait. He'd be in time, he told himself. The destiny he'd chosen for himself was laid out before him, and nothing was going to stop him from achieving it.

With a final squeal, the excavation elevator crunched to a stop at the gallery level. Frost led the way onto it, then triggered the return to the bottom of the temple.

Blade tried to sit up, looking like a corpse rising from its deathbed.

Karen knew he wouldn't have made it without her help. His grip on her wrist was weak.

"Get out of here," Blade ordered.

"I'm not leaving without you," Karen told him, fighting to help him get to his feet. It was like lifting wet cement, his body weight shifting constantly as she pulled at him.

"You don't understand," Blade argued, pushing at her. "The Thirst—" His voice broke off into a groan of pain. He grabbed at his stomach.

Karen knew there was only one way out, if only she was strong enough to take it. She had known it as soon as she had seen the slits across Blade's wrists. She steeled herself. "I *know*." She took a deep breath, putting her hopes and fears all on the line. "Take some of my blood."

"No." He pushed at her again, trying to create distance between them.

She held his face in her hand, letting him see her tears, and made her voice rough. "It's the *only way*. You know that. We'll *never* get out of here alive if you don't."

Blade shuddered, his eyes blazing white with

the full fury of the Thirst on him. "I can't. I won't be able to stop."

And that was Karen's strongest fear, too. But she had to believe in him, believe in the man whom Whistler had put his faith in, believe in the man who had tried to save her from the vampire virus before he'd even known there was a cure. And she had to get him to believe in himself. *"Yes you will,"* she said. "The human side of you is stronger. I know it is. Whistler knew it, too. That's why he loved you as much as he did. That's why I can't leave you here now."

Slowly, he rose, too weak to do it without her help.

And she quietly held in the screaming terror that filled her mind when he turned those hungry eyes on her.

Standing in the open elevator cage, Frost watched the concentric rings of ancient tombs that lined the cylindrical walls of the temple as he dropped. He reached out and ran his hand along the obsidian stone tablets facing him, studying again the ancient glyphs cut into the stone with golden channels. All waited to be filled with Blade's blood.

Glancing up, he saw that they were gaining on the bloodfall. Above, the blood had already inscribed the glyphs on the tombs. The basso rumble that had started when the two blocks had closed over Blade grew more steady and louder.

Frost spoke quietly to Quinn, reverent in spite of his own nature. "Tonight we get to pay our respects to the human race. No more compromises, no more half measures. Tonight the Age of Man comes to an end."

Quinn, as always, never saw past his own needs, nor even a second past the moment. "Shit man, we're gonna be *gods*."

Frost looked at the man, wondering how the hell even Quinn could have missed what was truly happening, and what would take place. But it was no use. Quinn would never understand. "Of course we are."

A small crack sounded above. Looking up, Frost saw one of the glyphs that had been traced in blood suddenly split open. It was happening. They were on the event horizon of a whole new world.

Karen heard the renewed basso thunder from below and knew it couldn't mean anything good. The realization gave her strength to keep her head turned as Blade opened his mouth. She saw his canines elongate, growing needle points that gleamed in the darkness and against the pallor of his flesh.

Despite his emaciated and anemic appearance, his strength couldn't be denied. He closed his hands on her upper arms and pulled him to her.

She found she couldn't fight against him. She felt trapped inside her own body.

Almost hypnotically, his eyes drew hers, burning deep into her mind, burning away some of the fear that held her in thrall. Then he lowered his mouth to her neck, his breath hot on her skin for just an instant.

Then he bit.

She blocked the scream in her throat as his fangs sank deep into her neck, afraid that he would stop if she let it out. Then she grew afraid that he wouldn't as she grew weaker and a paralysis she hadn't counted on filled her.

He drank deeply, and she felt part of herself draining away, swallowed up and maybe gone forever. And he *kept* drinking.

CHAPTER

51

The blood reached the bottom of the temple first, but as the elevator touched down, Frost knew enough time remained. He strode from the cage, watching as single drops of blood fell from the edge of the twelve tombs that made up the lowest ring that circled the temple walls.

With unerring accuracy, the blood drops slammed into the foreheads of the vampire lords below. All of them were surprised, not expecting it. But they didn't move after they were hit.

Triumphantly, Frost strode to the dais, followed by Quinn and the guards. He motioned Quinn to stay at the perimeter of the dais, then went to join Mercury at the center.

"How's everybody doing tonight?" Frost asked the vampire lords. "You thirsty?"

None of them deigned to respond, their voices held in check by anger or fear.

Frost spread his arms wide, taking in them and their surroundings. He saw the fear in their eyes then as they touched the bloody splashes across their foreheads. The glyphs continued to split overhead, blood coming down to the lower levels with greater speed.

"I hope you're all *very* thirsty," Frost warned them. Mercury pulled his shirt open as Quinn roared with laughter. For the first time, Frost noted that his own heartbeat had acquired the rhythm of the basso thundering taking place within the temple.

It was going to happen, and no one could stop it.

Blade drank. When he was twelve, when the Thirst had first started making itself known, before Whistler had found him and introduced him to Kam's serum, he had drunk from animals. But never had it tasted like what he drank now.

His mind cleared of pain and dying, fueling itself with only the thought of drinking till he could hold no more. The taste was sweet hell, because, in some distant corner of his mind, he knew where it came from, knew the cost it came with.

Frost watched Mercury as she extended a forefinger, then willed the fingernail to grow. Inches long now, she used the razor point of it to carve the glyph into the flesh of Frost's chest. She worked slowly and deliberately, to get it right and to prolong the agony she must have known he was experiencing.

Strangely, Frost felt himself drawn to the pain, giving himself over to it instead of distancing himself from it. He shuddered in ecstasy, surprising them both.

Blade was dimly aware of Karen's head lolling back, her eyes open and glassy, seeing nothing. Then she reached ecstasy. Her breathing deepened and quickened, falling into a synchronous rhythm with his. Her fingers dug into him, pulling him closer, clawing downward.

As Frost remained standing while Mercury scored his flesh, he watched the lords look up, knowing they saw something. He looked up as well, his breath coming faster as the ecstasy continued to swell within him.

Twelve trails of blood crept across the underside of the moon dome, all heading for the center. And that center was just above Deacon Frost's head.

He watched the blood gather, willing it to come.

Blade drank Karen's blood, finding that he couldn't stop. He didn't even think about whom he was attached to or what it might be doing to her. He fed, not even surprised at how easily it came to him.

He heard his own heart beating, louder even than the basso thumping that filled the temple.

Debris pulled loose from the temple walls as the tombs cracked. Frost continued watching, but his attention was riveted on the blood gathering directly above him.

Taken over by a primitive joy that he didn't understand, Frost threw out his arms and stared at the moon dome a hundred feet above him.

Even at that distance, his vision sharpened enough that he saw the blood bead gathered there, trembling from the basso thunder that rocked the temple.

It had to fall.

Blade drank, thinking he'd never get his fill. Karen held on to him, giving everything she had.

And he was willing to take it all to satisfy that burning craving in his belly.

"Don't stop," she pleaded, holding him tighter.

Frost stared up at the blood bead, knowing it was too fat, too engorged to remain there. Mercury backed away, and he didn't understand the tears she had in her eyes. He was on the point of becoming; there was no sadness in that.

He kept looking up at the blood bead. It had to fall!

Karen no longer had the strength to hold on to Blade as he drank from her. She kept her arms loosely about him, but she knew she wasn't holding him anymore.

"My God, don't stop," she begged. Nothing had ever felt more wonderful in her life.

Frost watched the blood bead as it quivered. Even at a hundred feet, he knew this quiver was larger than the last.

It had to fall.

Blade took a breath, felt Karen take a breath with him. And he remembered how it had been in the car the night he had first met her, remembered how peaceful it had been to breathe with her.

It wasn't peaceful now; it was obscene. They were rushing toward a precipice, and only one of them was going to survive it. And that survival wasn't going to leave anything of Blade, the man— only the Thirst.

Gathering his strength, finding it all there and more, Blade released his bite and pushed her away from her. "NOOOOOOOOOO!"

• • •

The blood bead gave in to the pull of gravity, tearing free and beginning the plummet. Looking up, Frost saw it, and anticipatory delight ran through his body like an electric current.

Karen clawed at Blade, hating him for stopping the ecstasy that had filled her. It was more powerful, more potent than any feeling she had ever experienced in her life. She knew she was crying, could feel the tears coursing down her cheeks. "Don't stop!" she begged, throwing herself at him, baring her neck for him to take.

Instead, Blade gripped her by the shoulders, shoving her back.

It seemed like it took a long time for her to realize what she had been trying to do. Her senses and control returned slowly. She touched the raw wounds on her neck, then started shaking violently. "My God." She thought she was going to be sick, but her mouth, her throat, they were all too dry to produce anything.

The blood bead continued to fall, and Frost watched it, aware of its perfect shape. He waited, feeling the forces already at work within him. His destiny was in the making.

• • •

Blade rose to his full height above Karen with an easy grace. He wiped the blood from his mouth with the back of his hand.

Looking at his wrists, she saw that the slashes had healed. When she looked into his eyes, she saw an animal fury there that she had never seen before. How far over the line had the experience pushed him? How much was left of the human being that she cared about?

Before she could ask, a shadow moved behind him. She started to shout a warning, but Blade was already in motion, moving faster than anything she'd ever seen before.

Frost saw the blood bead, saw his own reflection within its depths as it neared to less than a foot away. He was power incarnate, a force that hadn't been seen since the old darkness had trod heavily on mankind.

And it was going to happen—NOW!

Blade fell into a natural defensive position in the bleeding chamber to protect Karen, but with the power swirling around inside him, being defensive was the last thing on his mind. He felt better than he ever had in his life. Whoever had made the mistake of entering the bleeding chamber was going to be one piss-poor individual.

Vanessa stepped from the shadows; the creature flicked her hot gaze over him.

CHAPTER

52

Frost closed his eyes and kept his arms out, his head back, waiting. The blood bead smacked into his head, creating a perfect red circle. His senses opened at once, stronger than he could have ever imagined. He even felt the planets aligning out in space as the power funneled into him.

Frost shook as the unseen force possessed him. A wind sprang up in the chamber, where no wind had ever been before, swirling around over the audience. A humming noise filled the air.

Without warning, one of the tombs burst open, followed by several others. BOOM! BOOM! BOOM! A cannonade rolled throughout the temple.

Frost gloried in the feeling of power that grew geometrically within him. Even after everything he had read, everything he had guessed at, he could not have expected this.

Mercury and Quinn drew back, along with the other vampires nearby. Their faces showed their apprehension. The pureblood vampire lords struggled to get away, but Frost's guards held them in place.

Frost wanted to laugh at them, but he was too busy growing, *becoming*. The occult energy released by the Day-Walker's blood shimmered over him.

And Deacon Frost was thrown headlong into the dark godhood he had been searching for.

Vanessa attacked at once, aiming a handful of elongated nails at Blade's face. He stepped aside, barely stopping an instinctive killing blow. She came at him again, shrieking her fury. Her fangs flashed toward his face, and he blocked again.

Knowing a defensive battle wasn't going to last against her because she was too quick and strong, Blade stepped into the next charge and flung her into the back wall.

Frost felt himself consumed by a hellish force, blasted by the spirit energy. His body turned loose of its undead frame, becoming something much, much more.

He looked out over the audience, hearing the fear in their voices and seeing the fear in their eyes.

They had every reason, he knew, to fear him. He was the most powerful thing any of them had ever seen.

The tombs continued to explode, raining stone and mortar out over the crowd. Then, incredibly, swirling transparent wraiths shot up from the tombs. Without pause, they aimed themselves at the blood-marked foreheads of the vampire lords.

The wraiths shot like spectral arrows, stabbing through the foreheads of the vampire lords. The men holding them prisoner stepped back in fear and shock.

The supernatural wind wound around Frost. He laughed crazily, caught up in the exultation that filled him. Vampire wraiths swirled around him, spooking even Quinn, who stepped back.

"Fuck," Quinn said.

The impact against the wall in the bleeding chamber didn't faze Vanessa. The vampire came back at Blade in full force. Shrieking and striking out, she clawed and bit at him.

The Hunter moved too quickly, brushing aside Vanessa's attack as he hardened his heart. Whistler had shown him the way, and Whistler had been the only truth and parent Blade had ever known.

And when it came down to it, Whistler had given his life fighting against the vampires. Blade knew he could do no less. He reached down, scooping up the broken femur that Karen had brought with her. Then he waited.

•   •   •

Surrounded by the whirling vampire wraiths, Frost watched as the pureblood vampire lords succumbed to the wraiths writhing inside them. The lords' bodies disintegrated, collapsing in on themselves.

Without warning, their pureblood spirits leaped from their screaming mouths. Frost saw them as almost invisible black ragged things, but they were more substantial than the wraiths.

Their spirits ripped from their bodies, the vampire lords exploded into clouds of black ash.

The freed spirits flew toward Frost, who let them come. He held his arms out, allowing them to penetrate his body again and again. But they brought with them an agony like nothing he'd ever known before.

He screamed, watching as Mercury turned away from him.

Vanessa came at Blade again. This time the Hunter caught the creature's arm and whirled Vanessa into the nearest wall. He pinned the vampire with his body and his free arm, looking into Vanessa's eyes.

"Erik," Vanessa said softly, almost pleading.

Blade didn't allow indecision to touch him. There was only one choice. With vampires, there was always only one choice.

He drew the femur back, then drove it straight into Vanessa's heart.

The creature screamed, shrill and loud.

• • •

For Frost, the agony he was trapped in as the pure-blood spirits ran through him so rampantly was exquisite. If he could have realized he was still standing, he wouldn't have known how he was.

Blade held the struggling, shrieking vampire up against the wall and rammed the femur into her chest again and again, willing it to die.

Acting in concert, the pureblood spirits ceased their attack on Frost. They turned and wheeled, quick as thought itself, and entered Frost's body through the glyph Mercury had drawn on him.

They didn't reemerge.

But the pent-up force of their entry slammed into Frost, knocking him from the dais and into the shadows of the catacombs surrounding the coliseum.

One final thrust by Blade with the femur sank the bone all the way through Vanessa's chest and heart. With all his strength behind it, the bone crunched into the stone wall behind the creature, embedding in the rock.

He backed away from Vanessa as her claws continued to rake the air for him.

The vampire gave a final shriek as she died, then exploded into a ball of fire.

Smoke hung heavy in the air over the chamber. Frost saw it, but he saw it differently than ever before. It was as if someone had plugged new senses into his head.

Mercury led the others forward, hesitation in her every move. "Deacon?"

Then he realized he was standing with his back to them so they couldn't see his face. *He was seeing behind himself.* It was incredible. And he knew the human name she had called him by was wrong. It didn't fit what he had become.

Blade made himself watch as what had once been his mother burned, distancing himself from the emotion. With a last flash, Vanessa turned into a cloud of ash that drifted down over him.

He'd lost her again—for the final time.

And the man who'd caused it was going to pay.

Frost watched as Mercury took another hesitant step forward. "Deacon?" she called softly.

"Not anymore," he said, and his voice pealed over the crowd.

• • •

Blade grabbed his armor and ran from the bleeding chamber. He'd ascertained that Karen was going to live, but it didn't look like she was going to be of help anytime soon.

No matter what else happened, Deacon Frost wasn't going to get away. There was going to be a *reckoning*.

He ran down the stairs, pulling on his armor as he went. His reflexes, his speed, everything was greater than he'd ever remembered.

Turning another corner, he realized he was on the upper gallery overlooking the central dais and the pit surrounding it. He spotted Quinn and Mercury below. Wherever they were, he knew, Frost wouldn't be far behind.

Without hesitation, he flung himself over the railing and into the air. He somersaulted, finishing pulling the armor together as he fell. Then he landed on the central dais, surefootedly as a predatory cat.

"Frost!" Blade challenged.

Standing partially hidden in the shadows of the catacombs, Frost followed the sound of Blade's voice. "There's no way out for you," the vampire told the Hunter.

"For either of us," Blade replied, his eyes glowing with the power that filled him.

The vampires shifted, finally starting to close on Blade.

"Who dies first?" Blade asked.

CHAPTER

53

Blade looked at the number of vampires in front of him. Whistler would have thought him insane for issuing such a challenge. Smart money would have been to hustle out of the cavern and live to fight another day.

But Whistler wasn't there, and Blade had never felt stronger, more ready for a battle. He also wasn't sure if he would be able to return to anything close to human.

He spotted his sword, embedded in a nearby wall.

"Take him out," Frost commanded.

In a heartbeat, guards stepped from the shadows surrounding the dais, all armed to the teeth. They encircled Blade, drawing closer as they drew the cordon tight around him.

"Me first," Quinn growled, moving forward.

The vampire still wore Blade's wraparound sunglasses. "I owe this fucker." He pulled a wicked gutting knife from his boot. Offering his second new hand up for viewing, he said, "Grew another hand for you, sweetmeat." He tossed the knife across to the new hand. "And now I'm gonna kill you with it." The creature charged headlong at the Hunter.

Blade met the rush head-on, surprised at how fast and strongly he moved. He dropped and kicked out, sweeping the vampire's legs from under him. Still on the move, he spun behind Quinn before the vampire could get up. "Let's see if you can grow a new one of these!" He hooked a finger through the metal ring at the end of his jacket sleeve and pulled out a retractable garrote. In less than a heartbeat, he twisted it around Quinn's throat. He tightened the wire and decapitated the vampire.

The headless body turned to ashes, and Blade caught up his sunglasses before they had time to fall. He slid them on, turning to the rest of his opponents. He picked up Quinn's gutting knife and moved automatically into a practiced kata. "Next?"

A group of vampires attacked en masse.

Going with the initial movement and adrenaline flow coursing through him, Blade launched a spinning-wheel kick that caught the lead vampire full in the face.

The creature's neck snapped like a brittle

branch, the head going back to lie on his shoulders. The body dropped.

Mercury came at him, blades gleaming in her hands. Blade met her attack, blocking the vampire's steel with his, then launched a snap kick that connected with Mercury's face. The blonde's head jerked back more than Blade estimated, so he missed on his knife-thrust follow-up. The blade skated inches from Mercury's throat. Caught off guard, the creature scrambled to safety.

Another woman took Mercury's place in the fray, this one carrying two pistols. With his heightened senses, Blade knew she was one of the familiars Frost had on hand. She lined up her pistols on the Hunter.

As she fired, Blade rolled out of the way. The bullets wouldn't kill him even if they penetrated his Kevlar, but her shooting sent the other familiars dodging for safety, which put them in the way of the vampires. He slashed out with the gutting knife, hamstringing a vampire at his side. Then he kicked upward, knocking one of the pistols from the woman's hand.

The pistol spun across the floor, out of reach. Staying on the move, Blade trapped the woman's other arm, stripping the second pistol from her hand. Rising, he flipped her over his shoulder, throwing her into a small knot of vampires that had rushed him. He plucked the pistol from the floor and came up firing, aiming at everyone in front of him.

The heads of three nearby familiars exploded as the hollowpoints blew through them. Surprisingly, a nearby vampire turned to ashes as well, letting him know the ammo had to be silver and garlic rounds. Evidently Frost had armed his own men with the antivampire rounds.

Blade whirled again, ducking beneath a vampire that had thrown himself through the air. Reaching up with the knife in his other hand, the Hunter gutted the vampire, running the blade through the creature's heart.

Another vampire caught him in a viselike grip and lifted him from the ground, holding a shotgun barrel tight against his throat, intending to break his back.

Blade kicked the bloodsucker's knee, breaking it and sending them both tumbling. Blade was on his feet first, the gutting knife naked in his hand as he sheathed the pistol in his waistband.

He launched himself at his opponent in a somersault, using the newfound strength and ability that had been given to him. He caught a fistful of the vampire's hair, and flipped over his back. The Hunter landed on his feet behind the vampire, then forced his knife through the creature's spinal column. He yanked the head, tearing through the remaining flesh. The corpse turned to ashes, revealing the other creatures rushing at him.

"Blade!"

Recognizing Karen's voice, Blade looked up and spotted the woman standing on the upper gallery. Moving quickly, he dropped a shoulder and butted into the lead vampire, sending it crashing back into the three others following closely behind.

Blade yanked the abandoned shotgun from the dais and tossed it up to Karen. There were extra rounds for the shotgun on a bandolier around the butt. Then he turned his attention back to the fight, his blood singing through his body. He drew the pistol and fired it dry, killing familiars as well as vampires. When it was empty, he used it as a club for a time till the blood made it too slick to hold on to.

The moves came naturally to him as he fought the crowd. He blocked a sweeping roundhouse, then snap-kicked the vampire in the face as he knifed two other vampires closing in from the side. He felt like he had a radar system going off in his head, knowing where he was, knowing where each of his opponents was in relation to that position.

He heard the crash of Karen's shotgun often. Not everyone she shot was a familiar, but enough of them were hit to give pause to the rest. Blade concentrated on the undead.

Even with so many of their kindred down and dead, the vampires still came on.

Blade cut and slashed at them, not stopping with only the knife. His new strength worked just as well, allowing him to punch through ribs and rip the dead hearts beneath.

Then he noticed that Mercury was missing.

CHAPTER

54

Karen reloaded the final three shells she had on the bandolier around the shotgun's butt. She racked the slide, then fired down into the crowd again. The numbers facing Blade were much less than they'd started out, but she wished she knew more about who were familiars and who weren't. It was frustrating to shoot vampires who only staggered, then returned immediately to the fight.

The man she shot staggered back, his head going to pieces. He didn't incinerate which meant he wasn't a vampire, but the head wound—if not lethal to begin with—was definitely debilitating.

Her own head still ached, throbbing with the ordeal she'd gone through, and her neck was burning as though acid had been injected into it. She fired her last two rounds, but evidently both rounds hit vampires, because the targets only staggered a moment.

Frustrated, Karen tried to think of anything else she could do to help. Then she noticed movement on the periphery of her vision. Before she could run, Mercury sprang from the shadows, reaching out for her throat with razored claws.

Mercury landed on top of Karen, pinning her to the floor. The blond vampire closed her hand, shutting off Karen's air. Her opponent's strength was so much, and Karen had so little to give after everything she'd been through that she almost gave up.

Straddling her, Mercury toyed with her, like a cat playing with a trapped mouse. The smile on the blond vampire's face was absolutely feral.

Karen struggled to get away, knowing she couldn't. But as she moved, she felt a cylindrical object in her pocket. She remembered what it was and reached for it. Her hand searched for it, finally finding it in the folds of her clothing. She fisted it, bringing it out, just as Mercury opened her mouth wide to reveal the gleaming canines.

The blond vampire leaned in to bite, going for the kill.

And Karen sprayed her full in the mouth with the silver nitrate/garlic vampire mace Whistler had given her.

Mercury broke away at once, coughing, gagging, and howling with pain.

As Karen watched, the blond vampire's head

suddenly exploded, then her body turned to ash.

Karen pushed herself to her feet, gasping for air. She stumbled over to the railing and stared down, fully expecting to see Blade at the bottom of a pile of vampires.

Managing to break free of the crowd of opponents still standing before him, Blade leaped over a vampire that dove at his feet. The Hunter landed near the section of wall where his sword was. He fisted the pommel and yanked the gleaming sword from the rock.

Using both hands, Blade cut a swath through the men swarming toward him. The sword whirled like a live thing in his hands, like it was fluid death instead of a steel-spined razor. His vengeance was undeniable and unrestrained. Everything that moved was a target. The sword licked out hungrily, taking arms and legs, heads and parts of heads. Vampires died in gusts of dark ashes, swirling over the bodies of dead familiars. The sword twirled madly, wreaking havoc, not pausing as it cleaved through living and undead flesh either one.

In moments he stood alone, breathing hard. Blood and perspiration covered his body and drenched his clothing and armor.

"Blade!" Frost's voice rang out through the chamber.

Looking up, Blade spotted Frost in the center of the dais. The vampire brandished a katana sword.

Frost inscribed a salute in the air. "Let's do it," he said.

Blade moved at once, racing toward the dais. He somersaulted and flipped through the air, landing perfectly.

Frost swung at once, bringing the katana around in a blinding arc that would have taken the Hunter's head off.

Only Blade wasn't there when it arrived. He flipped back out of reach, avoiding the deadly blade by less than an inch. He came down on his hands, pushed and tried to regain his feet, only to have two vampires attempt to waylay him.

Blade whirled the sword, carving deep into both of the creatures and sending them scampering back to safety. He spun to face Frost, bringing the sword into the en garde position. He blocked the next sword swing, sparks crashing as steel rang on steel. Then he riposted, ripping the sword through the air only inches in front of Frost's face.

"You're good," Frost said, turning the dagger aside.

"Wait till I get warmed up," Blade said, pulling back as Frost swung the sword.

The vampires around them stepped back, widening the circle around the combatants, no longer as willing to chance stepping in and taking a swipe at Blade. The edged steel flew too quickly, changed directions too fast.

No matter how fast Blade pushed himself,

Frost seemed to get faster. It was like the vampire was plugged into an unending source of energy. Blade started taking more chances, trying to slip the sword and score. Frost brought the sword down on his shoulder, cutting deep into the muscle and bone.

A smile twisted Frost's lips. "Come on, Blade! Get it up! You're not fighting Deacon Frost anymore!"

Controlling the pain the way Whistler had taught him too, knowing that the wound was part of the risk he had chosen to take, Blade rose to the challenge. He didn't think about the sword's movement anymore—he became the movement, became the blade itself.

There was no fear, no hope, no friends, and no enemies. There was only the blade and the unforgiving net of steel he wove around himself.

Sparks jumped along the lengths of both swords, grating hisses of razored edges echoed around them.

Blade parried and riposted, blocked and slashed, cut and thrust. Frost's defense was immaculate, a perfect rhythm to everything Blade had to offer. The Hunter's lungs ached, burned from their need for oxygen. Salt from his own perspiration stung his eyes.

He concentrated on the void. He was movement, perfect and pure, better than anything Frost could ever be.

Then, in a flash, he saw his opening as Frost

pulled the katana back. Blade stepped in, slashing at the vampire's exposed arm.

The sword blade cut entirely through Frost's arm at the elbow. Blade drew back, regrouping, not letting the triumph touch him yet.

The katana fell from Frost's grip as he dropped to his knees, but the severed hand spun through the air, turning to ash and blowing away almost at once. The vampire stared at his stump, awe and disbelief staining his pained features.

Blade took a fresh grip on his sword and stepped in to deliver the coup de grace that would literally part Frost from his undead existence.

Blade wasted no time, putting all his increased strength into a swipe across Frost's midsection. The Hunter had expected the sword to grate on bone, to hang on sinew, and to slow through muscle as it cleaved Frost in two.

Only the sword passed cleanly through Frost, slicing him neatly in half.

Frost's upper body separated from his lower, toppling backward. Startled at first, a sudden confident smile lit his features. Bloody strings leaped from Frost's two halves, taking the place of the intestines and internal organs that Blade had expected to see come spilling out.

The bloody strings pulled Frost together again like rubber bands, and the two halves of his body joined into one once again with a rushing liquid *GLOOP!*

"You're too late, Blade!" Frost roared. More of the bloody strings jumped from his severed arm and quickly knitted him a new hand. The skeletal foundation was laid, then filled out with sinew, blood, and flesh. When it finished, not even a scar remained to show the miraculous healing.

The vampire stamped his foot on the katana on the ground. The sword spun through the air, the hilt thudding into Frost's waiting new hand.

Blade backed away, giving ground as Frost lifted the katana into an en garde position. How the hell was he supposed to kill Frost if he couldn't touch him?

Katana in hand, Frost launched a snarling attack at once.

Blade concentrated on the gleaming razor's edge of Frost's sword. Maybe he couldn't touch Frost, but the sword was definitely tangible. However, seeming invulnerability hadn't been the only transformation Frost had received. His strength was incredible, way beyond anything the Hunter had even after the recent feeding. And Frost was so *damn* fast, faster than anything Blade had ever seen, living or undead.

Sword crossed sword, and sparks flew into the air. The cacophony of grating metal erased even the sound of Blade's heart beating frantically in his ears as it tried to supply his oxygen needs. Black comets threaded through the Hunter's vision, blotting out his peripheral vision and reducing the combat to a narrow tunnel that balanced on a turn of the wrist, a quick shift of a foot.

Blade didn't try to connect with Frost's body, only weaving the most creative defense he'd ever entertained in his life. His swordarm muscles burned like they were on fire, like napalm had been injected into the tissue. Then it began to go numb and his movements slowed.

Without warning, Frost trapped Blade's sword, holding it clear of their bodies. The vampire drew his hand back and slammed it into the Hunter's face, knocking him backward like he'd been caught in a bomb blast.

Blade's lungs emptied in a rush as his feet left the floor. He flew through the air, flailing to find a balance, but driven so hard by the blow that recovery proved impossible. He smacked into the temple wall behind him, hanging for just a moment while the centrifugal force created by the blow finally gave in to gravity. Then he fell.

Frost leaped high into the air, propelling himself at Blade, flipping in the air with the uncanny grace of a trained acrobat. He landed on his feet in front of Blade, the katana shifting into the en garde position.

Weakly, Blade forced himself to his feet. It hurt to move, hurt to breathe. But there was no fear in him. He let the hate take over, focusing on it, remembering how Frost had taken his mother from him twice. First before he'd ever been born, then again when Blade had been forced to kill her himself.

His arm came up, and his moves felt more sure. Frost moved into the attack, and Blade met him swordblow for swordblow. Steel rang out, filling the temple cavern again, echoing long and hard in the shadows that twisted around them.

The Hunter dug deep in himself, dredging up all the old hate, all the skill that Whistler had given him, the things he'd learned on his own. He was more than human, more than anything he'd ever been in his life. Karen's blood flamed through him, giving him strength.

Frost swung at his head, the blow coming edge on, the movement barely picked up in Blade's failing peripheral vision.

Blade pulled his body into motion, making the defensive step and mirror thrust to block the katana. When it hit, the blow felt like it tore something loose in his elbow and shoulder.

Before he could recover from the agony that burned through his arm, Frost seized his wrist in a viselike grip that felt like it was going to shatter the bones.

"I don't think so," Frost snarled in savage triumph. He released Blade's wrist, moving so quickly the Hunter couldn't block the slap that nearly took his head from his shoulders.

Blade flew backward, turning a cartwheel in the air, and landed on his side. His lungs worked in vain to suck in oxygen.

"You lose, stud," Frost announced, coming closer, the katana dropping into position.

Even then, the hate inside Blade wouldn't allow him to give up. He'd fought all his life, and his hardest opponent had always been that dark nature that lurked within himself. As he turned his head, refusing to simply give in and die, he spotted the bandolier of EDTA injectors hanging in the shadows high above him.

He went into fluid motion, his mind recognizing that the bandolier still held the blue-filled glass EDTA capsules. Frost might have thrown them over the edge above, but they'd survived the impact, lodging in a deep crack in the temple wall fifteen feet overhead.

They offered a final hope.

Ignoring Frost's approach, knowing he was setting himself up for an all-or-nothing gamble, the Hunter lunged, fisting the sword and set the booby-trap. He threw it, hoping his flagging strength was up to the task.

The sword flipped end over end, drawing Frost's attention as well. It missed the bandolier by a foot, then flipped around to land handle first in the crack above the EDTA injectors. The sword edge gleamed, well out of reach now.

Frost howled with laughter. "Looks like you're losing your touch."

The familiar SNAP of the booby-trap going off brought a smile to Blade's lips. He watched as the embedded blades within the swordhilt snapped out and split the crack wider.

When the splitting crack reached the bandolier, the EDTA injectors slipped free. They tumbled down in freefall, dropping toward the Hunter, the sword following close behind. Blade reached for the bandolier instead of the sword, trusting his honed reflexes. He caught the bandolier inches above the hard stone of the temple floor just before the sword clanged against it.

Then he tucked himself into a roll that brought him to his feet. Frost was on his heels, giving up any defense he might have made in order to pursue the offense, swinging the katana with all the incredible strength he possessed.

Only Blade wasn't there when the katana struck sparks from the stone floor. Slipping one of the EDTA capsules from the bandolier, the Hunter stepped into Frost before the vampire could recover. Setting himself in a martial arts stance, Blade rammed the EDTA capsule deep into the undead flesh of his opponent.

Frost didn't even register the blow.

But the capsule stayed put.

And hope dawned again in the Hunter. Pressing his last advantage, Blade launched into a flurry of kicks and blows, fisting the EDTA capsules when he could. Frost fought him, swinging the katana.

Avoiding the blow, Blade swung in a roundhouse kick, connecting high on Frost's chest. Frost flew back up the ramp leading to the dais, falling backward. He rose to meet Blade's attack, but the Hunter didn't let up. Blade planted another EDTA capsule under Frost's ribs. A third went into Frost's chest.

Unable to withstand Blade's vicious, all-out assault, Frost was driven backward in disbelief. The vampire protected himself as best he could, but the EDTA capsules continued sliding into his body.

Blade had the last EDTA capsule in hand when Frost slammed up against the temple wall behind him. The Hunter lifted the capsule in his fist, breathing hard. "Some motherfucker's always trying to ice-skate uphill." He drove the last capsule home, burying it deep inside Frost's face. The Hunter stepped back, waiting.

The effects of the EDTA in Frost's system was immediately apparent. The vampire's face turned crimson around the embedded capsule, and the crimson spread, taking in all of his head. He clawed at his throat as his head started to swell, doubling in size, then tripling, like a blood-engorged tick.

"NOOOOOOOOO!" Frost forced the agonized scream through his closing throat.

But the agonized denial was lost in the climatic KA-BOOM! that filled the cavern. The explosion reduced the vampire into a billion whirling globules that formed a swirling crimson mushroom. Then those globules began to atomize, disappearing.

Blade wiped a fleck of blood from his cheek as he stood there for a moment, gazing down, thinking he should have felt something—more. Instead, there was only a hollowness, and a grim reminder that Whistler was gone. No one to share the victory with.

Then Karen stumbled to the edge of the gallery, drawing his attention. "Blade."

Almost no one, he corrected himself. "Let's get out of here," he said. He leaned down to pick up the sword, and took the lead as they walked out of the vampire hell.

Dawn came at its appointed time, hanging in the sky like a molten fireball. Blade paused at the construction site entrance to the underground temple and watched it, somehow feeling it was important that he see it for himself.

Karen stood beside him, shielding her eyes against the morning glare as she bathed in the sun's rays. She looked whole, healthy. "I never imagined I'd be so happy to see the sun rise," she said, then turned to glance at Blade. "I need to get back to the lab if I'm going to cure you."

Blade regarded her briefly, then turned to stare out across the city in the distance, thinking about the other vampires who were even now cursing the sun and its hold over them. New victims had been claimed during the night, some of them being turned to rise again and multiply the menace that was already out there.

He thought about helping her secure her fantasy, but realized she'd been through too much to ever completely believe that she'd be safe again. And who knew? Maybe a little warning might save her life as well.

"It's not over," he told her. "Keep your cure."

Her surprise showed in her face.

"There's still a war going on out there." And he knew that was the right answer for him. The Thirst was a part of him, had been the crucible that had helped make the man Whistler had guided and taught. He would find a way to deal with it. He took out his sunglasses, flipping them open and putting them on. He grinned at the sun, defiant in spite of the agony that filled his body. "I'm the Day-Walker. I need their strength. If you want to help me, find me a new serum."

She looked at him as if she couldn't understand him. "Why?"

Blade looked at the sun, enjoying the warmth of it on his face. "Because it takes one to kill one."

"But I thought we stopped them."

He shook his head. "There'll be others. And when they rise," he lifted his sword, the sun's rays splitting along the razor edge, "I'll be waiting for them."

EPILOGUE

The man and woman walked toward the grimy steel door at the end of the alley, hunkering inside their thick coats to avoid the cold wind and the falling snow. She giggled at something he said, something he'd thought sounded cute. He was dressed in gangster black, something that represented his profession, and a tip of the hat to the American movies that had helped him create his present persona. The woman was beautiful, her skin so perfect in the moonlight.

Night had quenched the day hours ago, and the snow had pierced the darkness, delivering an artificial diurnal cast to the cityscape. The lighting underscored the basso throbbing of the bump-and-grind music coming from the room beyond the steel door.

"Where are we going?" the woman asked in Russian.

"It's a surprise," he told her.

"I like surprises," she replied, smiling broadly at him to show that she did. "Cigarette."

The man reached inside his coat and brought out a pack. He shook one out and offered it to her.

She took it, shivering from the cold but obviously wanting the nicotine more.

He patted his pockets, not finding a lighter or any matches. A man in a heavy hooded fur overcoat passed by. The Russian gangster called out to him, causing him to pause. "You have a light?"

The hooded man stopped, turning to face the gangster, his hands deep in his pockets. He didn't say anything and the shadows hid his face.

"Do you have a light?" the gangster repeated.

The hooded man maintained his silence and his stare.

Angry, the gangster stepped forward and reached for the man's hood, intending to yank it down so he could see the face underneath, get some clue for why the man acted the way he did. "I asked you for a light."

Hands moving so quickly the gangster didn't have a chance, the hooded man opened his mouth and exposed gleaming fangs. The gangster had only a second to realize the doom that reached out for him, then his throat was torn out, staining the snow crimson in a gust of arterial flow.

Even as the gangster fell, the hooded man

turned his attention to the woman. She screamed and tried to run. The hooded man had her before she'd gone two steps, his speed incredible.

She turned her face to him, prey frozen in hypnotic fear of the predator. Instead of biting her, though, he plucked the cigarette from her lips.

"Catch you at a bad time, Comrade?" a voice behind him asked.

The hooded man turned easily, chuckling at the irony of the situation. He heard the footsteps of the woman tearing out behind him, shushing through the snow. He recognized Blade easily. The Hunter stepped out of the shadows, drawing his great sword with slow deliberation.

Taking a Zippo from his pocket, the hooded man flicked it to life with equal deliberation. As he bent his head to breathe flame into the cigarette, the glow revealed his face.

His whiskey-aged voice was exactly the way Blade remembered.

"Well, this is gonna be interesting, isn't it?" Whistler asked.

MEL ODOM lives in Moore, OK, and has written dozens of books in a variety of fields. Serious die-hard collectors will remember him as the author of *Harte: Of Darkness*, a four-issue comics series about a vampire private eye who worked occasional jobs for the Roman Catholic Church.

When he's not writing, Mel attends lots of sports activities, cheering on his children. He has five of them, with his wife, Sherry, and has even been brave enough to take on the coaching mantle from time to time. He also loves to travel and hangs out on the internet too much. For those interested, his e-mail address is denimbyte@aol.com.